Nearly Human
Marked Book 1

Meredith Spies

Copyright 2022 by Meredith Spies

All rights reserved. No part of this book may be reproduced or used in any manner without the prior written permission of the copyright owner, except for the use of brief quotations in a book review. All characters and situations are products of the author's imagination and any resemblance to persons or situations living or dead, past or present, is purely coincidence.

Huge Thank You To

Editing by Cate Ryan (www.cateedits.com)
Cover and Promotional Art by Samantha Santana (www.amaidesigns.com)

Potential Triggers

Mentions of assault, depictions of violence between a supernatural creature and a human, references to child abuse, drug use, nonconsensual medical procedures, mild body horror consistent with shifter fiction, descriptions of cadavers in a forensic setting, descriptions of hoarding, mentions of stalking, mentions of torture, mention but no description of past sexual assault.

To Jinn... I... love you... Best... braintwin... ever...

Chapter One

There were three werewolves ahead of me at the deli. Three. It was weird, to be honest. They were the least subtle werewolves I'd ever seen, making a display of tilting their heads and sniffing the air. One of them even licked his damn lips, making it hard for me to keep from laughing aloud at their antics. They weren't weres I recognized, none of the handful I knew were scattered throughout Hitchens County or further afield.

That... was unsettling. To the weres who knew me here in the county, I was harmless. Annoying, but harmless. To the ones elsewhere, I was a curiosity. Close to prey but no fun to play with. These weres had a tense, studied indifference that felt dangerous in ways the others didn't. More immediate. Closer.

Nerves sizzled to life in my gut, and I considered, for a moment, turning and striding out of the deli. Just heading back to work and the stack of files I had waiting on my desk. The lurch of hunger-induced nausea in my belly put paid to that notion in a heartbeat, though. Working with cadavers—even on paper—was never a good idea on an empty stomach. Moving up to the counter, the weres laid in an order for more food than even three of them could eat, supernatural metabolism or no. The three of them craned their necks, peering at faces in the line behind them and in the small booths and tables all around us. The weres could smell me. The almost-wolf part of me would be a giant flashing neon light to their senses, but I wasn't one of them, and any minute now they'd either figure it out and leave me alone or do something damned foolish.

They huddled together at the pick-up window, murmuring in low voices that rumbled beneath the deli's cheerful pop hits from the nineties.

"Hey."

Here we go. "Yes?"

"You look familiar." He was the tallest of the three, and possibly a direct descendant of Paul Bunyan. He had to crane his neck to peer down at me. I fully expected a few clouds to drift by his forehead at any moment. Wildly curling coppery hair did nothing to curb his wild man image, despite the (even I could tell it was) expensive suit and Cartier watch. "You one of the Dorian clan?"

I smiled and shook my head in my best 'sorry, can't help you' gesture. "'Fraid not." It was my turn to order, but they weren't moving. The other two had turned and were affecting casual poses, but they looked about ready to leap at me.

I hadn't been *close* to any weres in almost ten years. The only ones I'd been in any proximity since I left home had been far less friendly. Because of them, the tiny, feral part of my back brain that recognized apex predator behavior was pointing out the tense legs, the way their fingers were curled and ready to grab, the unwavering stares. That scared bunny brain of mine was shrieking at me to run like hell and not look back; head for the nearest hole in the ground and hide.

I made an aborted motion toward the counter, freezing when none of them moved. The teenager taking orders was wide-eyed, half-turned toward the kitchen, unsure which way to go, what to do next. She wasn't like them, like us, at all, had no trace of Other on her, but even normal humans knew when a predator was hunting close by.

"Um, sorry, y'all, but I'd like to get lunch before I need to be back at work so..." My heart raced, aching in my ribs. I knew they could hear it. The soft susurrus of panic rising.

"You sure you're not one of the Dorians? Maybe you're a MacIntyre." Big Red leaned a bit closer, the spicy scent of his cologne only underscoring the earth-musk-sweat-salt scent I always associated with werewolves with their blood up. "You look like I should know you. You got the look of the Dorians on you," he added, squinting. "Dark hair like them. Big eyes like them." He bared his teeth in a grin. "Short little shit like them, too."

The other two moved slowly down the counter, eyes still on me as they eased toward the pick-up window. The short line behind me had gone quiet. They were expecting a fight, I realized. They thought these guys had a beef with me, maybe I'd popped off to them or something, and they were waiting to see me get hit.

"I'm not kin to Dorians or MacIntyres," I said, my tight smile making my lips ache.

Big Red took a half-step to one side, his smile curling nastily as I eased past him. I knew what he was doing. He wanted me closer, wanted a good, deep whiff of me as I passed by. Fuck my life.

I tried not to wince away when he inhaled, not bothering to be quiet about it when he huffed that deep breath, sucking in my scent. The girl behind the counter had gone a funny pink, her mouth working but no words coming out as Big Red pressed closer behind me, inhaling again. "That's enough," I said through clenched teeth. "I don't know you. You don't know me. Now get off me or I'll have to call someone."

Red eased back. "You're talking brave for someone who sounds like they're a few seconds away from a stroke," he said with a low chuckle. "You still look familiar," he pressed, though he took another step back, then another. His friends were holding bags now, huge grocery sized ones, and a to-go tray of drinks sat perched on the counter, waiting. He kept his eyes on me as he reached for the tray, only looking away when he had to turn to the door. He looked back once more as he and the other werewolves hit the sidewalk.

Nervous as I was, it was difficult to be intimidated by a man carrying six gigantic Styrofoam cups of soda.

I offered the girl behind the counter a friendlier smile than the one I'd had pasted to my lips moments before and placed my usual order, thankful that I was a creature of habit when it came to my meals and didn't have to think about it. I rattled off the items, having the exact amount ready to go thanks to weeks upon weeks of Thursday lunch breaks at the same deli.

As I edged down the counter to wait for my order, my phone buzzed in my pocket. "Shit!" My heart kicked back into high gear for a minute as I fumbled the phone free of my jacket, the sudden vibration making me have the ridiculous thought of *fuck, they got me!* before I could stop and use reason. "Landry Babin," I managed, only slightly out of breath, catching the call before it went to voice mail.

"Thank God," Reba Summers groaned on the other end of the line. "I've been looking everywhere for you! You left your work phone in the lab, you know. I could get a raft of shit from on high for calling your personal number during work hours!"

"Shit, I'm so sorry," I muttered. I grabbed my order as it came over the counter, tucking the cup of sweet tea carefully into the crook of my elbow so I could manage my phone, the food, and the drink all at once as I headed out the door and back toward my office. I wasn't used to carrying two phones, and the county had a strict policy about using personal phones for official business. Reba had taken to patting me down whenever I left for lunch, but today, she was elbow deep in payroll paperwork when I took my break. "What's the problem?"

"An all-hands situation." She blew out a harsh breath. "Two

bodies, rush order from the sheriff down in Tuttle. They're hoping..." Reba trailed off. "Well."

"They seem to forget we're not psychics or miracle workers," I said, crossing the street and breaking into a quick stride, mindful of my tea. "I'll be there in five."

"Our guests aren't going anywhere," she pointed out. "I'll tell the sheriff you'll be here soon, though. He's called three times since you went on break."

"Next time he calls, send him to my line. I'll deal with him myself."

"Thanks, Doc. See you in five."

I shoved my phone back in my pocket and groaned. Eating on the run—literally this time—was one of my least favorite things. I loved my breaks. I cherished them. They were necessary to keep me from losing my shit.

Working as a coroner for Hitchens County wasn't exactly high stress—the county itself was small, and my job, for the three months I'd had it, consisted mainly of signing off on autopsy findings for elderly decedents who'd died natural deaths and the occasional accident of the auto or home variety. The last murder in Hitchens County had been in 2014, and that had technically been an accident when Flora Guerne shot her cheating husband in the head, not the knee as she'd intended.

Allegedly intended, anyway.

The part that drove me absolutely spare was the number of people who seemed to think I was some sort of magician and could not only determine cause of death but everything from the exact time of death down to the second, to the mood of the deceased at the time of death (honestly, if they were awake, they were probably pretty upset, but if they were asleep, I'd have to say they gave zero fucks). I juggled my lunch around until I could eat my sandwich without dropping my drink, wolfing it down in four bites before reaching the office doors and pausing only to dig my key card out of my trouser pocket.

Belmarais, the seat of Hitchens County and where my job as

coroner was located, might have been a small town, but they were dedicated to their high-tech gadgets in the government buildings. I had two cards to swipe in order to access the maze of the morgue and labs, and a third card with just my title and picture on it over the county seal. That one, Reba told me on my first day, was just for show. I tossed my paper bag and sandwich wrap into the trash bin at the curb, turning back to swipe the first of my cards. The hairs on the back of my neck stood up, the irony of my hackles rising not lost on me.

Big Red was just a few storefronts down, watching. Not even trying to hide it, either. Openly standing on the sidewalk in front of Rudy's Treats and Eats, staring at me as I let myself in to the old building that housed the coroner's office. His two buddies were nowhere to be seen, but they had to be close by. Werewolves rarely traveled alone.

The bunny part of my brain was vibrating itself into a tizzy, but I forced my hands to move slowly, keeping as normal a pace as possible as I keyed myself into the building and made sure the doors were shut and locked behind me before moving on to the next set of doors. The feeling of being watched—no, hunted—was painful. Every part of me ached with the need to run. I was sweating buckets—that slick fear-sweat that smells sour and lingers—and my mouth was dry. Everything was so *much;* the lights were too bright, my hearing too sharp. Lucky me, my special abilities included heightened prey response. Super sexy, no? It's just what a guy wants in a date: a short stack who gets jumpy any time there's a loud noise and has a tendency to bolt if you look at him wrong.

I made it down to my office in the lab area in record time, bypassing the public facing office I kept for official visits and meeting with bereaved families on the ground floor near the main entrance. Reba glanced up from a stack of files, her pierced brow arching toward her hairline. "What'd you do? Run down here from the first floor?"

"No," I laughed, wheezing a bit. I didn't run, but there may have been some power walking involved. "Did you get back in touch with the sheriff?"

"Mmhmm. He sounded damn pissed off that you hadn't miraculously teleported here from your lunch break and Quincy'd the bodies with your coroner superpowers. By the bye: Justin still isn't back yet."

"Third time this week." I sighed, shrugging out of my light coat and heading for the small changing room just off the lab. "Are they in the fridge?"

"Bagged, tagged, and slabbed."

"Reba..."

"You know I wouldn't say that in front of families." She sighed. "Go on, before Sheriff Stick Up the Ass calls *again*." She groaned as the office line rang. "Speak of the devil—"

"And he shall appear," I finished, already grabbing a fresh set of scrubs as I ducked into the changing room. When I came out, I took a deep breath and tried to brace myself for what I was going to see. Reba hadn't given me much detail, but if there was a rush, it was likely a murder or something equally problematic for the sheriff's department, something with a family demanding answers now.

Tuttle was the size of a pin head, across the Red River from where I'd spent my first few years in Hubbard before moving in with my Aunt Cleverly. The sheriff had, for as long as I could remember anyway, been a fusty old man with a mustache big enough to hide a small child. I was always surprised he could stand upright with that damn thing on his face. By all rights, he should have suffocated under its weight before I graduated from medical school.

He had always fancied himself to be above the nitty gritty his position should entail, big on delegating responsibilities to his deputies, including things that shouldn't be delegated either by law or just by basic human decency. If he was calling my office and getting shirty with Reba, something about these deaths must have his ass on the line.

I snapped on a fresh pair of nitrile gloves and chose the body nearest me. Both bodies were still in the black bags used by the coroner's office down in Tuttle, and both had bright orange tags looped through the zippers, showing chain of custody and identification for the cadavers. I didn't have to open the bag to smell the decay. New, too faint for most humans to detect, it was mingled with the stench of blood, urine, and loosened bowels as well as something sharp and animal.

Something definitely not human.

I blew a harsh breath out through my nose, grabbing the small tub of mentholated cream I kept on the desk in the corner. By the time I got it smeared under my nose, had my safety glasses on and voice activated recorder set, I had just about put Big Red and his friends out of my mind. They were still there but only as ghost-thoughts, barely a worry as I unclipped the orange tag and pulled the zipper on the first bag down far enough to reveal her face.

"Jessica Raymond, age twenty-two, time of death listed as approximately 0600 hours per the coroner in Tuttle. Note: Contact Jim Blakely at Tuttle coroner's office to ascertain how he reached this time of death. Did not indicate on intake paperwork. Coroner indicates severe trauma to chest, abdomen, and upper right thigh. Suspects mauling by dogs or possibly feral hogs."

I pulled the zipper the rest of the way down and nearly gagged in my mask. "This was not a pack of dogs, or a hog. Ms. Raymond's remains indicate predation occurred." The coroner, I knew, had not taken any samples from the body. He'd just had them bagged up and sent over. She was lacking any indication of even a preliminary postmortem. "God damn it, Blakely," I muttered, not caring that the recorder was going to pick that up. Reba would leave it out of the transcription later.

I took pictures of the wounds for our records, not trusting that Blakely had gotten enough or even every angle that we might need. Even through my mask and the menthol cream, there was no avoiding the fear-blood-offal stench rising from Ms. Raymond's torn body. The sharp predator scent threaded through it was a red light, flashing warning that whoever—not whatever—had done this wasn't human, and it wasn't an accident. The wounds were huge, not an accidental bite gone wrong, and not the wounds left by an animal in fear for its own life and lashing out against a perceived threat. She'd been torn into deliberately.

Deep gashes then ripped further, relatively straight slices into soft flesh ending in shredded flesh where she'd been pulled apart. "Not an animal," I muttered, a twisting certainty already lodged in my awareness. "Whatever did this did it with precision and intent. Her internal organs show evidence of predation, particularly the liver. Lower intestine has been pulled free of mesentery." The smell clotted in my throat. I wanted to race through the rest of the exam, but I forced myself to go steady, to follow protocol. I closed her bag back up and added a tag from our office to the orange one on the loop holding the zipper closed half an hour after I started my exam.

The rasp of the zipper triggered the recorder, the tiny light flickering and waiting for more input. I closed my eyes and swallowed against the rising panic in my throat, trying to force down the nausea and knowing it was a losing battle. I had never lied on a report in my entire career, but it was as good a time as any to start. "Correction," I said, voice shaking only a little, "animal attack, not of human origin. Without further evidence, it is impossible to tell what animal attacked Ms. Raymond, though if I had to make an educated guess, I'd suggest dogs; coyotes are not known for approaching humans in this area."

After a few seconds of silence, the recorder shut off with a soft click. Nausea filled my mouth with saliva and made my throat burn as I turned to the next victim, tagged as Thomas Raymond. His remains were much the same as his... wife? Sister? Torn abdomen, predated organs, torn upper thigh, ripping beyond the initial slice into the soft meat of the stomach. I made my observations quickly, failing to note for the recorder the animal-sharp-*panic* stink clinging to the bodies. This wasn't a pack of feral dogs.

My body was tight with fear, metallic tang of blood on the back of my tongue like a promise of what was to come if I didn't flee *nownownownownow*. I was shaking, my stomach cramping. The urge to give in to those damned heightened senses had me perched on a knife's edge, on the ledge of a skyscraper, clinging to a bridge, but I knew if I gave in once, that would be it. I'd never stop running.

Reba found me an hour later, face down on the work desk tucked into the corner of the exam room. Both bodies were very similar in their destruction, down to the sharp-sweet-bitter animal smell that lingered on the edges of the wounds, a very faint miasma rising from the remains. "You up for company?" she asked softly. "I can stall him for a bit if you need to regroup, doc." When I raised my head, she was looking over her shoulder into the exam room where both bodies had been carefully placed in refrigerated drawers for the time being. "No shame in needing a minute or two... or ten." She went on, voice low and quiet. "You're only human."

I smiled, tight and thin. "Rumor has it." Blowing out a breath that made my lungs ache, I pushed myself to my feet. "Give me a few minutes to clean up. I'll meet the sheriff in my upstairs office first." Reba's face underwent a weird little twisting shift of expressions and ended up stuck somewhere between nervous and polite. "He's already down here?"

"Mmhmm. New guy wants to be all proactive and shit." Her eyes were wide, pointedly glancing toward the exam room door. "Don't worry," she added when I groaned. "He showed up after you got done puking in the changing room."

"Ah." I smoothed down my scrub top and considered changing, but even if he wasn't already waiting, the sheriff would no doubt want to see the bodies and I would only have to change back again in a few minutes. "Okay. It was just so much," I said, my face hot. Let her think it was the carnage, not the knowledge. But something she said suddenly pinged for me. "Wait, new guy?"

"Yeah, Sheriff Michaels retired last year. Quite the scandal, apparently. Involved one of the church deacons and a gallon of bacon grease. They have an interim guy right now until the next election."

"Bacon grease?"

"Not what you think."

"How do you know what I'm thinking?"

"It's the same thing everyone thinks when the words scandal and bacon grease are in the same sentence."

"I'm gonna need to go poke out my mind's eye just to stop seeing that mental image."

"Mmm. Hey, do you remember someone named Ethan Stone?"

Yikes. Emotional whiplash hurt like a broken bone. "Why?" Reba's eyes narrowed just enough to let me know she knew I was about to lie to her. "I think I went to high school with him." *Werewolf. Werewolf, werewolf, werewolf...* My lungs tried to stop working, my heart tried to explode. He was the reason I knew, the reason I believed.

"Huh. Yeah, he said something like that."

"What? Why was Ethan Stone talking to you about me?" Oh my God, could I sound more fourteen?

"Because he's here to see you."

"Oh, Christ. Ethan Stone *and* the sheriff? Christ."

Why the hell would Ethan Stone be all the way out here? Last I heard, he'd moved to Dallas for college, and that was eons ago. Not that I'd checked back in with my Aunt Cleverly in Tuttle on the regular and asked or anything. Nope.

Reba's snort was somewhere between amused and pitying. "No, Doc. Ethan Stone *is* the sheriff."

Fuck. I sat back down behind the desk, my face going from tomato to chalk in just a few heartbeats. "Oh. Um. Hey, Reba? I'm gonna need another minute after all."

"Yeah, that's what I thought. I'll tell him."

Get your shit together, Landry! "What the fuck is today, Werewolf Wednesday?" Between Big Red and his buddies, the victims in my exam room, and now Sheriff Ethan fucking Stone showing up, I was starting to wonder if there were any normal humans left in the world. All I needed was for Reba to come in and announce she'd been Changed, and she'd need three days around the full moon off every month for the foreseeable future.

That's bullshit, the thing about full moons and about being Changed by a bite or scratch or something. And I only know that because of Ethan, who'd found it hilarious that it was such a *thing* in their lore and wished sometimes he could be openly were just so he could claim to need a few days off a month for *personal reasons*.

Fucking Ethan fucking Stone and his quick smile, strong hands, and golden tan skin that never seemed to burn. The constellation of freckles across his nose. The rough-soft way he'd kissed me all that summer, and how he loved to press me against that shit-brown car of his. And fucking hell, he was in my waiting room and would be in my office and *fuck*. Of all the fantasies I'd had since the summer I turned seventeen and Ethan fucking Stone decided I was worth his notice *finally*, meeting over two werewolf victims was never involved.

You're a grown-ass man, a doctor for crying out loud, and this is about the two poor victims in the exam room, not your wet dreams when you were a teenager. Get. It. Together.

Two deep breaths, smoothing my hands down my scrub top, and I was ready.

Ish.

Kind of.

The best thing to do, I decided on the extremely short walk from the exam room to the waiting area, was lean heavily on professionalism. It'd been over ten years, I reminded myself with each step. He moved on long ago. Probably before I even cleared the city limits.

Professional Polite Face firmly affixed, I stepped into the small, cold waiting area and held out my hand toward Sheriff Ethan fucking Stone. His back was to me when I entered (ha, don't think it, Landry, don't think it... too late), but he was still gorgeous. I didn't have to see his face to know that.

It had been over a decade, but he hadn't gone soft around the edges like a lot of guys in our age ranged tended to do. Ethan was still built like a brick shithouse. He had always towered over me even as teenagers, being easily six foot two by the time I left Tuttle. It looked like he'd grown a few more inches on top of that. I found myself standing straighter, an entire ballet corps of butterflies staging avant-garde productions in my stomach as he turned around. God damn it, still the most beautiful boy—no, man—I'd ever seen.

His green eyes went wide at the sight of me, and I had a niggle of satisfaction that he still found me somewhat attractive, even after so long. Ethan stared, lips parted, and that little satisfied feeling bloomed into a full-grown rosebush of smugness. He wasn't looking. He was *looking*. "Landry." He sounded warm and pleased. "Love the Hopper print," he said, gesturing at the picture hung over one of the sofas. "Reba here tells me you decorated the waiting area yourself. I like it. This shade of blue is really calming. Goes well with the green sofas."

The flutter in my belly called me a liar when I tried to remind myself that I didn't give two good damns about Ethan Stone anymore. So that left me with my one good option: lie my ass off by acting like I didn't know who he was, and hope he got in and out of my office before I made a fool of myself. "Sheriff. I understand you're here regarding the two bodies I have in my exam room. Come on through, and I'll—"

"Don't pretend like you don't remember me," Ethan said, a familiar (oh God, so familiar) smile curling the corners of his lips. "This how you're gonna talk to me after everything in high school?"

Shit. "Um."

"I thought you were being cagey," Reba sing-songed. She edged closer to me, nudging me with her elbow. "He said he didn't remember you, Sheriff, but Doctor Babin can't lie for shit." She laughed her trilling, sharp laugh and elbowed me again.

Ethan's smile was as slow and sweet as ever. I felt dirty—and not in a fun way—even noticing. He had his hands folded behind his back, parade rest, and was grinning down at me like we'd just seen one another yesterday and not years ago. Not after a shouting match that woke up his mama and brother and sent me crying back to my house.

"Well," I said, my voice a bit too high, too breathy, "you're here about the Raymonds. If you'll follow me, I can get the chain of custody handed over to you, and I'll give you my findings. Oh, Reba—"

"Already on it!" she said, her transcription equipment plugged in and ready to go. "I'll have it ready within the half hour."

Ethan was still smiling at me, but his brows were ever so slightly lower now. He was thinking hard. I knew that face. Oh Lord.

"Follow me, Sheriff," I said, plastering a pleasant, albeit businesslike, smile on my face. At least I was hoping it was pleasant and businesslike. Judging by the expression on Reba's face, I may have overshot and landed squarely in 'digestive problems forthcoming' territory.

I didn't look back, just barreled on ahead back into the lab and exam area, not stopping until I was past the tables and behind my small working desk. I grabbed my freshly printed findings from my desk. "Here are the hard copies," I said, trying to breathe. My chest was tight, like being in a wave pool and just on the edge of drowning, that weird little moment of panic where your brain tells you you're about to die. It wasn't just because Ethan fucking Stone was less than five feet away from me and certain parts of my body wanted to reduce that distance to eight inches or so (ahem). That stupid annoying bunny brain problem was back in full force.

Nausea nibbled around the edges of my awareness, my body exhausted and sick from spending a good part of the afternoon on high alert thanks to Big Red and the gang and now, Ethan fucking Stone—sorry, I mean *Sheriff* Ethan fucking Stone—was there and smelled *good*. Yeah, his aftershave was great and all, but I mean on a damn near molecular level. In a way Reba wouldn't be able to detect even if she climbed him like a tree and shoved her face in his neck (yeah, I saw the looks she was giving him, and she wasn't the only one who had a hard time hiding shit). It was imprinted on me, a part of me, weaving around inside me for years now. I'd be able to find him if I were blindfolded in a cavern under the earth just by smell alone.

I couldn't hear his pulse like he could mine (damn it), but I knew his was faster than average. Not because he was nervous. Because of what he was.

He sniffed, drawing in a deep breath through his nose that he had to know I'd notice, a small frown twisting his lips.

"And I'll email the digital copies to your office shortly," I added, suddenly aware that we'd been quiet for too long.

Ethan took the file folder from my hand (thank God it wasn't shaking yet) and tucked it under his arm. "Landry Babin," he murmured. "It's Thursday."

"Um..."

"Earlier. I heard you." He made a halfhearted gesture toward his right ear. "You know. The whole... senses thing." His brows were even lower now. I was surprised he could keep his eyes open under that glower. "Werewolf Wednesday. Who else has been around? I thought... well. Who else? Was Jessup by?"

"Jessup?" I jerked back, bumping into the edge of my desk. All pretense at businesslike behavior forgotten for the moment, I crossed my arms across my belly and didn't quite meet his eyes but managed to stare at a spot somewhere near his chin. "I haven't heard from Jessup since I left home."

"Hm. So, who was it then?"

A lie tickled my chin. He doesn't know about Big Red out

there. Maybe he gave up on trying to scare me, figured he marked his territory well enough and went on back to wherever he was going all dressed up. Maybe Ethan does know about him and is testing me, seeing if I'm gonna keep secrets still.

I tipped my chin up to meet his verdigris gaze and gave him a flat lipped smile. "You're not the only werewolf I know, Ethan." His eyes flared for just a brief second, something like interest or maybe possessiveness bright and clear. I didn't dwell on it, just filed it away for later so I could obsess instead of trying to sleep (because who was I kidding, thinking I'd just toddle off to bed tonight and *not* freak out about Ethan freaking Stone being in my lab?).

I grabbed a pair of gloves off my desk and snapped them on as I headed for the drawer holding Jessica Raymond. "I'm not going to pussyfoot around," I said, wincing inwardly because 'pussyfoot' totally negated the gruff, devil may care vibe I'd been trying to affect. "The Raymonds were definitely attacked, but you and I both know it wasn't a pack of feral dogs or even a wild hog." I unzipped the bag and a flicker of triumph shot through me when he winced and withdrew, turning his face toward my desk and breathing hard through his nose. Then guilt crept back in; I was using the demise of this poor woman to get one over on my ex... um. Whatever he was. "They both smell," I said. "They smell like werewolf, Ethan. There's no doubt in my mind."

Why hadn't he picked up on that himself before now, I wondered. Was he not involved in the original case? But he was the sheriff in a very small town. He'd have to have been there, at least to see the crime scene in situ—

"Shit." He sighed, closing his eyes. "Shit, shit, shit."

I closed her bag back up and reached for the other occupied drawer, only to have him wave me off. "The Raymonds, their folks, are screaming murder. The coroner is calling it a dog attack. We got a feral band running around down near the Thompson place." Glancing up at me, he added, "You remember that place, right?" His tone was noticeably different, softer but heavy.

The crap on my desk suddenly needed rearranging, and it was absolutely impossible for me to meet his gaze just then. Ethan wasn't asking if I remembered the creepy ass old farmhouse on Randall Road with the burned-out mattress in the yard and the overgrown acres that had once been a truck farm. He *wanted* to know if I remembered sneaking off in the middle of the night, being stupid with him, running across the narrow band of nut trees that made the southern border on the Thompson property, meeting him near the sluggish creek that was more mud than water. Hot, greedy hands and mouths, the damn near animal sounds as we'd pulled at clothes and nipped at skin, no words at all. His stare felt like fingers over my jaw, trying to turn my head. I dropped a box of paperclips, breaking whatever spell that was as they scattered down the desk and floor. "Fuck."

He rocked back on his heels; the intensity gone by the time I finally glanced back at him. "So, the thing is." Ethan sighed, raking his fingers (good God, stop staring!) through his thick, dark (oh my God, why doesn't he ever get it cut? Doesn't he know what I think about when I see it's long enough to grab?) hair. "The thing is the family's insisting on a full investigation. They want us to bring you out to see the crime scene."

"That's not my job. I'm not a CSI. Hell, I don't think Hitchens County *has* a CSI unit. Besides," I said, "there's literally nothing I could do, even if I came out and saw where the bodies were found. My job is here. I just verify findings, perform autopsies. That's it."

"That's simplifying things," he grumbled. He flipped open the file folder, but I knew he wasn't reading a damn thing. He was just staring down at the pages, thinking hard again. "Look, I know this is weird but—"

"Stop. Just... stop." God, it hurt to do this, but I had to. I didn't want to, but I knew it was the only way. "Being cool for the summer once years ago doesn't mean we have to, I don't know, act sweet now. We're both grown men with real life jobs, and duties and responsibilities, none of which involve making nice with one another because of a few mutual hand jobs when we were teenagers!"

Ethan didn't slam the folder down. He set it carefully on the edge of my desk and took two steps toward me. He wasn't crowding me yet, but he was close. I heard the faintest growling rumble low in his throat and smell the wolf on him, the sweet-sharp-musky-wild smell of earth, and green, and animal that no one else ever seemed to notice. *How could they not know about him? How? It's so obvious.*

"You're lying to yourself if you think that's all it was," he said in a soft, calm voice. "Now, I know for a fact you don't have a huge case load to deal with right now, and I know you're damn well aware how important it is we keep this"—he jerked his chin in the direction of the Raymonds— "quiet as possible. Come out to Tuttle tonight. See the scene. Shut the parents up, let them bury their children, and let us deal with tracking down who did this after the dust settles."

"It's a bad idea. Like, beyond bad. If I get caught out there—"

"I won't let that happen."

It was tempting, for all the wrong reasons. The biggest one being the word *us*. I knew he didn't mean *us,* as in me and him, but *us* as in the small clan of werewolves in Tuttle. Ethan and his family, the Dorians, the MacIntyres, and... maybe Big Red? Maybe that's why he and his sidekicks were lurking around? Had they come to see what they could find out? The idea seized hold of me, and for a few seconds, I didn't feel the fluttering in my belly, the way my heart seemed to go liquid and hot under Ethan's sharp gaze. "Did you come alone?"

Ethan jerked back, his face going through so many expressions so fast, it was almost funny. "Why?" he asked cautiously.

Was I mistaken or did he sound a little hopeful? I flatter myself.

"Look, I'll do what I can with the Raymonds," I said, pointing to the exam room and extinguishing the brief flare of hope in his eyes. "But I'm not going out to the scene. Not right now, not while things are still too high risk. You're right. You're not the only were I've seen today." It wasn't even close to quitting time, but I needed privacy for this conversation. "You got a few minutes before you need to head back to town? There's something I need to tell you, and I don't need Reba hearing."

Chapter Two

"So... Sheriff Stone..."

"No."

Reba made a hmming noise as she handed me the stack of death certificates to sign. "I need to get these out by tomorrow morning, so get your rubber stamp warmed up." She added a few cremation release forms and an autopsy request to the pile before turning back to her monitor and bringing up her transcription program.

I knew better than to say it, but I said it anyway. Her refusal to pursue the matter was just plain weird. "That's it?" I asked after she fiddled with the headset for a moment, took a sip of her coffee, and squished around to get comfortable in her seat. "You're not gonna bug me about Sheriff Stone?"

"What's to bug you about? You said no. And you also said you barely remember him from high school." She flashed me a sunny smile, shrugged, and hit play on the recording to transcribe.

"Okay," I drawled. *Five, four, three...*

"And, I mean, the fact you turned the color of skim milk as soon as you knew the sheriff was Ethan Stone, this guy you barely remember... who doesn't even bear mentioning."

Here we go. It was a bit of a relief, to be honest. I needed to vent, damn it, and Reba was great at this. I just couldn't let on the real reason why I was so annoyed with Ethan fucking Stone. Well, the current reason. I was sure there'd be more reasons soon.

When I told him about the three weres from earlier in the day, he grunted 'huh' and said he'd 'check into it.' He stopped just short of patting me on the head and telling me to be good and stop worrying. Okay, maybe he wasn't going to do that, but the idea that he *might* sure did take root fast and hard. "It was a long morning," I said, raising a brow. "And I'm naturally pale. I can't help it. My body freckles instead of tans."

"Hmph. Okay, then. I guess I don't need to mention him fishing for your relationship status."

Whoa there. "He what now?" The files could wait a minute. My patients weren't going anywhere.

Reba managed to restrain her smile to a bare smirk as I sat down in the chair across the desk from her. "When he showed up after your lunch break, he asked if you were back yet or still out to lunch with, and I quote, your 'boyfriend or husband or whatever.'"

My wince was mostly unintentional. "Yikes. Real smooth, sheriff."

"Don't you want to know what I told him?"

"The truth? That I was back and in the exam room?"

"Of course!" She pressed her pink-tipped fingers to her breastbone, the very picture of affronted professionalism. "I said, 'Well, sir, he's back there with the Raymonds waiting on you.'"

I nodded. "Good, good. That's good. I mean, whether or not I'm attached has no bearing on his visit, and it was really out of line for him to even try to find out."

"Mmhmm." She waited until I was back on my feet again and almost to the door adjoining the lab area before adding, "Oh, and I also mentioned that you were out to lunch alone because you just hadn't found someone to share your sandwich with."

Ugh. My face grew hot at the thought of that exchange. I could imagine Ethan's smug little smile, how it would crinkle the corners of his eyes. The beard was new to me, though. I wondered if that would soften the smugness at all, or just make it worse.

"You know, compared to you, Sheriff Stone's fishing expedition *was* smooth. That was awful, Reba!"

"Maybe so," she trilled, "but he damn near got a cramp in his jaw from grinning so hard at that."

"Get back to work!" Her laugh followed me into the lab, the heavy thunk of the door closing behind me cutting off the warm, liquid sound of her amusement. We only had the Raymonds on site and, until their next of kin made arrangements for their move to the funeral home or crematorium, there was nothing else I could do for them. Even with the drawers closed and locked, I could smell the faint tinge of were that had been on the bodies. It was nothing like Ethan's scent or even that of the handful of other weres I'd met over the years. It was sour. *Wrong*. Like someone had tried to synthesize the smell of a werewolf and missed by a margin.

I wanted to ask Ethan about that, if the wrongness of the scent had anything to do with the bodies themselves or if it was particular to the were who had killed them. Ethan had taken off like a shot, though, once I had dragged him out to my tiny little hatchback for privacy and given him a rundown of my lunch break. I'm not sure what I'd expected, but it was sure more than the response I got. Thinking about it made me angry all over again.

He came all the way out here from Belmarais, I thought, signing off on the cremation release forms, then took off like a bat out of hell before we could really discuss the Raymonds. I had questions, damn it! Like why didn't he twig to the fact that was no dog attack? If I could smell the wrong, so could he! I wasn't even a real werewolf, and I could tell one of them had been all over those poor kids. And why wasn't he more worried about that fact?

There were a handful of werewolves living within an hour's drive of Belmarais, last I knew, and even if he *was* related to most of them, they should all be suspects when two were victims turned up in the vicinity. Weres could be aggressive with one another, especially over perceived territory and clan wrongs or rights, sometimes dating back decades or more. But it was almost unheard of for them to kill another were. There were so few as it was, Ethan had explained to me once, that no matter how wronged a were was, the instinct to preserve what was left of the clans usually meant the most aggressive, violent fights ended in minor bloodshed and broken bones rather than murder.

I grabbed my stamp and began reviewing the death certificates, double checking the information against the files saved to the database. Three strange weres show up the day I get two were victims in my morgue, my ex (fine, yes, my ex; even though we'd never been officially anything, we'd been *something*) who also just happened to be a damn werewolf comes barreling into town and says he had no idea I was the new coroner on staff. Okay, to be fair, I had no idea he was the sheriff back in Belmarais, but I'd only just moved back a few months before and the job was kind of sudden and unplanned.

But Ethan had been just so weird about the three weres. Werewolves are rare. I mean, obviously, otherwise everyone would know about them, and they wouldn't have to be all sneaky and shit. But they're rare to the point of running into more than one outside of clan territory is downright unheard of. And the clans themselves are tiny. The one Ethan belonged to only had twelve members.

Running into a lone wolf (ha, I am so funny) wasn't necessarily unheard of, but again, rare. So rare that the very few times in my life it had happened, I wasn't sure who was more shocked: me, noticing a werewolf nearby, or the were knowing they'd been spotted. The few weres I'd run into outside of Ethan's clan had been experts at diversion, pretending they had no idea I'd recognized the wolf in them, acting like I wasn't a curiosity myself. Lots of tight-lipped smiles, careful not-touching, quick exits.

Except when they weren't. Except when they decided I might

be something fun to play with, a human that recognized them for what they really were.

That's what was so off about the weres that morning, I realized. They hadn't been surprised. Not really. Curious, surprisingly aggressive, but not surprised to be recognized. In fact, they'd done nothing to deny it when they'd realized they'd been made. Red had been about ten seconds from piss-marking the deli from the looks of things. His two quiet buddies would have bared teeth and growled if they could've gotten away with it.

I pulled the Raymonds back out from their temporary resting places, unzipping them both where they lay on the metal trays, side by side. After a moment's hesitation, I took my desk chair to the exam room door and wedged it under the handle. The building was old, only retrofitted in some places with security measures and nice lab equipment (well, as nice as a small county in East Texas could afford).

The door to the exam area didn't have a good lock to it. One solid push from someone strong enough could pop the latch easily. Reba wouldn't be able to shove the door open even if she got a full head of steam from across the waiting area and really threw her back into it. Still, I needed to hurry. There'd be no way to explain what I was doing if she *did* manage to open the door to check on me.

I returned to the Raymonds, closed my eyes, and tried to open the small space inside myself where I kept my otherness, the weird part of me that was not really a werewolf but sure liked to act like it could be. Those prey instincts ratcheted up, the first twinge of *hunter* skittering across my awareness as I bent close to Jessica and inhaled slowly, deeply.

The scent was even fainter than before. The odor of death and nascent decay barely held in check by the morgue's refrigerated storage drawers. I shifted to Thomas and repeated the scenting, memorizing the trace odor. The desire, the damn near *need* to run burned in my muscles, making them ache from forced stillness. I needed to run. The prey part of my brain was screaming. Get away from whatever did this, run like hell and don't stop till I couldn't smell this wolf, this thing, anymore.

Swallowing down hot bile and acid, I closed the bags back up and returned the Raymonds to their places in the storage unit. My skin was clammy, and I knew I stank to high heaven with fear-sweat, that slick and oily sheen that comes on when humans are truly afraid. Heart hammering dangerously fast, I sank down to the floor and put my head between my knees. The chair needed to be moved, I reminded myself. No time for hiding. Still, I thought, closing my eyes and trying to calm my breathing, it could wait a few more minutes.

"I THOUGHT YOU'D DIED IN THERE," REBA MUTTERED. A few more minutes had become sixty, and I'd only lurched to my feet when Reba had tried to open the door to ask me to walk her to her car. She'd glanced at the chair sitting where I'd shoved it aside before yanking open the door she was pounding on and grunting under her breath something about sniffing the embalming fluid.

"We don't have embalming fluid in the exam room," I reminded her, grabbing my bag and coat with hands that still shook a bit. My shirt stuck to my back with dried sweat, and the smell of the were was stuck in my sinuses as we locked down the office for the evening. Hitchens County was small enough where we got by with one coroner (that would be me), and Justin DuBois, who was technically my assistant but only took the weekend shift and occasional afternoons when the paperwork got overwhelming, and we needed more hands.

"So, you tell me," she snapped, though there was no real heat in the words. "C'mon, I'm late to meet Brian and I don't want to hear about how dinner got overcooked waiting on me."

We fell into step beside one another, saying goodbye to the

night guard at the front desk as we exited onto the sidewalk. Despite being a small town, all things considered, Tuttle was fairly busy for a Thursday evening. Every parking spot on the street was taken, and knots of people were already moving between the few restaurants the tiny downtown area had to offer. It was early evening, barely six, but music drifted from the small venue at the far end of Hyssop where it ran into Center Street. Reba was going on about Brian's newfound love of *Kitchen Challenge*, her voice soothing and a nice distraction from the sick feeling that had been crawling through my body after scenting the Raymonds. I couldn't do much, but at least I could know their killer if I ever ran into them.

It was something I could do that Ethan and most other weres I'd met couldn't. They might be able to scent one another, tell in broad strokes information about a fellow were, but they couldn't get the details like I could. It was one of the first things Ethan noticed when he realized I was haunting his steps at the end of our junior year. Not only could I smell *him*, but I knew things about him just from how his scent changed. I thought it was kind of gross and sad that my weirdness made me a good stalker. He thought it was adorable.

Reba and I reached the parking lot on Hyssop a few blocks down from the office and paused near her car. "You okay, Doc? I mean, really. You've been kind of twitchy since lunch, and... well. The exam room earlier..." She fidgeted with her purse strap, not quite meeting my eyes. "There's no shame in admitting something's wrong. Trust me. I know it's hard but... well." She glanced up quickly, nothing but concern and sympathy in her eyes.

"I'm fine," I lied.

And she knew it was a lie. Her worried expression pinched a bit, her lips pursing and eyes narrowing. But she didn't call me on it.

"I just need more rest. Still getting my feet under me. It's been kind of a big change, going from working as an assistant to the medical examiner in Little Rock to being the official county coroner back home." There. Redeemed the lie with a little truth. I tried a smile, and it must have looked as bad as it felt because she sighed and shook her head at me.

"I'm not telling you what to do, but I know for a fact this job came with some sick days built in, so if you decided to call in tomorrow and just have a mental health day, I'm not gonna say that's a bad thing."

"Reba, I promise, I'm fine!" My smile must have been more convincing that time around. She sighed, nodded once, and bundled herself into her car. By the time I made it back to the sidewalk, heading toward where I'd parked closer to the office, she was already peeling out of the parking lot, blasting eighties dance hits. Rolling my neck in vain, refusing to acknowledge that the knot of tension just below my skull might be lodged there permanently, I pressed the button on the fob unlock my car door, hissing as I dropped the key and had to bend to scoop it off the asphalt.

"Are you sure you're okay?"

My scream was definitely very butch and loud. Not at all a thin, terrified meep. I wasn't stupid. I knew, despite my muscles, I would lose a fight with Big Red. He towered over me by several inches and was built enough to make Ethan look like a stick figure. He'd also managed to approach upwind so I couldn't cotton to his approach. "The sheriff's department knows you've been stalking me. I told Sheriff Stone earlier."

"Whoa, easy dude!" Red threw up his hands, smirking uneasily. "I know I was a huge dick this morning, and I want to apologize!"

I pointed at him with my keys between my fingers, Wolverine-style. "Step away." He took a giant step backward. "Keep moving. I'll tell you when to stop." Red rolled his eyes but took several more steps back, stopping only when he bumped against an Econoline that had seen better days. "I'm going to take my phone out and dial the sheriff. You're going to stand there."

"I'm not stalking you." He sighed, hands still raised. We stared one another down as I fished my phone out of my hip pocket, belatedly realizing that I did not have Ethan's number programmed in. *Damn it. Old habits. Shit.*

I glanced down quickly, bringing up the number for the Hitchens County Sheriff's Department on my phone's browser app. Red stood exactly as I'd left him when I looked back up. "I don't care what you think you're doing, it's harassment. You and your friends in the deli this morning, showing up outside of my work, and now this? Hey! I didn't say move!" He had lowered one hand to his hip, shifting his weight to one side. "Hands. Up."

"I'm getting out my business card." He sighed. "I probably should have led with that, huh?" He slowly removed a brown leather wallet from his hip pocket, never breaking eye contact as he opened it and removed one card. "Here." I hesitated. He rolled his eyes again and dropped to a squat, reaching as far as he could and placing the card on the ground. "Read it before you hit send on that call." He pressed himself back against the van and lifted his hands again, waiting.

I inched forward until I could reach the card with the toe of my shoe, pulling it back across the gravel toward me. I quickly crouched to grab it and stood back up, putting distance between myself and Red again. "Oliver Waltrip, Private Investigator. Licensed in Texas. Okay. So, you're... what? In town with your sidekicks, trying to drum up business by scaring the shit out of locals?"

"Can I put my hands down?" He nodded in the direction of my Wolverine claws. "I mean, I know I could technically overpower you, take those away, and use them against you, but I want you to feel safe in this discussion, so I thought I'd ask before I dropped my hands and you got stabby."

"Just for that, I should make you keep 'em up." I lowered my keys, though I didn't put them away. "If you're a legit PI, you have a license. Show it to me."

He made a face, nose wrinkling and lips twisting like he'd tasted something bitter. "It's not like a fucking driver's license. I don't carry it in my wallet! You can check with the state licensing authority or, hell, come to my office in Dallas and I'll show it to you. It's in a nice frame on the wall near the door." Red—Waltrip, rather—swayed forward on the balls of his feet, stopping himself just before he had to take a step or lose his balance. "I know I was a dick earlier, but I had a reason."

Yeah, no. Not playing this. "Okay, well, that's awesome, but I'm not interested." I shoved the card into my hip pocket and brandished my keys again. "Stay there. You move, and I'll—"

"Unlock me?"

"I was going to say stab you with a dirty scalpel but sure, let's call it that. I'm leaving now. If I see you around here again, I'm calling the cops. I don't care how nice a frame your license is in back in Dallas."

I was loath to turn my back on him, but I had no other choice if I wanted to get in my car. He stood still, though, staring. My body screamed at me to hide, to go still, something, anything, just make the predator *stop hunting us.* Instead, I swallowed against the nausea, promised myself at least two cold beers once I got home, and unlocked my car. I threw my bag into the passenger seat before turning to face Waltrip once more. "I don't care how good you think your reason was. You fucking stalked and terrorized me. You and your little friends. I'm calling your licensing board and the cops to report you once I'm out of here and safe."

"That's fine," he said, voice infuriatingly calm. "I just need to let you know that I'm looking into the Raymonds. I have questions."

Shit. Shit, shit, shit shitty shit, shit. "I'm off the clock," I said. "Call tomorrow and the office secretary can schedule you an appointment." And I'd make damn sure I had Ethan on hand for it, too.

Red smiled, the expression completely transforming him. He looked good, damn it, and I hated that I noticed. At least when he was scowling or giving me that damned 'I'm humoring you' bland expression, he looked too gruff, too brutal. But smiling? He looked like one of those hot Scottish guys who throw giant logs around for fun. Damn it.

"I'll do that," he said.

Tilting his head to one side, he inhaled slow and deep. My legs didn't move, no matter how hard I tried. I wanted to get in the car and drive off while he did his little dominance display, sniffing the air for my scent and posturing to show off his larger size, but that stupid bunny part of me just stood there, frozen somewhere between fear and—goddammit—interest.

"I've never been wrong before," he finally said. "And I don't think I am now, not really, but this morning, I could've sworn you were like me. Now..." He sniffed again, not as deep but twice as loud, making it obvious. "Now, I'm not sure we're as much alike as I thought."

"Well. On that odd little note," I said with a forced laugh. "Make the appointment. I'll answer what I can but keep in mind, even though my patients are dead, they still have privacy rights." I moved then, final-fucking-ly, and got into my car, locking the door before I started the engine. I didn't look back at him again, but I knew he stared at me as I tore out of the parking lot.

Friday flew past. I was proud of myself for not asking Reba about Waltrip calling until almost the end of the day. Sometime during the early part of my shift, two hearses from Tuttle Family Funerals and Crematorium arrived, and the Raymonds went home. The rest of my hours were filled with paperwork, phone calls, and inventory checks. Justin had skipped out on those, too, apparently. Reba muttered about writing him up, but so far, he hadn't done anything fireable. Just shitty.

Anxiety is the better part of valor or however the saying goes. Rather than going to grab lunch, I dove headfirst into my backlog of administrative paperwork to avoid seeing anyone, even Reba. At ten to five, I gathered up my bag and a few journals I wanted to read at home, shut down my computer, and headed for the reception area. Reba was already waiting by the door, texting with impressive speed considering the length of her nails.

"Hey, I meant to ask. Do I have any meetings scheduled next week?"

"Just the usual weekly one with the hospital folks on Monday at St. Dymphna's Memorial and a lunch thing with some funeral director group on Tuesday at La Cheval over in Tyler." She looked up from her phone and frowned. "Were you supposed to? Did I miss something?" She started to head back to her desk, but I stopped her with a hand on her shoulder.

"No, it's okay. I was just double checking. It's been a weird week."

She waited until we were past the night guard and almost to the sidewalk before asking slyly, "Expecting a call from the sheriff? Were y'all gonna *meet up*?"

"Good Lord! If you bat your lashes any hard, you're going to achieve lift off!" Reba snorted but elbowed me, winking. "The Raymonds' deaths are going to have a lot of questions heading our way."

"Oh, that's so true." She sighed. "I feel so bad for not thinking about that! Do you think whoever owns those dogs will be charged with murder?"

We'd made it to our cars, parked next to one another today. There was no sign of Waltrip lurking in the parking lot, and my senses told me the only other creatures nearby were definitely of the non-predator variety. Safe.

"Folks at the sheriff's department said it looked like wild dogs," I replied carefully, not wanting to lie and dig myself a hole. "If it was wild dogs, there are no owner to charge. Poor things will be put down, though."

Reba tutted, fishing her keys from her cavernous purse.

"Well, it's a damn shame, is what it is. Those kids are barely older than my sister, and I can't imagine her..." She shook her head. "I know it's part of the job, but some of these deaths are just a little too close to home."

We parted a few minutes later, her heading toward what passed for downtown Tuttle, and me heading for my tiny house on the outskirts of the city, just before it turned into miles of forest interspersed with small farms. It was early enough in the evening that traffic was light, even for Tuttle, and I made it home in record time, pulling into the open carport next to the house.

As soon as I stepped out of the car, my senses went on high alert. *Freeze, hide, get under the car, don't move!*

"Shit." The word came out as barely a tremor of sound. Next door, the sound of Mrs. Hudson's TV blaring the evening news out of Tyler was loud through her open window. I could smell the chili mac she was making for dinner and the sweet-sour smell of something slightly off in her kitchen. Milk a little too close to being bad, maybe. She was humming, moving around, talking to someone in another part of the house.

I closed my eyes against my better judgment and tried to focus, filtering her out and letting my senses reach for whatever was hunting me, sending my awareness into overdrive. I breathed in slowly, letting the evening smells wash through me, picking them out one by one. Grass, hot car, drying earth, my herb garden, a cat pissed in the roses again, cold charcoal in the grill, wood rot sneaking through the walls, rodents, asphalt...

And there. There it was. Fading fast. Sour-animal-hunter-*wrong*. The smell that had been on the Raymonds.

The killer. The were. They'd been here, outside my house.

The smell wasn't strong, maybe a few hours old, meaning they'd crept around while I was at work. Taking a step toward my back door, I stopped myself mid-stride. *Don't be stupid. You know how this goes. Call the police first!*

And tell them what? Hey, I'm kind of a werewolf but without the cool parts and my super senses tell me a killer was sneaking around my house. Oh, how do I know? Well, I sniffed two corpses yesterday and—

Yeah, calling the cops would go well. Okay. I had to do it myself, I reasoned, taking another step and hating how my pulse made my ears ache with its intensity.

Or... you know, you can call a specific cop. And see if he'd be willing to come check this out. And, you know, hang out and talk. Reconnect.

"Great. About to be murdered and I'm considering a booty call." Next door, something clattered in Mrs. Hudson's kitchen, and I jumped, jerking my head around to see the source of the noise. Mrs. Hudson started cussing up a storm at Bitsy, her mutt that liked to jump on the kitchen table, and I blew out a long breath. Until I checked my house out and knew it was safe, being calm was a pipe dream. Raking my fingers through my thick blond hair and making it stick out in just about every direction, I muttered, "C'mon, Landry. You got this."

Great. I was talking in third person. The hallmark of someone who's 'got this.'

I made it all the way to my front door before a car crunched up my gravel drive, stopping me in my tracks. A low-slung, shiny, dark-blue car that looked way too fine for Tuttle pulled up behind my little Fiesta, the driver giving me a wave as he shut off the engine.

"Well, fuck me," I muttered. "Speak of the devil and he shall appear."

Chapter Three

"**O**h, thank God!"

Ethan paused, still half in his car. "I honestly wasn't expecting such an enthusiastic greeting. Accusations of stalking maybe but not praise to a deity." He stood fully, holding up a cardboard carrier. "I brought a local IPA, thought maybe we could have a few drinks?"

"I need you!"

His grin was slow and familiar, and very, very hot. "Very definitely not expecting that." Folding his arms, he leaned against his truck and nodded at my house. "Like the color scheme you've got going on here. Really works with the midcentury style of the house." He nodded, pleased with what he was seeing. "A lot of people get these post-war VA homes and start stripping 'em down to modernize the exterior. Glad you kept the aesthetic." He flashed me a bright smile. "Now, what's this about needing me? Care to elaborate?"

My face was a lovely shade of beetroot, heat spreading up my chest to my neck before suffusing across my cheeks. Ethan's quick grin did nothing to help my embarrassment. And if my previous experiences with Ethan were any indication, there was no way he was going to let me forget the double entendre *or* my blush.

"I need your help," I corrected, baring my teeth in a parody of his grin. He laughed but got the rest of the way out of his car and came to me with an easy lope that would have looked ridiculous on almost anyone else. He stopped just out of arm's reach and fell into an easy posture, hip cocked and arms loosely folded. I wasn't fooled, though.

He wasn't waiting. He was *waiting*.

His gaze flickered from my house, curiosity evident in his expression, to Mrs. Hudson's where the clatter and rush of the dinner hour was now in full swing, then back to me, his brow quirking in a silent question.

"I think whoever killed the Raymonds was here earlier."

He startled, jerking up straight so fast, I was surprised nothing popped. I told him quickly what I'd noticed, and he gave me a curt nod, striding away from me and toward the back of the carport where it opened into the small yard I shared with the Hudsons. He was gone less than five minutes, leaving me standing alone and awkward in my own driveway. He came jogging back with a grim set to his mouth, brows drawn and expression dark.

"Is your house unlocked?"

"Uh, no? I mean, I locked it when I left this morning but—"

He cut me off, holding out his hand, wiggling his fingers. It took me a second to realize he wanted my keys.

"You could use your words like a big boy, you know." I dropped the ring into his hand anyway. Ethan sighed gustily and started picking through the keys before I had pity on him. "The silver one with the pink dot of nail polish on top."

He hesitated for a moment, glancing up at the house and then back at me. "I know I'm going to hate myself for this in a minute but come inside with me. You'll be able to tell me if anything is off."

He honestly thought I was about to let him go in there without me? "To be frank, I was planning on following you in," I admitted, brushing past him closely enough to get a good, hard hit of his smell, bergamot and sandalwood and salt-sweat-skin. *Get it together, Landry!* "Just let you flush out the killers first."

"Thanks," he drawled. "Glad to be useful."

The déjà vu hit hard. We'd had a very similar conversation That Summer (yes, it was worth the capitals). I had gotten home from work, a part time thing at the dinky little Dairy Queen knock-off in Belmarais, to find my house standing wide open from front door to back when no one was home. I'd turned my bike (because I was that kid) around and high tailed it to Ethan's, begged him to come back with me and check out the house. *"I don't wanna call the cops. Aunt Cleverly would flip if they got all up in her shit and there wasn't anything wrong."* Ethan had thrown on his shirt (and he was *that* guy, never owned a shirt he didn't take off and throw in the corner as soon as he could) and made me put my bike in the back of his truck.

Back at the house I shared with Aunt Cleverly, he'd walked around the outside, making me stay back at the truck before telling me to follow him into the house and see if anything seemed out of place. We'd gone through every room and cupboard, even the tiny little closet where the water heater lived. Nothing was gone or moved. Ethan had declared that the door probably didn't catch on the latch as Cleverly left for her shift earlier that day and the wind had blown it open, but I couldn't shake the uneasy feeling someone had been there, looking around.

We'd gone back to his place, ignored his brothers, and hung out in his room till my aunt was home from work. And by hung out, I mean we had hot, sweaty monkey sex for hours with the enthusiasm only newly out teenagers who just figured out what their dicks were for could muster.

The walk through my house was haunted by the ghosts of that moment in time. Everything was still locked tight, Ethan using the key on the deadbolt to let us in. Not a thing was out of place, down to the sock I'd aimed at the laundry basket that morning and missed. Still, I couldn't shake the feeling.

"You ever go into a room, and you know someone was just in

there but left like the second you walked in?" I asked once we rounded back into my small kitchen. Ethan took a seat at the table as I headed for the fridge, accepting the beer I held out in his direction. "That's what I feel right now."

"I'm not trying to downplay your concerns," he said carefully, taking the open beer I offered him, "but I think it's possible you're projecting a bit."

Sinking into the chair across from him, I tried not to be annoyed. It's possible I failed, because my next words made the scowl between his eyebrows deepen. "You think I'm crazy again?"

"Landry, I never thought you were crazy. Never." He didn't quite meet my eyes, looking at my shoulder instead. "I said some shitty things but that was... Hell, a lifetime ago, almost. I'd hoped you'd have moved past that by now."

"Wow. That's kind of shitty, you know?" I took a deep pull of my beer, wincing at the acrid, sour bite of it. "Are you over it?" I asked, cutting him off when he spoke. "I mean, that whole thing? Not just us fucking like rabbits."

"Which part?" he asked, setting his beer aside and leaning forward, forearms resting against the table. He pinned me with the intensity of his glare. "The part where you lost your shit and told me to go to hell? Or the part where you broke my heart and took off to fucking Baltimore before I got back to town?" Ethan blew out a rough breath, leaning back to scrub at his eyes with the heels of his hands. "I guess we can safely say the answer to that question is no," he murmured. "Sorry. For about a second before I opened my mouth, I really thought the only thing I was going to say is 'yeah, no big deal, water under the bridge' or something bro-y like that."

"I think having our dicks in each other's mouths for the better part of four months put us past bro status some time ago." I took another pull of my beer, staring at him over the bottle. He smirked, shook his head, and ducked his face away. I could see the pink tinge to his ears and felt myself unbend just a tiny bit inside. "I'm not going to apologize for everything. I thought..." I trailed off, rolling my mostly empty bottle back and forth between my hands. "I believed you when you said I was just an experiment."

"Jesus, Landry. You know—"

"No, I didn't. Hell, I trailed around after you like a hungry dog after a bone for the better part of middle school and high school. Everyone knew I had a thing for you. When you got interested in me, I jumped on it because, hell, it was every damn wet dream I'd had come true."

Ethan set his bottle down carefully, lips parting on something unspoken before he shook his head, closing his eyes like he wanted to block me out but couldn't.

"When I told you about me, about..." I gestured vaguely at my temple. My little 'problem' had been a mental one—or at least I thought so back then. Like my mom, like my grandma. None of us Babins were right in the head, and everyone in Belmarais knew it and loved to remind me about it. "You didn't freak out on me. You treated me the same as ever. I thought I'd died and gone to heaven." I laughed, raising my bottle to my lips. Damn thing was empty. How'd that happen?

Ethan raised his brow again, damn it, and glanced from me to the fridge. Daring me to get more liquid courage. I sighed and settled back in my chair. Best to get over this and get all the dirty laundry aired before we had to work together again.

"The most beautiful boy I'd ever seen, the one I had been dreaming about day and night since I figured out my girls-are-yucky phase wasn't a phase, not only liked me back but didn't think I was one of the headcase Babins? Didn't tell me all this weird shit happening to me was my brain being broken? Shit, I thought I'd hit the lotto."

Ethan huffed, something between a laugh and sigh. "I thought you were a were, like me." His beer was empty, too. I knew he wasn't feeling it at all. A benefit of being were was a very fast metabolism. Beer buzzes never lasted longer than a minute or so, if even that long, and even then, it would have taken a tremendous amount of beer, not one bottle of the shitty light beer I kept in my fridge. Still, I blamed the alcohol for the look he gave me, all blown pupil and unwavering focus. "I thought you were being coy with me whenever I hinted around about it. I didn't realize you had no idea."

"Not until Tyler." I sighed.

"Fucking Tyler."

Apparently, everyone in the Stone family had thought I was a were, too. I just thought they were being antsy around me because of my family's reputation, but they were being paranoid about a new wolf in town, one from a family with no history of weres in the bloodlines. Tyler, bless his little heart, decided to force my hand one day, make me prove I wasn't trying to encroach on pack territory or something. Walked right into the den where Ethan and I were definitely not having a sneaky grope underneath a blanket, no sir, and shifted right in front of me. Looked me dead in the eyes and shifted. Everyone on the block heard my scream.

That was the beginning of the end as far as Ethan and I went. He pried it out of me, the details about my little problem. Heightened senses, the increased prey reactions—what I referred to as my scared rabbit brain, my ability to tell when someone wasn't 'right.' Ethan's acceptance of my differences became strained, stilted. He never shamed me for them, but he started testing me, it seemed. Pushing my buttons.

It all came to a head when he snapped at me, accused me of being afraid of my wolf side, holding myself back. We started to excel at makeup sex, tearful fights always ending in orgasms. Even then, I knew it wasn't healthy, but I was seventeen. No one has ever accused seventeen-year-olds of making great decisions.

Ethan was caught in the same tangle of memories as me, apparently, because he reached across the table and tapped one finger against the back of my hand where it rested next to my empty beer bottle. "You were never an experiment for me. I know what I said, and it was shitty. But you were never... It was never like that. I didn't need to 'find out' if I was gay or not. I knew I was."

"To be honest, I thought maybe the experiment was whether or not you could be with someone who wasn't like you." I nodded, eyes prickling. It was something I'd figured out a long time ago about Ethan, that he'd lied to me that day about just using me for sex. He wanted to hurt me, to hurt *us*, but I never understood why.

Now or never.

"Why, then?"

"Jesus, Landry." He sighed, letting his head fall back against the top of the chair. "You scared the hell out of me. Out of all of us. There you were, oblivious as all get out, waltzing into the middle of a pack of weres without a care in the world. And when I figured out you weren't one of us, even though everything in me was screaming that you were?" He shook his head, the finger on the back of my hand pressing down a bit more firmly. I was a butterfly, and he was the pin. "My family was on my ass about you soon as I told them you weren't like us. My father—he went 'round to every damn pack in driving distance. Wanted to talk to the heads of families in person, see their faces to make sure they weren't lying to him when he asked about you."

"I remember Aunt Cleverly getting pissy about your dad," I murmured, unable to look away from where our bodies touched, however minutely. "Said he was full of himself and needed to get his head out of his ass." Ethan made a choked, amused noise. "I know she didn't think y'all were anything other than plain old human. I know your father didn't ask my God-fearing, church-going aunt if she had a werewolf in her spare bedroom."

There was that sound again. Definitely amused. "You know how many weres are God-fearing church goers?" he teased. "And if I recall correctly, he asked her if you had some sort of, in his words, 'mental defect or some shit.'"

"Seriously? Cleverly must've loved that. She was always worried people would think I was weird, or she'd messed me up somehow." My aunt hadn't exactly been overprotective, but she'd definitely been cautious, making sure I was as aggressively normal as possible in the eyes of the community. Afterschool job, check. Hobbies, check. Dinner at a decent hour, check. Homework, chores, neat appearance, check, check, check.

Ethan grunted softly. "He was convinced by that point you were just refusing to accept your true nature and had somehow gotten stuck."

"Stuck?" I finally looked up at him. He looked away so quickly I knew I'd almost caught him staring. "Half were, half human? Like Eddie Munster or something?" I laughed, turning my hand palm-up without thinking. He froze for just a split second, long enough for me to realize what I'd done, but he didn't pull back. Ethan uncurled his fingers and laid his hand against mine. It was the most awkward, heart-flutteringly wonderful hand holding I'd had in a while.

"We do not speak of Eddie Munster," he sniffed. "Besides, he was supposed to be fully werewolf." Ethan made a face, and I laughed again. Our amusement petered out after a few seconds, though, and we sat in hesitant quiet for several more before Ethan spoke again. "But when I finally got back..."

"I'd graduated." I sighed. "I couldn't stand it there after you'd gone."

His expression shuttered, but he didn't move his hand away. "From what I was told, you drowned your sorrows with Patrick Morris pretty damned quick."

"Patrick Morris?" My lips curled in disgust at the very mention. The man had been mean as a rabid dog when we were in high school, and the years hadn't improved him. "Who the hell told you... Oh, wait. Your brothers?"

Ethan had the good grace to look mildly ashamed. "Yeah. Tyler and Stephen both said they saw you and Patrick at the lake, down by Breyer's Cove."

Slowly, I curled my fingers around his palm. His hands had always been larger than mine, rougher too, and that hadn't changed at all over the years. He tensed in my grasp before slowly relaxing against me. Nervousness rolled off him in waves. He shifted his weight, a subtle movement but obvious to me, rocking onto the balls of his feet as if ready to flee. Or pounce. Ethan's gaze darted from my mouth to my eyes and back again before settling at some indistinct point on my face. There was the faintest hitch to his breath. I wondered how my own uncertainty felt to him, if it fluttered like hummingbird wings or crackled like static.

His sizzled along my awareness like water on a hot griddle, popping and rushing as he took deliberate, slow breaths. His dark green eyes were narrowed, his body tense. He was waiting, poised.

"The night you left and every damned night after, I stayed home. Until the day I left for college, my entire life consisted of going to school, going to work, coming home, repeat."

"So, what you're saying is... I've been an ass for going on fifteen years now."

"Hey. Don't be like that." I leaned forward, squeezing his fingers in mine. "You've been an ass for much longer than that."

Ethan's snort of laughter broke open the dam between us. I pulled on his hand, and he rose to his feet, tugging me with him. We stepped into each other's arms, a hard embrace that didn't erase the awfulness of the past but dulled the sharp edges a bit. We'd been much younger than, less sure. I started to say as much to him, or something like it, tilting my head back to speak without a mouthful of cotton shirt in the way, but he was already leaning down. It was muscle memory, déjà vu, nostalgia, need, all of it bundled up into one burst of realization the moment before his lips brushed mine.

That's what Ethan looks like when he wants to kiss me, I remembered. Oh, and that's what my nerves do when I see that face. Hello, tap dancing butterflies.

I couldn't close my eyes, even though I thought I should. His were closed, after all, lashes dark crescents against his tan skin, the faintest traces of freckles drawing my eye as I hummed a surprised sound of pleasure against his mouth. I parted my lips against his, taking his breath into me when he sighed. Ethan started to pull away but thought better of it, letting go of my hand to grasp my hips, holding me against him as we swayed gently in my kitchen, the kiss deepening.

Part of me was desperate to wiggle free, to run and just keep going until he was so far behind me, he'd never catch up.

When we were younger, I thought that was some sort of guilt, growing up gay in a conservative little town giving me internalized homophobia. But now... now I knew it was whatever made me almost.

Almost were, almost not human. Almost afraid of this.

Ethan made a guttural sound, not quite a growl but close enough that I smirked. His fingers tightened on my hips, and he rocked against me. Someone was obviously more than happy to see me, I thought, unable to stop smiling into the kiss. He nipped my lower lip and I gasped, drawing back just a little. His teeth flashed in a wild grin, hands moving up my back to tug me back into the embrace before I could go far.

Arousal was thick in the air, not a scent but an awareness. A feeling racing in my veins and heating my blood. Ethan was feeling it too. He wanted to chase, to hunt and play and *take*, and good Lord I wanted to let him.

"Landry"—he breathed against my neck when we finally came up for air— "tell me to stop if you don't want this. I won't be mad. I promise, I won't. Don't do this just for old time's sake, or... or, I don't know, to hurt me later. Please just tell me and—"

I hushed him with a breath against his ear. "We're different now, huh? We're not going to use this to hurt one another, right?" He nodded, eyes squeezed shut. It was a visceral thrill, seeing this big, strong were damn near begging me for... Well. For whatever we'd do. I didn't know if sex was going to happen just then, but it was definitely in the future for us, if we kept our heads out of our asses. "Do you? Want this, I mean? Or is this... I don't know, nostalgia run rampant? A chance to have our goodbye and pretend it never happened later?"

"I want this," he said, voice heavy. "I want *you*. I've always wanted you."

I pressed against him again, ducking my head to kiss the curve of his jaw. "That's good. Very, very good. Yes…" He laughed shakily against me and slid his hands up my back, one hand reaching the curls at the base of my skull and tangling there. "We should at least go into the living room, though. I'm getting a crick in my neck trying to make out like this."

Ethan released me but stayed close as I led him through to the small living area. The sun had dropped lower, bathing the room in dark golden light with thick shadows stretching from the corners. I tossed some of the pillows off the sofa and dropped to one end of it, Ethan stretching out along the other. It was always awkward, interrupting a make out session, no matter how old you are or who you're with.

We sat in heavy quiet for a minute, then two. Ethan was doing his best not to look at me, cutting his eyes to the side as he kept his face turned toward the small fireplace across the room, pretending he was interested in the scattering of family photos I'd set on the mantel. His long fingers drummed against his knee, the muscles in his forearm shifting, distracting me for several seconds, making it hard to remember what I was going to say. "You've done a good job sprucing this place up. A few years ago, whoever owned it was just letting it go to shit. Done a great job of restoring it…" He trailed off. "Very. Very midcentury modern."

"Um." There we go. Years of advanced studies finally pay off in your suave conversational skills. "So, why did you come over, anyway? I mean, thank you. Really, thank you. But…"

He finally looked at me again, cheeks pink. "Ah. Well. I don't have your personal number. Just the ones for the office. And… I'd already missed you." He rubbed the back of his neck, that dull flush spreading from his cheeks to his throat. "And apparently your home number is unlisted."

"I don't have a landline," I murmured. "Just my cell phone."

"Ah."

"Mmhmm." Welp. This got awkward as balls pretty fast. "So, you wanted me?" His brows shot up, and his expression cycled quickly from surprise to embarrassed to salacious in record time. "I mean," I said, a bit more loudly than I'd intended, "you drove all the way out here to see me, and I'm guessing it was something to do with the Raymonds if you were trying to catch me back at work…"

I couldn't look at him, not while he was giving me *that* look. It made me want to giggle like a teenager and hide my face.

Ethan cleared his throat, twisting onto one hip and facing me. He was trying, bless his heart, to look serious and all business, but his lips were still swollen, and judging by the way he was awkwardly positioned, he was trying his damnedest to keep me from noticing his erection. "Um, right. The Raymonds are insisting on an autopsy for both of the kids before they go through with the cremation."

I sat up straight, all hints of arousal fading fast. "What? They should contact the coroner's office, not you. Or at least through the funeral home. They shouldn't have taken them home."

Ethan couldn't have looked more uncomfortable if he'd tried. "They, uh… they're requesting a private autopsy. They want the remains sent to this private hospital north of here. Garrow Clinic?" I shook my head—the name didn't ring a bell. "The clinic sent word 'round to my office this evening, just at the end of my shift. You'd already left work, when I called." He slid me a sideways glance that reminded me of a puppy waiting to be chastised. "Sorry?"

"I'm not mad about it. Confused but not mad." I wished I'd brought my beer bottle with me because I desperately needed to fidget. "It's been days since they died. Any tox screens will be piss poor. Their organs have already started to deteriorate!" Ethan's face crinkled in disgust. "Sorry, I forget not everyone can talk about this sort of thing without being grossed out."

"It's just… I kind of knew them. Thinking of them deteriorating is just…" He blew out a breath. "Sorry."

"And it's expensive," I added. "The Raymonds weren't a very wealthy family last I checked. A private autopsy can cost over five grand conservatively. Especially going through a private clinic. And it'd have to be done by a pathologist, not just the family doctor."

"There's no way the Raymonds can come up with ten grand," Ethan murmured. "They didn't seem to think it was anything other than feral dogs when I spoke to them the other day, but this morning, there was a message waiting from Mrs. Raymond, demanding I call her immediately. She told me she thinks you were wrong on the cause of death and wants a second opinion. I guess she didn't like my reply, that she needed to talk to your office herself, because the people at Garrow called this evening."

It's in bad taste to laugh about the dead, but it's perfectly fine to cackle about the dead's family. "What the hell? First of all, the cause of death wasn't dog attack. It was blood loss due to massive abdominal and thoracic trauma. Secondly, what the hell?" I shoved myself to my feet, heading toward the kitchen to grab another beer. Make out time was long gone, apparently, because there was no way to get myself back in the mood after that news. Ethan grabbed my arm as I passed, though, and tugged me down across his legs. "Hey!"

"Hey," he repeated without any mocking to his tone. "I thought you weren't mad about this. It's not like, I don't know, cheating on your hairdresser with another one, right? Them getting another opinion on the cause of death?"

"It's not a good look for me, professionally, if the private autopsy turns up a different cause of death, but even a first-year medical student could tell you it's going to be damn near impossible to determine the cause was anything other than the blood loss due to trauma. And frankly it's unusual that someone would insist upon a private autopsy like this. You usually see it in cases where cause of death is less obvious, like a young person just dying in their sleep with no known pre-existing conditions. Not someone dead from an apparent animal attack." I held back my other thought: I needed to look up this Garrow Clinic. I'd never heard of it, and if they were doing private autopsies, I needed to know. The forensic pathology world wasn't so big as we couldn't find one another easily, and when you narrowed it down on a regional level, it got even cozier. I knew the pathologists in our area by name, many also by face, and not a single one of them worked at a place called Garrow.

Ethan shifted his legs, so I sat on his thighs rather than his knees, tilting them up so I tipped to one side. Leaning against his chest, my legs hooked over his, I smiled. "So that's what you'd come over to tell me?" It seemed like a pretty thin excuse, especially since I'd have found out myself on Monday when I had to sign off on my copies of the exam notes being sent to whomever they had performing the autopsies. But he was here, in my house, and maybe a little stalkery, but honestly, I was okay with that for the time being. Kind of. Mostly.

"I just want to be sure that you're not going to... I don't know, get fired or something."

Aw, damn it. He was being sweet. And I wasn't ready for that.

I wiggled a bit, turning on his lap until I could look him in the face. "I'm an appointed official. It'd take more than someone wanting a private autopsy to get me removed from the position. I may get some shit from the county about it since this is the first time it's happened under my watch, but unless they find something grievously wrong with my report, I'm fine."

Ethan studied me with an unfamiliar expression on his face before wilting back against the sofa a little, pulling me with him. "We should talk more about... Well. Everything. Before."

"Everything before or everything before we do anything?"

"Both," he chuckled. "Fucking hell, I missed you, Landry," he breathed, pulling me down so my head was under his chin and his arms were around me.

"There've been others," I murmured. Both a question and a fact.

"Mmm. I'd have been shocked if there hadn't been."

I had to ask. "Is there anyone now?"

"Ah, no. The job doesn't really allow a lot of time for dating."

"Ah." Reluctantly, I slid to my feet, offering him an apologetic grimace. "Sorry, but if we're going to have this conversation, I need to be somewhere that's not your lap."

Ethan nodded. "I'd say it's an old habit but..." He shrugged, looking sheepish, and got to his feet.

We headed back into the kitchen, Ethan taking up his seat at the table and me heading for the coffee maker. I felt unexpectedly shy under the glare of the kitchen light, and the domesticity of the moment was weird for us. I fussed with the coffee maker, painstakingly measuring grounds, then spent an inordinately long time choosing mugs, arranging creamer and sugar on the table, and generally trying to avoid the moment.

"I guess I'll go first," he said when it had been quiet for too long. "I'm not going to lie and say I'm not still attracted to you, but I know we're not going to just jump back in the way things were."

"We were teenagers," I reminded him. "And hormonal."

"You know there was more to it." The soft burr of his voice sent a wave of *want* through me, and I knew it was obvious. He straightened in his chair, his gaze hooded as he regarded me across the table, coffee finally poured but ignored. "But we're grown men now. We can't... we can't just listen to the wolf in us like that now."

"Wolf in you, maybe," I replied, my tone unintentionally tart. "Mine's defective." I added too much sugar to my coffee, needing something to do with my hands under his intense stare. I was exposed—bare and open in front of him in ways that had nothing to do with sex.

"We're coming back around to this again," he muttered, shaking his head.

A spark burst to life in my blood, igniting my temper. I dropped my spoon on the saucer, unable to keep from glaring at him. "Don't belittle me," I snarled. "You know what this has done to me, to my life. Hell, we *just* talked about this not an hour ago!"

"We touched on it," he growled. "And you sounded like you'd made peace with how you are."

Words and anger choked me. No, not anger, I realized as the heat crept down my spine and sweat slicked my neck. Embarrassment. Shame. The old wounds of being different. Too weird for the humans, too weird for the weres. Not being able to *tell* anyone what the hell was going on in my head, all day every day, since my earliest memories.

I closed my eyes and let my chin drop, exhaustion creeping in on me. "It's impossible to make peace with it when it informs every single moment of my day, Ethan. I'm not like you—"

"Yeah, we've covered that. Ad nauseum."

"Look at you, college boy," I teased without mirth. "But I don't think you get it. It's not just a neat trick, being able to smell that were on the Raymonds or knowing how fucking turned on you are when I bite your neck. All day, every day, I am *aware*. My brain is constantly spitting out red alerts, telling me I'm in danger. Any predator in a thousand yards loves me. I stink like fear to them. Like easy prey."

"No, you don't," he snapped, smacking one hand down on the table. "You don't!"

"Not to *you*!" I was shouting. The Hudsons could probably hear me, I realized, but I couldn't stop now that the floodgate was opening. "Do you know how many werewolves live in the Baltimore area? Including the suburbs? Twenty-two. I met each and every one of them within a week of arriving. Do you know how many places there are to hide in the greater Baltimore area where a werewolf can't find you?"

Ethan's expression grew closed off, carefully blank. "None."

"None," I repeated.

I could *taste* those memories, smell the dry dust and wet mold of the places I tried to hole up to avoid the three small clans in Baltimore. They were aggressive, more than Ethan's clan had been. The difference between the two was stark. Where the Stones and the other weres in Belmarais had been reserved but trying to interact with humans, the clan in Baltimore gave zero fucks about how humans perceived them. They were violent, indulged in vices that would've killed most humans, horded wealth and power. I could never prove they'd killed anyone, but the way they hunted me down night after night, slowly appearing in my daytime life as well... I had to leave the city before I found out for sure.

"Ask me how many weres live in Denver. Or Houston. Or Charleston."

Every part of me ached to run, to flee from the predator at my table. *Wolfwolfwolf!* It was starting to drown out all coherent thought, making my breath sharp and hard. My heart raced, my pulse thumping all the way down in my palms and the soles of my feet. I wanted to climb out of my skin, turn myself in knots just to get away from Ethan, and he wasn't doing a damned thing but looking at me with that blank, guarded face.

"I didn't even have to try," I spat. "They would find me within a day, maybe two, of arriving. It's a fucking miracle I finished college. Hell, it's a miracle I made it back here without one of them deciding I was *too* tempting after all."

Ethan pushed himself up hard enough to make the table skid a few inches, his chair tumbling backward and clattering to the floor. "I never heard a damned word about this. Why didn't I hear, goddammit?"

"Ask your father. Isn't he the one in charge? Isn't he the one who tells y'all all the pack news and shit?" It felt like I was experiencing full body whip lash as I dropped from *runrunrunrunrun* to *freeze*, the urge to flee transmuting into the need to hold as still as possible, the stalking wolf in my kitchen far too close to chance a break for safety.

Ethan stopped mid-stride. He raked his hands through his hair, the gesture becoming familiar now, and shook his head. "Dad's been in the home for two years now," he said, voice so low

I could barely hear him. "Had a stroke and just... didn't come back from it."

"Shit, Ethan." I stood but hesitated. I wanted to go to him; he and his dad had been close, or at least as close as the prickly old man would let them be. I settled for a weirdly friendly pat on the shoulder and a muttered, "I'm so sorry." With almost anyone else I knew, I'd have gone in for the hug and offered a compassionate ear, but I was pretty certain Ethan would have just gone stiff and brushed it off—his father brought that out in him, even if the old man wasn't in the vicinity.

"I'm in charge of the clan now," he said, slightly louder but still soft and tired. "And I haven't heard a damned thing about you in years. Not from Dad, not from the other clans. Why is that?" He turned to face me then, expression grim. "Why wouldn't they want me to know?"

I shook my head. "Ethan..."

"No. I'm not saying it's your fault. But something is wrong. Really fucking wrong. Someone like you on the loose? And the other clans knowing? Not just *knowing* but actively pursuing you?"

"Pursuing? That's definitely one way of putting it..."

"Landry, did any of them hurt you?"

The question was so plaintive, so unexpected, I recoiled a bit. "You mean like hit me or something? No. Just scared the hell out of me more than once. Well, except this one were in Little Rock. I was in a gas station on my way back to Dallas a year or so ago. She came out of the stock room, saw me, and damn near came over the counter to corner me and tell me to fuck off out of the city. She said she'd kill me if she saw me again." I held out my right arm and pushed back my sleeve. "She got me on the arm, a scratch but deep enough to scar."

Ethan grabbed my arm and scowled down at the faint pink mark. "No bites, though?"

"I thought you told me it didn't work like that," I reminded him. "It's inherited, not transmitted."

"Doesn't stop some weres from trying." He let go of me but didn't step back. "Or some humans."

"What? Wait, other humans know about y'all? I thought that was the biggest deal: no one who isn't were knows you're were. Are there just like a million of us who know and have to act like we don't know, and we could all be in the same support group right now if we just had each other's contact info or something?"

Ethan's lips pressed into an almost-smile before his expression fell again. "Since the earliest part of our history, there have been humans who know about us. How do you think we keep going? We can't all have kids with other weres, or the family trees would stop forking pretty damn quick. Some of us reproduce with regular humans. They're sworn to secrecy."

"Like a ceremony or something?" I couldn't help it; I laughed. "Oh my God, is there a secret handshake?"

"Fuck's sake, Landry," he growled, exasperated, but his eyes crinkled. He wasn't that mad at me yet. "Focus!"

"I'm trying, but you're making it difficult, because all I can think of now is some organization like the Boy Scouts but for humans who know about werewolves where we all meet up once a week to have a potluck and talk about near misses."

That was the mood killer right there. "Near misses? How many have you had, Landry?"

I stepped away then. Not far, less than a foot, but it did something to the tension between us, twisted it from a softening sort of awareness back to frustration, nearly to anger.

"Enough to know that whatever is wrong with me, whatever made me like this, is probably going to get me killed one day. Belmarais is safe because even though it's been so long, I know your clan aren't going to start hunting humans down. Never once in the entire time I lived here before college was there anything that would lead me to believe weres were truly hunting ordinary humans."

"Until the Raymonds," he murmured. "If they were killed by a were."

"They were," I said fiercely. "I have no doubt in my mind. If there's *one* thing my little problem is good for, it's sussing out weres. And the smell was all over them." I blew out a harsh breath, the scent-memory threatening to gag me. "And that were was here earlier, before I got home." There we are. Full circle. "And it's not," I added, "one of yours. Not unless you've got some new people in your clan that I haven't met."

"No, just... just us still. Everyone you knew back then."

"Then it definitely wasn't one of y'all. None of you smell like that. Whoever killed the Raymonds smelled *wrong*. Like if were scents could go bad." Just thinking about it made the sense memory grow stronger. The sour-bitter-wrong stench was thick in my nose, pouring down my throat. "Ugh, I need some water or something. Just a sec." I made it only a few feet before Ethan's hand shot out to grab me. "Hey!"

"Shhh." His grip was tight to the point of pain. Sharp points pressed against my bicep. Shit—he was changing or close to it. *Fuck fuck fuck!*

Slowly, I turned my head, hoping he wasn't on the verge of losing all control. It was a perilous moment, those first few seconds after a were shifted when their brains were muddled, and human was vying for control over wolf. If he was close, I might be royally fucked. I risked a glance up at his face and saw his eyes were golden, the pupils wide. Nostrils flaring, he breathed in deeply, grasp on my arm growing even tighter.

"Ethan," I said as softly as I could manage, "you're hurting me. Stop. Please."

Slowly, his grip relaxed, but he didn't release me entirely. "Someone's outside," he murmured. "Were."

The thought that it might be Waltrip crossed my mind, but I discounted it quickly. Just because Ethan decided to be a stalker and come see me didn't mean Waltrip would, I reasoned. Then again, he was a creepy asshole, so... maybe?

I tried to ease away from Ethan's grasp, but he kept his fingers curled around my arm. "It's probably just the were from town the other day," I murmured, my tone as calm and even as I could make it. "His name's Oliver Waltrip. He's a PI. He came to my work the other day and wanted to arrange a meeting about the Raymonds." I decided discretion was the better part of not pissing off the werewolf in my kitchen and left out the details about the parking lot encounter with Waltrip. Still, it didn't help.

"What?" Ethan breathed, voice thick and tinged with a growl. "He's still in the area? I had Tyler and Rosie look everywhere and not one damn trace of the weres you described turned up. We thought they were up from one of the other cities nearby..."

He trailed off and sniffed the air again. "Stay inside, Landry. Fucking hell. Just... stay inside and lock the doors." Ethan let me go, pushing past me in a blur of motion. My back door slammed, and I lurched toward it, slamming the bolt home. The only thing my flimsy wooden door would do against a determined were was buy me a few seconds while they broke it down, but a few seconds could make all the difference. I was kidding myself, but it was all I had.

The smell was thick in the air; it hadn't been my sense memory, I realized, but actual scent. The were that had been all over the Raymonds was outside my house, close enough for their stink to get through the minute crevices and cracks, close enough for Ethan to finally pick up on it. I knew I should get away from the door, go find something to defend myself with, but I was frozen in place.

The faintest sounds came from outside: thumps as something hit the side of the house, the clatter of a garbage can lid falling, a short bark, all muffled by the house and shrubs outside. It felt like an hour but was likely just a few minutes before a hard knock fell on my front door. "It's me," Ethan boomed.

Ethan shoved the door open the second I unlocked it. He shouldered me aside and reset the lock in the knob as well as the deadbolt. Eyes still shining gold, he physically set me to one side, picking me up with his hands at my ribs, before prowling through my house. "Um, hello?" I started to take a step after him, the feeling of my personal space being invaded somewhere between embarrassment and annoyance, but he snapped out a growl and disappeared into the dark recesses of my house's only hallway. "You can seriously just turn on the hall light and see everything," I called. No response. "Why am I standing here?" I muttered.

"Because I asked you to," he called from the back of the house.

"Sure, *that's* the part you hear? And you didn't ask. You shoved."

"I carried," Ethan retorted, striding back down the hall toward me. He stopped in the middle of my small living room and looked, for just a moment, comical among my belongings. He had always been tall, but the years had filled him out and made him, if I looked at him just right, seem giant. More than.

The moment flickered and faded, leaving me staring not at a larger than life were next to my sofa but a frustrated, visibly tired Ethan with wild eyes and fists clenched at his side till his knuckles where white.

"Right. So. I already know you're going to fight me on this, but you're not staying here tonight."

I'd already decided that for myself as soon as I realized the murderous were had returned. But hey, I'd throw Ethan a bone and pretend like I was going along with his idea. "Okay."

He jerked, blinked, and cocked his head. *Nice doggy...* "Okay?"

"I'm stubborn, not stupid." I was also shaking, hoping he wouldn't notice, and trying not to give in to the urge to just climb him like a tree and let him hide me from whatever the fuck was just outside my house. Instead, I made myself stand straight and shouldered past him, maybe bumping him a little on purpose, and headed for my bedroom. "I'm assuming I'm allowed to pack. How long should I plan to be gone?"

"Uh, let's start with the weekend," he said, sounding like he was still standing in the living room.

"Did you at least get a look at the were? I'm assuming they got away. No offense. I just figure that otherwise we wouldn't be just standing here talking while I pack my bags." I grabbed handfuls of clothes from my drawers, adding in a few work shirts and some slacks at the last moment. "Hello?"

"Just checking the windows," Ethan said, startling me. He'd come down the hall so quietly, his appearance in my doorway went unnoticed until he spoke. "Sorry. Didn't mean to set you off."

"I know." My voice shook on the words, and I knew he could smell the nervous energy roiling off me. Something like fear, adrenaline maybe. "The were?" I prompted, tucking the book on my bedside table into the side pocket of my bag.

Ethan hesitated, worrying his lower lip for a moment as he looked up at me from beneath lowered lashes. "That's the thing." He sighed after a moment. "I could smell them, but I didn't *see* anything out there."

Chapter Four

Belmarais wasn't a far drive from Tuttle but it sure as hell felt like it. By the time Ethan had agreed to let me follow him in my car rather than riding together, and half browbeat half convinced me that it would be safer to stay with Aunt Cleverly than a hotel in town, it was nearly nine o'clock. I'd been up since five and was drained. Driving down mostly narrow, blacktop roads with swamp on one side and dark woods on the other was its own kind of exhausting. The roads had by and large lost their center stripes, Hitchens County deeming it too expensive to replace them. The lack of lights meant the edges of the asphalt blended in too well with the shoulders and the slopes into trees or marsh on either side.

Ethan drove slowly, barely sticking to the speed limit even when I tailgated him. "I know the way back to town, damn it," I shouted, knowing he couldn't hear me even with his supernatural hearing. "Move it, Gramps!"

I backed off a bit as we rounded the long, banked curve just before Belmarais, putting a bit more space between us for safety's sake despite my petty desire to annoy him. For a moment, he was far enough ahead of me on the curve that I didn't see his taillights. Out of the corner of my eye, I saw movement, sensed something running alongside and just slightly ahead of my car on the swamp side of the road. The shock of movement where there'd been nothing but darkness and ill-formed shapes for miles made me jerk the wheel to the left, away from whatever that had been. I slammed on my brakes as I swerved toward the heavily wooded side of the road. "Shit, shit, shit! God damn it!"

The headlights glared through the pines lining the road, making pools of white-yellow light between the thick trunks and picking out the underbrush. Nothing moved there. I was afraid—no, terrified—to look in my mirrors and see what was behind me. The sudden glare from oncoming headlights made me shout, my heart leaping in my chest as I shifted into reverse and eased back onto the correct side of the road.

It was only Ethan, I told myself, not whatever I thought I saw a few moments before. I wanted to tell him not to get out of his car, but he was too fast, throwing on his emergency blinkers and all but leaping from his car to the driver's side door of mine. I hit the button for the window and called out as it lowered, "I'm okay. Just got spooked by a deer or something."

"Liar," he chided. His jaw clenched around something he didn't want to say. "Just a few more miles. You sure you're okay?" When I nodded, he looked up, over the roof of my car, and into the swamp. "Come on. Just watch my lights, got it?"

"Don't baby me," I said, trying for sass and falling short. Ethan grunted, not quite a laugh, and trotted back to his car. He swung it around to face back the way we were heading and got in front of me in less than a minute. He was moving fast, I realized, because he was scared. Not the fear that prey feels for a predator, not like mine. The fear a predator has against an unknown, an intruder.

I stuck close to his car, dangerously so, even on that long, final curve. The woods thinned the closer we got to Belmarais and the swamp receded from the roadside. Soon, a few signs dotted the shoulders. Advertisements for restaurants in town, a craft store, churches. The first tiny little bar on the roadside was a relief. The battered, formerly white-painted icehouse had its front doors propped wide, the metal shutters rolled up so the handful of regulars inside could enjoy the evening without dying from the heat in an unairconditioned space. My shoulders relaxed a little at the sight of Billy's. It had been there since my parents were babies, if not before, and seeing it open and lit up like always broke up the creeping shadows in my thoughts.

As soon as we were past Billy's, Belmarais began in earnest. It was late enough that the only things open were a few fast-food places, the two other bars in town, and the tiny movie theater just past the city limit sign. Ethan dropped to a crawl as soon as we were inside the city—it wouldn't do for the sheriff to be ticketed for speeding in his own jurisdiction—and I fell back again, still keeping Ethan in my sights. There was no chance whatever I saw in the swamp was still following us, if I had really seen anything at all, but I couldn't shake the hunted feeling.

A cupric tang filled my mouth, and I knew I smelled sour. It didn't take were senses to smell fear-sweat on a person. By the time we turned into my Aunt Cleverly's drive, I knew I was a mess. I had gone from wanting to tear Ethan a new one for strong arming me into staying with her to wanting to make a beeline for my old room and lock every door between me and the outside world and not look back.

Ethan intercepted me as I got out of the car, his hand on my elbow when I would have made a break for the front door.

"Looks like Cleverly's out," he murmured, nodding to the empty parking spot beneath the carport. "I'll stay here with you till she gets back."

It was a sign of how wrought up I was that the idea of being alone in the house with my former (maybe soon to be renewed) flame didn't even make me perk up a little bit.

"I'm grown, Ethan," I pointed out. "I don't need a babysitter. Besides, I know where Cleverly keeps her shotgun and the shells. I'll be okay till she gets in. In fact, I should call her and let her know I'm here, so she doesn't freak out when she finds me."

Ethan's brows were drawn, and he looked like he was tasting something bitter, but after a long moment, he nodded. "Alright. But you're not disappearing on me tomorrow morning, you got me?"

"It was just a deer," I muttered, rolling my eyes. It had to be just a deer; it had to be.

"Sure. Okay, it was just a deer, and you got spooked by it, that's fine," he allowed, though his tone was calling me a liar. "I want you to come with me tomorrow to talk to the Raymonds, though."

"Uh, no. Nope. That would be hugely unethical. That would definitely get my ass handed to me by the county."

He shook his head. "Not... in an official capacity. For some reason, I can't pick up on the smell of this were that killed the Raymond kids until they're right up on me just about. I want you to come while I meet with them to see if you can, um, pick up on anything."

I stared in disbelief. "Are you asking me to sneak around the Raymond place while you keep them distracted?"

"I'm asking," he said, a faint grin tugging at the corners of his lips before he managed to tamp it down, "for you to come with me and maybe stretch your legs a bit while I talk with them."

"Stretch my legs discreetly?" A flutter of something electric sparkled through my chest. Ethan grinned at me, quick and small, picking up on my excitement. "I shouldn't be so into this idea, should I?"

"I'm not going to judge." He winked, stepping back toward his car, letting go of my elbow. "I'm meeting them at eleven. Be ready to go by ten. It's not far, but the roads are still messed up since the last flood."

I nodded, watching him watch me as he got into his car, started it up, and backed down Cleverly's long, gravel drive. As he swung out onto the road, I remembered the thing in the swamp, racing alongside, and I couldn't stop the shudder that racked my body. Even with neighbors close by, I was alone and exposed.

Letting myself into the house (I still had my old key, and Cleverly would never change the locks so long as she lived because that would require, well, change), I made sure every door and window to the outside was locked tight before calling Cleverly to let her know I was there, leaving her a voicemail message before shooting off a text just to be sure I covered all my bases. She wasn't exactly a stereotypical gun toting granny type, but if she missed my car in the shadows off her drive and came home to find a man in her house... Well, she did keep guns in the house and did know how to use them.

It was after eleven, and Cleverly worked the late shift at Bluebonnet Biomedical out near Lindale as a phlebotomist. She wouldn't be home till well after midnight, so I made myself at home by changing into my sleep pants and an old shirt that had managed not to make the move from there to anywhere else I'd lived, checking the locks again (paranoia saves lives), and making a cup of hot tea.

The familiarity of Cleverly's house, the home I'd grown up in from age six onward, was a stark and unsettling contrast to what I'd left behind in Tuttle just hours earlier. My childhood bedroom (thankfully, redecorated since I'd moved out and not kept as a shrine to all things Brad Pitt as I'd left it, though I did hope Cleverly had kept that one shirtless picture I'd had over my bed... reasons) made me feel seasick, off-kilter. Even though I truly felt at home with Aunt Cleverly, it was disorienting being there so late at night without the sound of her puttering around.

The only change she seemed to have made was a new dedication to those little plug-in air fresheners—she had one in every outlet, it seemed, those fancy sorts that looked like flowers or lit up like nightlights. She had something going that smelled like it might have been trying to be lavender, but it had a chemical tang to it that made my throat itch and eyes sting a little. I wondered how she could stand it for a moment before remembering she wasn't like me, not when it came to things like that.

She'd also left out a banker's box on the table, full of file folders that were stuffed to bursting. I fought the urge to take a peek, see what my aunt was up to—she never left her private papers out, or hadn't as long as I'd been living there. Maybe she was having financial problems, I thought. From the little bit I could see of the papers peeking out of their folders, they looked like some might be receipts or invoices. *Did she need help?* I wondered. *Should I ask her?* An entire fantasy of my poor aunt being scammed by one of those people who preyed on the elderly spun out as I waited for my tea to cool. The fact it culminated in Ethan swooping in for a heroic kiss as we saw the scammer put in jail for going after my aunt made me snort, blushing with embarrassment even though no one saw what I was imagining. *You're just tired,* I scolded myself. *Stop being so damned dramatic.*

I took my tea back to my bedroom and stretched out on the fancy, blue satin comforter Cleverly had put over the old, beat-up queen size mattress. A brief, powerful, fantasy of Ethan stretching out next to me blazed to life, but I tamped it down hard and fast. We'd gotten carried away earlier—enjoyably so, but still. There were far too many things to hash out before I let myself indulge in any fantasies of Ethan, much less any more actual hands-on situations.

I must be an official adult now. I was actually contemplating scheduling a relationship talk around a murder investigation. Wait… does that make me an adult, or a member of the Addams Family?

I wasn't quite asleep but seriously considering it, my body slowly unwinding against the familiar lumps and bumps of my old mattress, when my phone chimed with its familiar text alert.

Unknown Number: *Mr. Babin, I apologize for contacting you so late. This is Oliver Waltrip. At your earliest convenience, please contact me at this number to arrange our meeting.*

"Huh."

Three things occurred to me in rapid succession: how did he get my private cell phone number, why was he contacting me so late, and should I tell Ethan? A very stubborn voice in the back of my brain pointed out that Ethan was *not* my keeper, and this was none of his business, not really. Waltrip had questions for me, and if he needed to speak with the sheriff, he would contact Ethan himself.

The less stubborn part of me was a tiny bit louder. There is a murdering werewolf out there somewhere, somewhere nearby, and Ethan is trying to find out who it is. Don't hide this shit.

I read the text again. It had not, in the minute since my last reading, changed. Damn it. At least he uses complete sentences and proper punctuation. I don't think I could take any of this seriously if he used that chat speak shit. And he'd have to get off my lawn.

I glanced at the bedside clock. Five till midnight. Ethan would be home or back at the office by now. I could call him. "Shit! I forgot to get his number! Damn it!" *And if you call the office and he isn't there, what would you say to whomever answers and wonders why the off-duty coroner for Hitchens County is calling in the middle of the night if it's not an emergency?*

My phone chimed again, startling me out of my roundabout thoughts.

Aunt Cleverly: *Glad you let me know! Be home around 2, staying late! Luv U Bunches! Talk in a.m.!*

I didn't bother to text her back. Mostly because of the chat speak.

I scrolled back up to Waltrip's message, and gnawing curiosity got the best of me.

LandryBabinMD: *How did you get this number, Mr. Waltrip? This is my private number. Any communication pertaining to business related matters needs to be done through official channels. Thanks for understanding.*

I set the phone on the nightstand and made myself close my eyes. Belatedly, I realized I'd left the overhead light on, but I knew if I got up, I'd use it as an excuse to stare at my phone and wait for a reply. By the time I finally dozed off, the phone had chimed three more times.

"You look like shit."

Coffee so strong it could strip paint, waffles of dubious provenance, and affectionate insults. Felt like home again. "Morning, Aunt Cleverly."

"Now I know you weren't up when I got home, and it's dang near nine now, so you must have had at least seven hours. What's got you looking so hang dog? And why," she added, pouring me a cup of her death brew, "are you creeping into my house in the middle of the night when I know you have a perfectly fine place in Tuttle? Not that I mind. I love seeing you, Landry."

She shifted her plump bulk against the counter, hitching one hip up so it rested near the toaster and letting her feet dangle as she flashed me her sweet smile. My aunt was one of those women who seemed to be everywhere in the small-town South: powdered, perfumed, dumpling-soft, ageless, and sharp as a serpent's tooth if she thought you were up to no good. Ethan had called her an attack cupcake once when she'd gotten after him for tracking dirt into the front hall, and the mental image had stuck. She was a soft pink confection that could and would take you down and make it hurt if she had to. I had the feeling that I was on the verge of being tackled and held down till I spilled my guts if I didn't talk fast.

I took the coffee she held out to me and braced myself for the bitter bite, swallowing hard against the urge to spit out that first mouthful of her too-strong brew. "Oh, just... long week at work," I choked out. Her very plucked brows arched upward, her familiar 'bullshit' expression. "The Raymonds," I muttered, lifting one shoulder in a shrug. That wasn't a lie; I was there because of the Raymonds but let her think that I was rattled by their deaths because it was close to home rather than... Well, rather than the truth.

Aunt Cleverly clicked her tongue. "That was a mess. Those

poor kids! I've been saying for years that that Thomas place needs to be razed! It's a... what's it called? Oh, Sheriff Stone said it the other day!" She gave me a pleading look as if I'd know anything Ethan said when I wasn't nearby.

"A den of inequity?" I hazarded around a mouthful of overcooked frozen waffle.

She narrowed her eyes, then snapped her fingers as it came to her. "An attractive nuisance! There're always people out there doing drugs and"—she dropped her voice to a whisper— "fornicating and fellating and such!"

"Oh my God," I groaned, dropping the rest of my waffle. "I could honestly live the rest of forever not knowing you know what fellatio is."

"Lord, you kids didn't invent it. You didn't even perfect it." Hopping off the counter, she took my coffee from my hands and drank it down in a few deep gulps before putting the cup in the sink. "Now, I've got to run and meet the Higgins sisters for our weekly stitch and bitch, but after that, I want us to have a nice, long chat." There was no arguing with Aunt Cleverly when she gave me *that* look. "I'm supposed to go meet up with Sheriff Stone in a bit, discuss the Raymonds. Their folks are having a private autopsy done," I said, cutting off Cleverly when she spoke. "Not unusual, but there are... things to discuss." Yeah, that sounded legit as hell. Go me.

Cleverly's expressive eyebrows lowered, and she stared hard at me, apparently trying to read my mind. "Okay." She sighed after a long moment. "Well, when you get back from your meeting with Sheriff Stone, text me." She started toward the hall closet, just off the kitchen, where she kept her purse and coat, but paused in the doorway. "I know it must be strange, seeing Ethan again after all this time," she began, offering me a small, sad smile. "I'm sorry I didn't let you know when he got the position of sheriff, but I didn't think you'd ever come back to town if you knew."

I sighed and crossed over to her, folding my arms around her familiar, soft contours and hugging her tight as I dared. "Nothing could keep me from seeing you, Aunt Cleverly. Even a shitty ex-boyfriend."

She snorted, tugging away before patting me on the arm. "Nothing could keep you away except that job, huh? And what was the excuse before that?"

"Interning? Medical school? Working for the Dallas coroner's office?"

"Mmhmm. Dead people are just more interesting than your dear old aunt, sure, sure!" She laughed as she said it, but it still stung. She called her goodbyes as she headed out the front door and, for a long moment, I stood in the silent house, the rush of her presence fading with the tea rose smell of her perfume.

"Jesus Christ." I sighed. It was too early for this level of stress. As if he knew, my phone chimed again. I knew without looking it was Waltrip. The three texts I'd ignored the night before had all been suggestions of times to meet up on Monday or Tuesday. I hadn't responded yet, though I knew I should just remind him to contact me through the office and maybe just block his number now that I had it. He had been (kind of) nice to me in the parking lot, but that didn't change the fact he'd menaced me in the deli and in front of my office.

Waltrip: *Dr. Babin, I'm waiting for your response.*

Fuck it.

LandryBabinMD: *You haven't answered me regarding how you came to have my private number. And I am unavailable for meetings until Wednesday. Please contact my office and go through the appropriate channels.*

Waltrip: *I'm a damned good PI. That's how I got your number. And I spoke with Dr. DuBois this morning. He informs me that your schedule is clear for meetings Monday afternoon and Tuesday morning, barring any emergencies.*

Fucking hell, Justin! Of all the days he decides to show up to work.

LandryBabinMD: *Dr. DuBois does not have any say over my* *schedule. Please contact Reba on Monday, and she will arrange a time for us to meet at the office.*

No response. I was relieved. Confrontation was not my usual bag, but I was spoiling to go at Waltrip with metaphorical claws out and fangs bared. We'd spoken for fewer than ten minutes total and already, he got under my skin.

When Ethan's knock fell on the door, I jumped, wondering for a brief moment how the hell Waltrip found me in Belmarais before I remembered that Ethan was coming by at ten. And shit, it was already five past! "Just a second!" I shouted. running back down the hall to my room and grabbing my shoes. I threw open the door to find Ethan leaning on the wooden post of the porch, looking distinctly amused and too damn good in his uniform. "Sorry," I panted, bending to tie my laces. "I lost track of time and Aunt Cleverly's coffee tried to kill me."

"I don't know how that woman has an esophagus. Or stomach. Or how she can sleep!"

I jogged down the porch steps to meet him at the bottom where he leaned. "I think they're made of cast iron. Had them installed in the late seventies and just hasn't looked back. And I'm really not sure she does sleep. I don't think I've ever once seen her so much as take a long blink in all the years I lived with her." Ethan chuckled and we headed over to his car. "You know," I admitted as I shut the passenger side door behind me, "I half expected you to be the type with a truck."

"Seriously?" He wrinkled his nose at that. "You think I turned into a truck guy? It's like you never knew me at all."

I knew he was aiming for funny, but I shifted a bit in my seat to face him as he turned onto the street in front of Cleverly's house. "Well, we're not the same people we were at seventeen. For all I know, you did become a truck guy."

He sighed, rubbing at his forehead with one hand as he drove. "We're going to do this now?" he asked quietly.

"Not now, but soon."

"Okay. Yeah. Soon. Soon is... soon is good."

We were quiet for a few minutes as he navigated the usual Saturday morning snarl in front of the high school as people came and went from the sports fields.

"So, about today," he began as we broke free from the knot of mini-SUVs hauling kids to one practice or another. "I'll park down at the bottom of the drive. Give me about five minutes to get them talking and you can... do your thing."

"Do my thing? It's not a party trick," I reminded him. "I'll see if I can pick up anything, but I can't make promises."

"You're right. Sorry. I remember that it was hurtful whenever we'd test you and shit." He was blushing, and a tiny voice in my head (one that sounded a lot like my stubborn voice, somewhere in the same vicinity) cheered. *Good. You should be embarrassed about that,* I wanted to say. Instead, I just nodded, making some vague noise of acceptance. More quiet for another mile or so, and then, "Hey, listen, in the interest of full transparency here, I want you to know I went back out to the farm road last night."

For a second, I was confused. Virtually every road around Belmarais was FM something or other, the old farm to market road system that was so ubiquitous in Texas never more apparent than around a small town. But then I realized what he meant.

"You were looking for whatever I saw?" I asked, unable to keep the slight tremor from my voice. Just remembering the quick flash of *something,* the way my senses flared up and set off every warning bell in my body, was enough to make me shudder and need to curl into a ball.

Ethan reached toward me, hesitating for a moment before making a decision and putting his hand on my knee. He gave me a gentle squeeze, not at all sexual or even in the neighborhood of a come-on. "I wanted—*needed*—to know one way or another, Landry. Not just for you, but that was a big part of it. I'm the head of the clan now, and if there's a strange were in our territory, I need to know. Hell, I need to know if it's one of us going rogue or even just getting sloppy and being spotted. If it was one of us, and it wasn't you who saw, Christ, can you imagine?"

I shook my head again. "Was it?" I asked, my voice still too thin, too reedy. "One of your clan, I mean?"

The long pause was all the answer I needed. I knew the answer was no before he sighed and shook his head. "No. But it was a were. I could smell it. Not," he added hastily, "the one from Tuttle, not the one who killed the Raymonds. This was different. Not a familiar were but not that wrong smell from your place."

"Shit."

"That was pretty much my reaction."

We had reached a red light, and he took the opportunity to reach for my shoulder and tug me closer. I awkwardly leaned into his grasp, and we half-embraced across the center console. My eyes burned with the urge to cry, and I hated myself for it. I blamed the part of me that was broken, the not-quite-were part, whatever made me sense things so keenly. I couldn't help but think that if that damn part of me was working right, or didn't exist in the first place, I would just be mildly annoyed, maybe scared but certainly not sitting in a Buick and almost crying on my ex's shoulder at a red light.

Ethan reluctantly let go when the light turned green, and I scooted back to my side of the car, determined not to show my feelings even though I knew he could pick up on all the signs without even trying. "What are you going to do?" I asked when I was sure my voice wouldn't shake. "And what the hell were you thinking, going out there alone? Don't think I missed the part where you didn't mention taking your brothers or anyone else in the clan with you, asshole."

"Ah, I missed our pet names," he said, smirking faintly. "I'm not exactly a pup, you know. You've seen me."

"I saw you when you were seventeen," I reminded him. "I have no idea what you're like now when you shift. For all I know, you're still a scrawny thing I could take down with a solid thump to the snout."

He had never been a scrawny thing, even as a teenager. When he shifted then, he was still obviously young, not quite done filling out, but he was big. Bigger than any wolf I'd seen in a zoo or on television. His size was past intimidating and well into fearsome in a primal way.

"If it helps, I was also armed."

"Because you can carry a gun while you're a wolf."

"Landry! For fuck's sake, trust me a little!" He turned sharply down Wallace Road, a narrow road that had once been neatly black topped but was now more pothole than not.

"I can't just turn that back on after fifteen years!" I said, nearly shouted really. "And just fucking accept that I worry for you, okay? I know you can hold your own but Christ, Ethan! There's apparently some new weres in the area, someone killed the Raymonds, and that fucking Oliver Waltrip is texting me and—"

"What?"

"Oh. Yeah, sorry. Forgot to tell you," I shrugged. "He wants to meet to talk about the Raymonds. Apparently, he's investigating their deaths."

"Whoa, whoa, whoa." There was no shoulder to speak of, so Ethan pulled to the right as far as he could without getting the car stuck in the thick, tall grass. He shoved the gear shift into park and turned to glare at me. "He's *what*?"

Shit. My own fault, really, for not leading with that information earlier but still... "First off, you have zero right to be mad at me about any of this. Secondly, he didn't outright say the Raymonds had hired him, but he pretty heavily implied it."

"I'm not mad at you," Ethan growled. "I *am* feeling like we're standing in front of the fan and it's about to get hit with a raft of shit, though."

"So, what are we going to do about it?"

He huffed a laugh. "Duck or get splattered." He shifted back into drive and eased out onto the rutted road. We bounced along for several seconds before he asked, "So how come Waltrip has your number, but I don't?"

"Oh, Lord."

"It's a valid question! I mean, I don't work with PIs at all, but

I'd think that if he wanted to speak with you in a professional capacity, he should be contacting your office and not your private number."

The jouncing of the road made it hard to tell if Ethan was laughing at me or not, his words bouncing up and down as we hit every damn pothole ever created. "That," I said, wincing as I bounced off the door, "is exactly what I told him."

Ethan didn't say anything, but he made a face I remembered well. The *I think that's bullshit but I'm not going to say anything aloud* face he tended to wear any time one of his brothers bragged about dates or sports back in high school. Then, it was cute. Now... Well. It was still cute, but I wasn't going to tell him this time.

Before much longer, he pulled off to the side of the road again. This time, there was a bit of a shoulder, mostly sandy gravel, and a large pecan tree overhanging the edge of the road. "Five minutes," he said. "Then be quick about it but..."

"I know, I know. Party trick."

Ethan didn't dignify that with a reply, instead unfolding himself from his seat and shutting the door quietly behind him before walking quickly up the Raymonds' drive, leaving me alone with the rattling crickets in the tall grass to serenade me. Five minutes dripped past and finally, I let myself out and stood, eyeballing the house from my spot on the roadside. I could only make out a bit of it—the corner of the garage, the peeling sideboards of part of the front, a bit of the porch—but there were no voices.

My senses weren't clanging for danger. Keeping to the tall grass, I picked my way from the road to walk parallel to the house, staying about a hundred feet out. If anyone looked out the side window, they would no doubt see me staggering through weeds and half-dead grass, not exactly the subtle perusal Ethan had been hoping for. Following the curve of the side yard toward an unkempt, unfenced backyard, I left the relative safety of the overgrown field and took a moment to breathe, to drop my guard and let my senses loose in earnest.

Nothing. Not even the hint of were or even a dog nearby. I moved as slowly and quietly as possible toward the house, ducking beneath the set of windows overlooking what had once been a rose bed. Several bikes were decomposing against the back patio door, and an old smoker with a hole rusted through it leaned precariously against an overfilled trashcan. The stink off the rotting trash made me gag, bile sharp in my throat. Pulling my shirt up over my nose, I hurried past, cursing the damned heightened olfactory ability when my mouth flooded with the rotten aroma.

Lurching ungracefully toward the farthest corner of the house, I nearly missed a whiff of our mystery were tangled with the fug from the trashcan. The smell was distinct from the wet, hot stench of rotting garbage. It came with warnings, with gooseflesh racing down my body and my senses growing even sharper, reminding me I was prey, being hunted.

The warnings weren't sharp, though, not paralyzing. They were cautious. *Hey, you might want to look out. There's something nearby. Don't hide yet but be ready.*

I took a step toward the trash, the source of all bad smells in the world apparently, mentally bracing before taking another deep whiff. The thread of the odor was steady, not fading. Whatever the source was, it was in the disgusting pile of garbage baking in the midday heat.

I took another step, wishing I'd thought to bring gloves or a hazmat suit or an intern. *Okay, Babin, you stick your hands in dead people for a living. You can do this. Then again, dead people aren't disgusting.* A low hum settled in the base of my skull, more feeling than sound. *Is that flies? Oh my God, am I about to get swarmed? Ethan can do this his own damned self...*

I retreated several steps, glancing up at the sliding glass patio door to make sure I was well out of sight. The humming only grew in intensity, making my teeth ache. My muscles tensed just a fraction of a second before I realized what was happening: someone was coming. A hunter, a predator, probably a were, was coming and I needed to go *now*. No footsteps, nothing to indicate which way was the wrong way to flee, but the humming, the twitching in my legs, was painful, the need too great to ignore. For the first time in a very long time, I stopped thinking. I let my body take over.

Without thinking about *why*, I bolted back toward the garage. I didn't bother to stay low or try to keep quiet, though part of me realized I was moving faster than I ever had before, light on my feet as I sprinted around the corner and reached the side door leading into the garage itself. It was peeling plywood, warped from weather and age, and looked as if it would fall apart as soon as I touched it, or worse, screech on old, ill-used hinges. But luck or some interested higher power was on my side and the door swung open as soon as I turned the knob.

I shut it behind me, my heart jack-rabbiting hard enough that I felt it in my damn ears of all places, the humming fading back a bit. It didn't go away entirely, but it died down to a low buzz rather than a tooth-rattling vibration. I lurched away from the door, nearly going face-first into a pile of what seemed to be broken lawn equipment. I could smell old motor oil and dust and that peculiar garage smell that lingered in old ones, a mix of metal and dirt, and grease and sweat. Darting around the dark shape of the pile, I brushed through a cobweb strung between ceiling and floor, barely managing to bite back a shout of disgust. Sure, I'd run around after werewolves and worked with cadavers, but spiders? Nope.

The garage was one of those one car types, barely big enough for the family sedan and you were shit out of luck if you wanted to use it for storage *and* parking. The Raymonds had apparently opted to use the space for junk piles. I picked my way through or around five before finding myself against the door leading into the house itself. I was, I realized belatedly, stuck.

When I bolted, I hadn't thought about the why's and where's,

I just ran where my feet took me, looking for somewhere safe, somewhere *away*. Now, I was stuck in the Raymonds' garage and had no idea what to do next. Outside was danger, was something my brain identified as hunter-predator-stalking-death. Inside was... well. More danger but of a different sort.

Ethan was inside, and, as much as I hated to allow the tiny little thought to even be alive in my head, the part of me that was not quite were and definitely not human? It clung to the idea of Ethan as my protector. It wasn't anything as crass and twee as 'my alpha, my mate'—yeah, those stories are... not quite reality. Having known weres for quite a while? Not even close to realistic. Whether it was some weird imprinting or the remnants of teenage memories, but the same little voice that screamed at me to hide was now poking and prodding at me to find Ethan, to let him help me.

Pressing myself against the inside door, I strained my ears for any sign of voices on the other side. Even with my better than typical hearing, there was nothing to pick up. My fingers curved around the sticky metal knob, and I turned it, holding the door closed for a moment to see if anyone came—if anyone saw it twist and stormed over to yank it out of my grasp and threaten me or worse.

Nothing. Not a peep.

THE DOOR OPENED INTO A SMALL LAUNDRY ROOM. It stank of rust and mildewed clothes with a healthy undercurrent of wet dog and rancid cat piss. The smells had been a confusing jumble of awful through the door but now, standing in the middle of the source, I could pick them apart easily and wished I had typical olfactory abilities. Whenever I got home, I decided, I was going to burn my clothes and take a shower with the strongest smelling soap I could find just to purge the nasal assault that the day had been from my memory.

The door leading from the laundry room to the kitchen was

open about halfway, and I could see a wedge of the room. Linoleum that had been trendy in the late seventies, a butcher block table that looked out of place with how shiny and clean it was, an open dishwasher full of dirty dishes, and the very edge of a carpeted area on the other side of the room. The house seemed quiet as the proverbial grave.

I eased my way into the kitchen, sucking in my stomach and holding my breath as I scooted through the narrow opening in the laundry room doorway. Old cooking grease, something dairy that had gone off, and overripe fruit overlaid the miasma of the laundry room as it followed me. The buzz in my skull had faded just a bit more, the urge to flee down to a very manageable level, but something was still off. I had never experienced that before, the rattling hum in my bones. It was either a new manifestation of an old issue, or something had changed.

Awesome.

There was no trace of the were we were looking for in the kitchen—not even a hint of any were, really. I stood beside the doorway leading to the carpeted area; it was a narrow corridor opening onto a sunken living room, I realized, chancing a quick peek around the corner. How retro-awful, considering the carpet looked like it hadn't been vacuumed since before I was born and was a dirty brown color that smelled like it was more dirt than carpet fiber. Still no voices. No sign of Ethan or the Raymonds.

Fear of a different sort bubbled to life in my chest. Had something happened to them? Had they done something to Ethan? I gritted my teeth and made a decision. Before I could talk myself out of it, I stepped out into the corridor and started toward the den. It was empty save for two folding chairs, the type you'd see at a church potluck, and a card table set between them. To my right was another hallway, shorter than the one leading to the den, with three closed doors down one side and an open door leading to a bathroom at the far end. "Fuck, fuck, fuck..."

I closed my eyes for just a few breaths, listening, but still nothing. Swear to God, Ethan, if you are dead, I will find a necromancer and raise you up so I can kill you myself.

The first door opened to an empty bedroom. And I do mean empty: Not a single stick of furniture, no bits of debris on the floor. Even the carpet looked like someone had taken a rug shampooer to it in the recent past. I could smell the faintest tinge of wet polyester and mildewed foam padding, reminding me of the time Aunt Cleverly had to have her bedroom re-carpeted when a pipe burst one Thanksgiving.

The next room had bunk beds on one wall, and two cots shoved against the other. There was barely room to move between the beds. I had to turn sideways to fit, so I couldn't imagine a larger adult doing much more than standing in the doorway. The cots were small, child sized I'd dare say, bare of any bedding. The bunk beds, however, were neatly made with plain sheets that made an effort at being white but veered more toward gray. More of the wet carpet smell and bleach this time. The bedding, I realized. Someone had made an effort with the laundry for whomever slept in there.

I eased back into the hall and tried the last door. It squeaked when it opened, and I froze. After a moment, I stuck my head in and nearly recoiled in shock. It was beyond a pit. Floor to ceiling boxes, most of them battered and stained, blocked any windows that were in the room. The bed was covered in black plastic trash bags and torn fast-food wrappers. The floor was hidden under a thick layer of filthy clothes and what looked like used sharps and nitrile gloves. There was no way in hell a person could even get into the room, much less sleep in there.

I started to close the door when it hit me. Mingling with the stench of the bedroom, the burn of bleach from next door, the lemony tang drifting from the bathroom was that smell of the other were. It wasn't strong there, either, but it was woven into the disgusting bouquet of odors wafting from what had at one time been the master bedroom. The urge to flee wasn't as great, either, but it stirred in me.

No. No, no, no. Just fight it, goddammit! My tongue was heavy, like it was trying to slide back and choke me, as I crouched carefully in the doorway. Had the were been in here, or was it just something that had been in contact with them? Maybe some of the clothes?

I fished my phone out of my pocket and turned on the flashlight feature, unwilling to chance turning on the bedroom light itself. The bright glare of the LED from my phone slid over the islands of clothes and glitter of the discarded sharps. Some of the clothes bore dark, rusty stains I knew were blood. Most were just filthy, torn, worn all to hell and back.

I duck walked back a few inches and scanned the snowdrift-like ridge of trash where the opening of the door had made a fan of empty carpet. Gingerly, I tugged the packet of tissues out of my pocket. So, sue me, I like to be prepared. Some people find that an attractive trait. I made a thick pad out of most of the tissues and used it to pick up a few of the needles, still attached to the hypodermics. It wasn't going to be the best sample I'd ever collected, but maybe I'd be able to find out whether someone just had shitty hygiene with their insulin delivery or if they were up to something horrific.

Somewhere outside, a woman started shouting. Not screaming, shouting. She didn't sound afraid but rather angry.

I'm guessing that's Mrs. Raymond, I thought. I turned off my light feature and shoved my phone into my hip pocket. The sharps, still wrapped tight, went back into the plastic baggie with the rest of the tissues. I darted into the bathroom and took a very quick look around. The place was spotless. It looked as if it belonged in a different home altogether. Hand towels were neatly folded and hung on racks, fancy soaps sat in porcelain dishes, the grout and mirrors were as clean as the day they were installed, and on the counter sat a small stack of white boxes, the sort sometimes used for pharmaceuticals.

I took a look at the label and found it was something I'd never heard of: Lycaon. There were no listed precautions on the outside, and the box itself was still sealed. They all were. The woman's shouting was getting closer, and now I could pick up on the low tones of Ethan's voice and a second man who sounded just as pissed as the woman but wasn't shouting, just loud. The box had a lot number embossed on the bottom, but no expiration date. I flipped it over, looking for some indication as to its use, whether it was possibly tied to the sharps in my pocket and all over the bedroom floor. In tiny font, on the bottom of the back of the box, was the name of the company that produced it: Bluebonnet Biomedical.

The same place my Aunt Cleverly worked as a phlebotomist.

Down the hall, a door slammed open, the shouting now clear as a bell. "You can get the fuck off my property, sheriff. How's that for a statement? You're not gonna charge them boys with murder, then you get the fuck out of here and I'm gonna call the county on you. How about that?"

"If you contact the sheriff's department main office, Linda can give you the information you'll need in order to file a complaint."

Mrs. Raymond sputtered a string of invective regarding Ethan's parentage and his mother's preferred bed partners, none of which sounded zoologically possible. Mr. Raymond sounded weary, but angry when he spoke. "I know you got a job to do, Sheriff, but these are our children. If you're not gonna take us seriously, we're going to have to go over you."

"I understand," Ethan said. He paused, and I knew, knew down in my bones, he'd realized I was in the house. "I, uh, appreciate you showing me your memorial for the kids," he said. "And before I go, I'd like to see it again, if you don't mind."

Mrs. Raymond snarled. "I *do* mind! You'll sully their memories!"

"I understand."

The window over the toilet was small, but not so small that my skinny ass couldn't fit through it. I pried it open carefully, wincing when it creaked softly. Ethan was talking again, offering to look up the contact information the Raymonds would need for a complaint, trying to keep them at the front of the house. Bless his heart.

I stuck my head out and looked both ways. It was, for the moment, clear. The low buzz in my skull was ramping up again, though, and my mouth was tasting of pennies. This would have to be fast and probably graceless, I thought. I shoved the box of Lycaon into my back pocket and scrambled through the window, landing awkwardly on the hard ground outside. The whiff from the trashcan reached me there, and I was fairly certain that, at some point soon, I'd be sick all over the place.

I ran again, light and fast, this time down the broken concrete and gravel path on the opposite side of the house from where I'd begun. I hauled ass across the wide driveway and nearly dove into the tall grass on the other side, tripping and stumbling back toward Ethan's car.

My breath came in ragged, heaving gasps once I managed to crawl back into the passenger seat, shifting to get the box and needles out of my pockets before I crushed my evidence. Evidence of what? I wasn't sure, but I had a horrible feeling that whatever the Raymonds were up to and however it involved this strange were, the drugs were related.

Ethan jerked open the driver's side door before the heaviness of heat and adrenaline crash could overtake me fully. "Keep your head down," he muttered, barely moving his lips. "They're still outside and fucking pissed off."

I nodded, glad I'd laid my seat back after getting into the car a few minutes earlier. "Tell me when it's safe."

Ethan made a bleak, sound low in his throat but kept otherwise quiet as he got us in motion, heading away from the Raymonds as fast as he could without being a dick about it. Finally, when the jarring and jolting of Wallace Road smoothed out into the better maintained county road, he let out a long, rattling sigh. "They're fucking nuts," he said. "They want a private autopsy because..." He glanced at me where I laid back in the car seat, half-turned onto my side to see him. "Well. They're homophobic, and they remember you from when you lived here."

"Are you fucking kidding me?" I groaned. "Of all the stupid reasons..."

"Well, that's not entirely it. Jessup let slip that the pathologist they sent the kids off to works for some lab."

I sat up. "That's not how autopsies work." I sighed "Even a private one."

Ethan shook his head, fingers tight on the wheel as we stopped at the traffic light just on the edge of town. "I suggested that this whole private autopsy thing seemed a little sus. As soon as I said it, he clammed up, and the missus lost her shit." He glanced at me, looking older than before we'd left. "They've got this *shrine* sort of a thing set up in the line of trees between their property and the big old field on the other side of the ditch. It's intense." The light changed, and he fell quiet for a few minutes, navigating traffic past the high school again. "It's massive. Pictures, lights, this massive stone bench thing..."

"That sounds like grief," I said quietly. "I don't see as much of it as a funeral director, or even as much as you in your line of work, but I've seen my fair share over the years and grief... it makes you want to lionize your dead. Make their lives matter somehow. And things like that? It's not so unusual. It's a way to keep them alive, so to speak." I fingered the box on my lap and frowned. "What did Mrs. Raymond yell at you about?"

"Everything," he said with a mirthless laugh. "It's my fault her babies got killed, my fault. Well. My fault you did the postmortem exam, and my fault I wasn't suitably awed by the memorial, and the wild dogs are also somehow my fault." He cut me another glance, his lips pressed into a grim line. "That one, I'll take the blame for. Any weres in the area should be my responsibility, whether they're clan or just passing through."

"About that..."

We were nearing Cleverly's house, so I gave him the highlights, including my wild flight into the house instead of away from it. Ethan's expression, already tense, grew so taut that I was worried he was going to snap something important in his neck and jaw. I held up the box in my palm like an offering. "I was going to talk to Cleverly later, fish around and see if she can tell me what this is."

"Landry..."

"I know, I know. Trust no one. I remember our *X Files* phase."

A very faint smile quirked the corner of his mouth. "It's not just a catchphrase; it's a way of life."

"Seriously?"

At my incredulous tone, the smile grew ever so slightly. "Not really, but it sounded kind of cool in my head."

"Ass."

"Seriously, though, Landry. Be careful. We don't know who this other were is, and your aunt isn't like you."

"Do you mean..." I tapped my temple. "Or just that she doesn't know about your sort?"

"My sort? Yeah, mostly that." He sighed. We were in Cleverly's driveway now, pulled off to the side so she could get back in if she arrived before Ethan left. "Don't even show her the box," he said urgently. "It might put her in danger too if she knows about this and it has something to do with this were and with the Raymonds' deaths."

I nodded. "I know. Of course."

There was an awkward moment of hesitation where we both just stared, the same question burning in our thoughts. Kiss or not? Ethan answered it for me with a half-lunge, half-lean that ended in a hug and bonked noses.

"I'll call you later," he said, his face turning a shade I liked to call Embarrassed Tomato. It revived the butterflies in my belly as I let myself out of the car, evidence tucked carefully back into my pockets, and trotted up the drive to the front porch. Ethan sat and watched me as I unlocked the door and let myself in. Impulsively, I turned back and waved before I closed the door and locked up. He grinned, quick as a fox, and waved back, shifting into reverse as I shut the door.

The box was heavy against my hip as I hurried down the hall to my old room and dug my laptop out of my duffle bag. I wouldn't be able to access the full complement of resources I had via my position as coroner, but I still had professional access to some databases and various sites that could possibly give me information about Lycaon. The name was familiar, pinging some distant memory from high school or college, but I couldn't pin it down. Maybe, I thought, I'd heard of the drug's development during one of my pharmaceutical classes. Or maybe I'd just seen the name on a flier at a conference and I was wrong about knowing the name from ages ago.

As my laptop powered up, I tucked the box and the baggie with the used sharps into my duffle bag, wrapped in one of the t-shirts I'd brought. I shoved the whole thing under the bed, feeling every inch the sneaky adolescent as the front door opened and closed and footsteps sounded on the wooden boards of the hall.

Wait. Footsteps.

Heavy footsteps.

My aunt was not a small woman, but those steps were too heavy for her. My first thought was Ethan had come back and had managed to let himself in somehow, and my heart leaped, but I knew, between one heartbeat and the next, that I was wrong.

The steps stopped outside my door, and I could smell him. Expensive cologne, salt sweat, cinnamon gum, and the earth-sharp-musk smell that came with Oliver Waltrip.

Chapter Five

He stood on the other side of my door for several long minutes. My heart hammered in my chest, everything telling me to flee, except I couldn't move. Fear froze my blood and locked my muscles. He knew I was in there. That's why he had come straight back without looking around the house. It's how he knew exactly where I was. He could smell me, not just my skin and breath and whatever products I'd used, but my growing fear and the adrenaline crash from earlier, and the spike my exhausted body was in the throes of as he stood there. Waiting.

I shifted my laptop to the pillow next to me and slowly reached for my phone on the desk by the bed. The floorboards creaked under his feet. My first thought was to text Ethan so Waltrip wouldn't hear me talking, but the horrible realization that I still hadn't gotten Ethan's private number hit me just as I started scrolling through my address book. *Fuck*. Note to self: Playing coy can get you killed by a werewolf. Stop it.

If he knows I'm in here, then he shouldn't be surprised if I call the cops, I reasoned, but still, I held off. Because I'm stupid, probably. His footsteps sounded again, moving away from the door, but he didn't leave. The front door didn't open. The rattle of drawers and thump of cabinets told me he had gone into the kitchen. I knew where my aunt kept her guns and the ammo, but I wouldn't be able to access any of it before Waltrip heard me. He likely wasn't there to murder me, but the fact remained he'd tracked me down, he'd broken in, and was apparently waiting for me and, from the smell of things, making coffee.

Waltrip didn't bother turning around as I stepped into the kitchen doorway. He was busy adding sugar and more sugar to his (my aunt's) coffee, humming under his breath something that sounded suspiciously like peak eighties Cyndi Lauper.

"I'm not armed, but I can be." I hoped I sounded calmer than I felt. Honestly, I was just glad my voice didn't shake. Much.

Waltrip turned to lean his backside against the counter, one of my aunt's Phlebotomists Are the Bloody Best mugs looking ridiculous and small in his hands and a pile of those plug-in oil burners at his elbow. "Thanks for that. Though, to be honest, you and I both know I could, ah..." He winked, shrugging one shoulder before taking a long drink from the mug. "These things reek, by the way. Burns the shit out of my sinuses. I could barely smell *you* and you've got a very distinct smell to you, Doctor Babin."

"So, you break into my aunt's house, drink her shitty coffee, unplug her air fresheners, *and* threaten me? How professional and charming." I had no idea what he would look like if he shifted, but he'd be huge. Maybe bigger than Ethan, if what I'd noticed in the past was true and weres body sizes translated between human form and wolf. He would be able to change and get to me before I even hit the front door. Granted, my experience seeing weres shift was limited to the Stone clan, but I had no reason to think other weres would not shift as quickly, be able to move from one form to another in mid-stride even. I'd seen Ethan do it a few times, mostly showing off for me, and he had been so quick that it scared me. I didn't even see the change happen. One moment, he was my boyfriend, tall and gangling and just starting to flesh out into the muscular adult shape he'd one day have, and the next, he was a massive fuck off wolf, dun-colored with golden eyes, a head bigger than my chest, a canine smile baring his teeth. His brothers and the other, more removed members of the clan had been much the same. At the time, I'd been in awe and not a little jealous. Now, remembering how they changed and moved, I was just scared. Waltrip knew it, too.

"To be fair, the coffee isn't so bad. She's probably just letting it brew too long, and it's getting burned." He gestured toward the pot with his elbow. "Want some? I made enough for both of us."

What I should have said was *get out*, or *I'm calling the police*, or even turned my back and gone straight to Cleverly's gun safe. What I did say was, "What the actual fuck is wrong with you?"

He barked a startled laugh, head thrown back, before shaking his finger at me like I was some naughty toddler caught with a crayon at the wall. "You've got a pair on you, don't you, Doctor Babin? You must," he continued, setting the mug down. "I mean, you had a relationship with one of us for a while, didn't you? Back when Ethan Stone was mister popularity at Belmarais High School, long time before you hustled off to med school and he decided to go into law enforcement. Ever ask him why he went that route? Wasn't he going to be a doctor, too? Or was that just a line he fed you to get in your pants?"

My chest ached. I could smell Waltrip so strongly, it choked me. It wasn't a bad smell, not like the strange were, but it was not pleasant. Not to me. It came off him in waves, like he was doing it on purpose. He smirked at me, eyes narrowed in assessment. I took a hesitant step backward and nearly stumbled thanks to my legs turning to jelly. *I'm not afraid of you,* I wanted to say. *I can't help this. It's not my fear; it's this broken wolf shit.* That would go well, huh? I could just spill my guts out to this asshole who had broken into the house, and he'd be totally understanding, apologize, stop trying to intimidate me, and just go on his merry way. Sure, Landry, sure. Waltrip's eyes widened, and his smirk became a grin. With measured steps, he paced toward me, stopping just out of arm's reach. "I know what it looks like," I said. "But I'm not scared of you."

He breathed deeply, rumbling low in his chest when he exhaled. "You smell like you're afraid. But I'm not going to hurt you." He sniffed again, frowning, his gaze growing fuzzy and distracted. "No other wolves here, huh?" he muttered, sliding me a glance that called me a liar. "Hm." His demeanor changed in a snap. He turned on his heel and strode back to the counter, picking up the coffee and leaning back, relaxed. "You sure you don't want any? We need to talk, and you look tired as hell." He took another sip and added, "I promise it's not poisoned."

"Of course not," I said, not moving any closer. "You'd lose your license if you poisoned me."

"Only if I got caught." He drained the coffee and poured a fresh cup, taking his time adding all the sugar before moving to the battered antique table in the middle of the room. "You don't have to sit down, but you might want to."

"I'm good."

"Hmm. Well, fine then. First of all, I should apologize for the dramatics, but..." he shrugged again. "I'm a frustrated comic book villain at heart, I suppose."

"That will go over great with the cops when they get out here."

"This is a small town, and you're the sheriff's favorite person at the moment. If you'd called them, they'd have been here before I finished my first cup." He saluted me with Cleverly's mug. "I'm here because I was in town, meeting with my client. They mentioned Sheriff Stone brought you in last night."

"How the hell did they know that?" His smell was fading, but my heart hadn't slowed. I wanted to sit down and just breathe, but so long as he was sitting in my aunt's kitchen, I was forced to stand, my body threatening to bolt whether I wanted to or not if he made one wrong move.

Waltrip looked me up and down slowly, clinically. "This is a small town, Doctor Babin. My client expressed concern because you work for the county. Being seen with Sheriff Stone, who is possibly involved with the Raymond murders—"

"That's bullshit!" *Huh.* Apparently, being angry and protective was enough to tamp down some of that damned fear response. I was still definitely afraid, but my anger was strong enough to push to the fore, driving me to be aggressive rather than trying to flee. "I know you can't tell me who hired you, but if it's the Raymonds, they're wrong. Sheriff Stone had nothing to do with those kids getting killed."

"You and I both know it wasn't dogs," he murmured, toying with the handle of the coffee mug. "And so does my client. My client is aware Sheriff Stone brought you to Belmarais last night and that you were seen with him earlier today."

"Is your client aware that sounds like invasion of privacy and stalking?"

"You were in public both times."

"Then it's just fucking creepy. Got it." Waltrip's chuckle was low and rich, and I hated him for having a nice laugh. "That doesn't excuse your little crime spree this morning."

"I was already heading here when my client called regarding your jaunt with the sheriff. They expressed concern that you are possibly being subverted to his cause."

"Tell your client to fuck off. I've known Sheriff Stone for a long time and—"

"You haven't."

"Excuse me?"

"Fifteen years is a very long time to go without speaking with someone, Doctor Babin. Even close family and friends can change dramatically in fifteen years, becoming unrecognizable."

"I get it. Your client, who may or may not be the Raymonds, think Sheriff Stone could have done something to prevent the death of their kids. And they think I somehow missed something on the postmortem, and these things are tied together into one big conspiracy against them. I really understand. Grief is a weird beast. It can twist your mind around in unimaginable ways.

Parents convinced the world is out to get them isn't the worst thing I've seen in my line of work. Hell, if I had kids, I'd probably be doing the same thing. I'd want someone to blame, and so do they." I rolled my eyes, adding, "Assuming we're talking about the Raymonds."

"Ten years ago, Sheriff Stone was in college. He was finishing his undergrad in sociology." Waltrip raised a brow at me, his smirk firmly back in place. "Did you know he majored in sociology? Or have y'all not gotten around to really talking yet?" My silence answered for me. He laughed, this time a lot less pleasant. "I get it," he mimicked, "I really do."

"Talk," I snarled. "Or I will be calling the cops and your fucking licensing board."

It was Waltrip's turn to roll his eyes. "You have no flair for the dramatic, Doctor Babin. My client has asked me to speak with you regarding Sheriff Stone's involvement. This case is a bit... outside of the norm for my agency."

It clicked for me then, and I felt more than a bit foolish for it taking so long. "You're not investigating this for humans."

He saluted me with the mug. "And my client is aware that you are not ignorant of the presence of weres both here in Belmarais and in the world outside of town."

I really did need to sit down then.

"Don't bother trying to lie about it," he said when I opened my mouth to do just that. "The Stone clan is well known to my client, and the existence of weres is no secret to them."

I chose the chair farthest from him, perching on the edge. "Mr. Waltrip, if you're going to be discussing the Stone family in any capacity, I feel you should have a representative here."

His smile was a curly thing, sliding between nice and feral. "Who would that be? The sheriff himself? He's the head of the clan now, isn't he? And I'm a strange were on his territory, talking to his..." There was that assessing up-down gaze again. I clenched my hands hard around the edge of the chair, refusing to squirm. "Well. His *friend*. I had no idea the Stone clan adhered so closely to old protocol, but I shouldn't be surprised. My client seems to think the Stones, the sheriff in particular, have quite a problem with weres who don't swear loyalty to them."

"Swear loyalty? Good God, this isn't the Middle Ages," I scoffed. "I don't know jack shit about were clan dynamics, but I know Sheriff Stone," I said, ignoring my better judgment and bullying forth, "and he's not going to make anyone take a knee for him. The Stones just live their lives. And your client needs to get counseling or something. Stop spending it on PIs who break and enter and steal and stalk and spend it on a good therapist instead." I pushed myself away from the chair, digging my phone out as I rose. "Now. You've wasted my time, you're on private property without the homeowner's permission, and if you don't leave in the next thirty seconds, I *am* calling 911."

Waltrip rose, calmly carried the mug to the sink and rinsed it out, gave me a curt nod, and headed for the front door, stopping only when he had his hand on the knob. "I was on my way over this morning to talk with you about my client's concerns regarding the postmortem findings. They seem to think the Raymonds were weres, and someone was trying to hide it."

My thumb hovered over the send button. "What?"

He widened his eyes, feigning innocence. "Oh, sorry, did you want to hear that part? I was just on my way out."

Anger boiled back up. I hated people playing games with me, at least this sort, and I wasn't going to let Waltrip intimidate me into being jerked around. "Fuck this," I snapped, pressing send. His hand shot out, grabbed the phone from me, and hit the power button. "They're still coming," I pointed out. "Talk fast."

"It's not like the movies, Doctor Babin," he grinned. "They'll have to figure out where the call came from first." He shook the cell phone back and forth. "Cell phones, a blessing and a curse."

Fucking Hell. "Talk, or I will scream till the neighbors call for me."

A dark expression skidded over his face, one that stirred nausea in my belly, but it was gone before I could identify it well.

His eyes did not flash gold like Ethan's, he didn't growl at me like the were who cornered me in Baltimore, but he changed. It was subtle, but it was there. He was *more*, somehow, his presence pressing against me even though he didn't move from his spot at the door. Before I could even squeak, though, it was over. He still loomed, but the predatory nature had receded. I wasn't safe, but the danger wasn't imminent. "My client is well aware of Sheriff Stone's status in the regional were community. They also feel he has reason to hide the fact the Raymond kids were weres, though not part of the Stone clan. Or any clan, for that matter. A clan master allowing rogue weres in their territory," he paused, eyeing me up and down again, less clinical and more pitying. "A clan master allowing rogues in their territory is a problem for the were community."

"They weren't weres," I protested. "The Raymonds. Not like Ethan. Or you," I added. "If anything, they were... they were like me."

Waltrip sighed gustily, pinching the bridge of his nose between thumb and forefinger before replying. "And like I said, this is a problem."

My mouth was dry. I could barely get words to form. "How much of a problem?"

"Enough of a problem that, if my client can prove Stone knew and did nothing, he'd have some severe consequences. More than I can share with you." He tapped the side of his nose like W.C. fucking Fields and winked at me. "Were secret, you know. Though," he added thoughtfully, tugging the door open, "I suppose you wouldn't."

"He wouldn't what?"

Waltrip didn't jump, but he definitely twitched. My aunt stood on the other side of the door, key poised to unlock it, smiling up at Oliver Waltrip like a shark who'd just scented blood. "Good afternoon," he murmured, cutting his eyes to me in a narrow glare. "Pardon me, ma'am. Let me get out of your way." He sniffed, nose flaring as my aunt wiggled past him, cocking his head at me like a confused dog for a moment before visibly shaking himself, though his gaze clung to my aunt for just a beat too long for my comfort.

"Oh, no! Stay, stay! I never mind Landry having friends over while he's here! Come in, come in!"

For one brief second, Waltrip and I were united in startled panic. Cleverly laid her hands on Waltrip like he wasn't well over six feet tall twice her width, pushing him until he moved back toward the kitchen. His eyes wide, he shoved my phone back at me and let Cleverly propel him toward the kitchen table. I followed helplessly, a faint twinge of schadenfreude percolating in my belly. Very faint, really, since Cleverly forcing him to drink her coffee and be social was nowhere near enough to balance out what he had done, but it was a start. Though, her coffee *was* terrible. She always either burned it or made it so strong it could reach out of the pot and slap you. I couldn't remember a time when her kitchen didn't have the tang of boiled, scorched coffee mixed in with everything else. I leaned against the doorway between the kitchen and the front hall, watching Waltrip watch my aunt. She chattered about her morning visits, the new bakery opening on the far end of town, and how they dared not to have kolaches on the menu. "In Texas!" she huffed. "Can you believe such a thing?" She tsked, taking down the good mugs, the ones she kept for company, before turning a bright smile to Waltrip. "How do you take it, dear?"

"Too much sugar," I answered for him. Cleverly shot me a look, one of her perfectly plucked brows arching up so high I was worried we'd need to send a search team for it.

"So, how'd the two of you meet?" she cooed.

Shit. I knew where this was going. "He's an acquaintance I met due to a work situation. He stopped by to pass along some information regarding..."

Waltrip had a gallery of smiles. The one he put on for my aunt was designed to charm the knee-high stockings off her. "Regarding a time-sensitive issue." He shifted his attention to me, the smile never faltering. "And I hate to sip and dash, but I really need to get back to Dallas by this evening. Client meeting in the morning." The emphasis on the word client spoke volumes.

"Let me walk you out."

Cleverly bustled along with us, getting between me and Waltrip as he rose and headed for the door. "Well, it's a shame you couldn't finish your coffee. Do you want it in a to-go mug? I have some of those travel mugs, and you can just give it back to Landry next time you see him. Maybe next week some time?" she asked, aiming for sly and missing by a wide margin.

Waltrip's startled look was back, fleeting but clear. "Ah, no, that's alright. Thank you, though, and sorry you went to the trouble. I'm sure Landry would *love* a cup, though. He looks like he's been running all over town this morning and could use a pick me up." He smiled down at Cleverly, stiffening ever so slightly when she reached up to hug him around the neck. I didn't have to see his eyes to know they were probably watering from the tang of her Jean Nate body splash.

"She's a hugger." I bared my teeth in a parody of a smile. Waltrip snorted softly. His smell was still strong, still unpleasant, but it was fading fast now that the door had been opened and we were getting some fresh air, the funk of those oil burners finally gone. I was steadier on my feet with each breath of the warm, fig tree-scented air that wafted in as Waltrip stepped down off the porch. He turned and gave me a long, steady look before nodding once, then flashing a smile at Cleverly. As he turned to head toward his truck, parked down at the end of the drive, a breeze blew softly through the door, and I smelled it.

The sour-bad-wrong stench of the strange were. The murderer.

Chapter Six

"I hope you can figure out what the hell is wrong with him," Cleverly huffed. "He's been pacing around like this for an hour now, and I'll be damned if I have to get my carpet replaced because he wore a hole in it!"

Ethan snorted softly, edging past her into the living room. "Oh, I love the change," he said, nodding at the clock over the mantel. "That turquoise enamel really picks up the patina on your new frames."

Cleverly blushed, of all things. *Blushed!* "Oh, thank you, Ethan. I have to admit they're not that new. Homegoods—well, back when it was Garden Ridge Pottery—had them on sale and I loved how they looked all antique! And the clock"—she shot me a purse-lipped glare— "has been there for ages now. It used to belong to my mother. It was just collecting dust in the hall closet, and I thought this room could use some color."

I stared back and forth between the two of them. "Seriously?" I muttered. "We're gonna talk decorating right now?"

"*We* aren't," Cleverly pointed out. "Ethan and I were."

Ethan smirked at me. "Hey."

"We need to talk." I glanced past him at Cleverly. "But I can't leave her here alone."

Cleverly pursed her pink-painted lips, glaring at us from the step leading down into her den. "Landry Babin, I am a grown-ass woman. I do *not* need you to protect me like I'm some frail old lady!" She would have stomped her foot if it didn't detract from her towering indignation.

Ethan caught my elbow and led me to the sofa. "He'll be fine, Miss Cleverly. He's just het up from a rough week at work."

"*Excuse me?*" I snarled. "I'm not a fu—freaking *child*, Ethan!" I jerked free from his grasp. How fucking dare he dismiss me like that, treat me like some sulking teenager? I glared at him, opening my mouth to read him the riot act, but Cleverly's sigh cut me off.

"I thought maybe he'd had a tiff with that young man who was here earlier. You sure it wasn't a lover's quarrel, Landry? You know I don't mind if you entertain here, so long as you're safe and don't flush condoms, I really—"

"Wow, okay, yeah, this is... this is awful," I yelped, shooting to my feet. The flare of hurt and confusion on Ethan's face was hard to miss, but he schooled his expression into polite amusement quickly enough that my aunt didn't seem to notice the moment. Was I an asshole for the flare of smug satisfaction at seeing that Ethan still cared enough to be jealous? Maybe. Probably. But I couldn't make myself drag out some coy fib to make Ethan get all growly and possessive—we didn't have the time and I definitely lacked the energy and skill. "He wasn't a boyfriend or a hookup or whatever, and there was absolutely no sex at all, and Ethan, for the love of God, please tell me you have a deputy or someone on hand that can keep an eye on my aunt when I go back to Tuttle!"

"Lan, listen, I'd love to set someone to watch over her for you, but that's not how the department works. You know that." He squeezed my arm gently, a frisson of familiar awareness curling through me at the contact. "Come on, let's take a walk around the yard." He shook his head when I started to protest. "We'll be right outside; we can have our talk and keep an eye on the house at the same time."

Seeing the concern crimping Cleverly's brow, the way she

squeezed her fingers together like she was praying, made me feel more than a little guilty for my outburst. "Let's go." Ethan didn't let go of me as we squeezed past Cleverly and out into the front yard. The smell lingered, so faint it was almost unnoticeable unless I really tried to pick up on it. It swirled through the air, delicate and thin, never strong enough in one spot to suggest someone standing in one spot, someone watching and waiting as we moved around inside the house. I wandered, tugging Ethan along with me, trying to inhale surreptitiously. He squeezed my arm again, not so gently this time. "I know what you're doing," he murmured as we stepped under the overhanging branches of a pecan tree. "Stop it."

"It's like picking at a scab," I murmured. "You know it's a bad idea, but it bugs you so much..."

"Exert effort."

I rolled my eyes. That had been one of his favorite sayings when we were teenagers. Any time he wanted me to try something that took more physical strength than I supposed I had, I'd hear him grumble *Exert effort, Landry. Stop waiting for it to happen for you, and just do it.* "Okay, let me talk first before you go off." I knew by the set of his jaw it was going to be physically painful for him to keep quiet while I spoke, but that was his problem for now. I told him about my morning since he'd dropped me off, his sharp huff of breath when I mentioned actually deciding not to call for help telling me exactly where the leaping off point for my chewing out would be. "And after he left, that's when I called." I sighed. "Cleverly thinks I'm on drugs."

"I'm starting to wonder myself." He finally let go of me only to start pacing himself. "First of all, fucking hell, Lan! How the hell have you survived this long?"

Embarrassment flamed hot on my face, the ugly flush spreading down my neck. "I made a decision—"

"Yeah, a fucking stupid one. He could have killed you, you ass!" Ethan stopped pacing in front of me, far closer to me than I had expected. I took half a step back and butted up against the tree, annoyance starting to override my earlier shame. "I had Tyler check up on this guy," he said, lowering his voice as if my aunt could hear us from a half-acre away, behind closed doors and over Judge Judy. "His PI license is legit, but there's no trace of him doing any actual work as an investigator. No known clients, no business accounts, nothing."

"What the hell does Tyler *do*? Isn't he still in college?"

"Stop trying to divert me," Ethan snapped. "He's shady as sin, Landry, and the fact he tracked you down—"

"He said that you could get in a hell of a lot of trouble for letting rogue weres run loose in clan territory."

Ethan jerked back like I'd slapped him. "Yes," he said after a long, sticky moment of silence. "That's true. I could. If there were any rogue weres trying to live here."

"His client says otherwise. They claim the Raymonds are rogue weres. And that you're helping to hide them." It was my turn to invade his personal space, stepping closer until I could smell the very faint tinge of his aftershave underneath the stronger scent of *him*. If there was one thing I would forever be grateful for when it came to this fucked up part of myself, it would be that I could smell Ethan like this, the warmth and rightness of him, something beyond just his skin and soap and sweat. It sparked its way down through me, settling low in my belly and glowing, a banked flame just waiting for the right touch to bring it to a full flame. Ethan knew, too, that I was scenting him, wanting him. He didn't move away when I got so close our chests brushed. Our roles reversed for a few moments. I was the predator this time. "What would happen to you," I asked softly, "if the Raymonds had been rogue weres? Who would be the one trying to punish you?"

He licked his lips, the pink tip of his tongue distracting me as it darted out, following its movement along his lower lip before he spoke again. "I shouldn't tell you, but it's bullshit, isn't it? Keeping this a secret from you now? I should have told you about it back then, but..." He shook his head. "I was stupid. There's an oversight committee."

The giggle that escaped me was as far from dignified as possible. I don't think it even existed in the same country code as dignified.

"Seriously? Fuck's sake, Landry."

"I'm sorry, it's just... How could this be so secret?" I shook my head. "Christ, Ethan, I can't even get an office Secret Santa organized. How the hell did y'all manage this?"

"Centuries of practice." He wasn't even a little amused, and I didn't blame him, but I couldn't stop giggling. "You're making this hard." He sighed, pinching the bridge of his nose. "If you're going to treat it like a joke, Landry..."

"I'm sorry," I gasped. "I think I'm freaking out." Hands over my eyes, I took several deep breaths. *Fuck, that does nothing...* I could smell Ethan, feel him so close, and the want was getting tangled with the *nope*. "I'm sorry," I managed, swallowing down more giggles. "I know it's not funny. It's just my entire world view just tilted to one side, and I wasn't ready."

"You can accept I'm a werewolf, that there are others like me, but the idea that we have community and governance among ourselves fucks with your head?" I peeked. He was smiling a little —it was in his voice.

"I think we both know there're no others like you." I sighed. My face heated, but I didn't care. Ethan cleared his throat, and the remembered touch of his fingertips skimmed over my cheek. "I'm sorry," I said again, "I just... This is a lot."

"Do you have to go back to work on Monday? Do you have any time off?"

"Um, the job came with some vacation and sick time, but it'd look hella bad if I took it now. I've only been there three months. I'm technically still in my probationary period for two more weeks."

Ethan grunted, staring past me at something only he could see, lost in some thoughts. His fingers had drifted from my cheek to my shoulder and held me in place, not a hard pressure but enough that I was loath to move for fear of losing the sensation. It was safety and good and need in a way that didn't leave me feeling gutted, desperate for more. Before I could give in and lean against his touch, Ethan's eyes cleared, and he fixed me with a hard, determined gaze. "Right. I can't set a deputy on your aunt without it being fishy as hell and also raising a lot of ethical issues. But I *can* set Tyler on her."

"Tyler. Your brother who thought frosted tips and tearing the sleeves off his t-shirt was the height of fashion? That Tyler?"

"I don't see what that has to do with him protecting your aunt and keeping an eye out for rogue weres."

"It speaks to his poor decision-making skills," I retorted. "Besides, he hates me."

"Tyler doesn't hate... Okay, well, he doesn't like you, but I wouldn't call it hate." He shrugged. "And he'll help because I'm telling him to. It's not a favor for his brother, but a clan matter at this point." His thumb rubbed a distracting circle on my shoulder. "So, this part, I have a feeling you might fly off the handle about but... are you sure that Waltrip isn't our suspect, Landry?"

I nodded, glancing toward where Waltrip had parked earlier. I'd walked around the spot when we'd first come out, and all I could pick up under the smell of slowly decomposing leaves and warm, sandy earth was the faintest tinge of motor oil and burned coffee. "I didn't smell it on him at all. Not even a hint. I didn't smell it until he was leaving, and the door was open."

"Fuck." He sighed. "I was hoping..." He squeezed my shoulder before dropping his hand to his side. "What about his two buddies? Have you seen them since the deli when they tried to scare you?"

"I prefer 'intimidate' and no. Not since that day." The low murmur of Aunt Cleverly's television drifted out over the front lawn. She either had the front door standing open, or it was turned up very loud for us to be able to notice it this far away, even with our increased hearing ability. Ethan made a low, considering noise that did more for my southerly blood flow than I'd like to admit, both of us turning to look back toward the house. "I think it's not a good idea, but if Tyler is my only choice, then yes, please turn Tyler loose out here. But I want him *actually* keeping an eye on Cleverly and the house! Without her knowing!"

"You do realize that's pretty creepy, right? I mean, I know I'm the one who's suggesting it, but hearing it out loud makes me realize how creepy it is."

"Do you want to explain werewolves to her?"

"Not especially. And I'm fine with it being creepy, I just don't like hearing it out loud. Makes me feel oogie."

We were walking back toward the porch, backs of our hands bumping like nervous teenagers afraid to just reach out and tangle our fingers together. "Oogie? Big, tough Sheriff Stone just said he felt oogie," I cackled.

"Who said I'm tough?" he groused, stopping on the bottom step to the porch, letting me stand on the second riser, making us just about even in height.

"Don't even try to pretend like you're oblivious to your public image." I poked at his bicep with one finger. "Guys who look like you don't just wake up one morning with muscles like that. Even"—I dropped my voice to a low whisper— "weres." I poked him gently in the chest, adding, "And the fact you're so aware of how you dress, how you look... Not in a vain way. Just like you give a damn. There's a difference between the big box store flannels the rest of us are wearing and your fancy mail order plaid shirts from freaking Maine or one of those hearty, cold states, you know."

He smirked. "So, you've been checking me out?"

"Considering we made out in my living room after seeing each other for less than an hour for the first time in fifteen years, you can safely say I still find you attractive."

Ethan's smirk blossomed into a full-fledged smile, one that made his dimples pop and his eyes crinkle. Goddamn, he was still the most beautiful thing I'd ever seen, and he knew it, too. The way he leaned in, breathing deep, he knew. The television was still blaring, the door open halfway, and from inside, the smell of Aunt Cleverly's cooking pushing away the smell of the rogue were. Ethan glanced past me, his smile softening. "Kind of reminds me of when I'd walk you home from your job at that awful burger place."

I looked over my shoulder at the slice of hallway revealed by the open door, how it looked unchanged since I'd left for high school, and then back at Ethan, the man in front of me who had traces of the boy I'd loved but was someone new, someone who had left behind that loud, and fast, and brash, and bright-burning teenager before either of us realized it. "It does?" I asked, my voice husky, barely a breath supporting the words. "It feels new to me."

Ethan closed his eyes for a moment, swaying toward me before exhaling slowly and opening them again. "I'm still on duty for a few more hours," he said regretfully. "Can I come by later? I want to... I want to learn about you again."

I raised my eyebrows and made a teasing, shocked face. "Sheriff Stone! Are you propositioning me?"

He rolled his eyes, his laugh low and rough. "Damn it, Landry, I'm trying to have a moment with you here!"

I reached out and fussed with his collar, with the stupid black polyester tie he had to wear with his uniform, twitching his smudged nameplate on his pocket. "Come by after your shift. I'm not leaving till in the morning. We can talk tonight. Or at least get started with everything we need to discuss."

Ethan nodded, walking backward a few feet before nodding once more and turning away. "I'll talk to Tyler before tonight," he called over his shoulder.

I waved, even though he couldn't see me, and watched as he got into the department's SUV and backed out onto the road. The television got quiet back in the house. Cleverly was moving around, fussing with something in the kitchen, but I stood on the porch a minute longer, staring after Ethan, my mind a tangle. I needed to make a list, I decided. More than one friend and coworker had told me, my reliance on list-making was annoying, my little sticky notes and torn out notebook pages thumb tacked to the boards around the office or apartment had been what I was known for in college, and later when I moved out on my own, sharing space with short term lovers or friends. It verged on obsessive sometimes, my need to list things out and find patterns, find the best order for things so I could be more efficient, so my life would go smoothly, even just for a few hours. *First, the Raymonds*, I thought, heading back into the house and closing the door behind me. Something smelled a bit burned, and I realized Cleverly must have opened the door to vent the smoke. I stuck my head in the kitchen, but she wasn't there. "Aunt Cleverly?"

"Back here," she called, sounding like she was in her sewing room. "Can you come help me with this?"

"Sure."

Why blame Ethan for hiding the fact they were rogue if they were weres? *Ooooh, maybe I'll make one of those web diagrams.*

I stopped in the doorway to the sewing room. It was empty. "Aunt Cleverly?"

"Over here, dear," she said, sounding very close. Before I could turn, everything exploded in pain, my vision going white as sharp, electric shocks shot down my neck and spine. I knew I was falling, but I couldn't stop myself. "Oh, dear," she gasped. "That looked painful!"

"Aunt... Aunt Cleverly?" I gasped, trying to push myself up onto all fours, trying to stand. I must have hit my head on something, I thought. What, though? The door was open; all that was behind me was an empty hallway and the guest bathroom. "What—" I managed to roll to one side. My aunt was frowning, bending toward me, her fingers reaching for my face. "My head..."

"Shhh, let me help," she soothed, dropping to her knees. "You're going to have a terrible headache later!"

"I have one now." Everything sounded so far away, even the mental alarm bells currently grating and screeching somewhere deep in my brain. "I think I need to go to the ER." *Am I having a stroke? Oh, God, is this an aneurysm?*

"Let me see your eyes, honey," she crooned. One of her palms pressed against my forehead, tipping my head back gently so she could look into my pupils. "They're even, so that's good." A sharp prick sparked against my neck. "Oh, dear, now they're dilating!" She tsked. "Oh, my."

I couldn't put the pieces together. I needed to make that damned list, I thought, everything blurring and stretching. "Call... call 911," I groaned.

The pain in my head was fading, being replaced by a heavy, thick feeling. This wasn't fainting—I'd fainted before, and it was nothing like this slow, sticky slide toward unconsciousness.

"Did I get a bee sting?" I asked distantly, reaching up to the burning spot on my neck.

"It's okay, Landry." She leaned in even closer. Her eyes were red, tears sparkling along her lashes. They seemed so bright to me as she pressed a kiss to my forehead and patted my hand. "We're gonna get you taken care of."

Chapter Seven

*H*urt wasn't a big enough word to encompass every sensation in my body, I opened my eyes to a dark-blue ceiling and faint hum of the telemetry at my bedside. I wasn't in any hospital I knew. Belmarais didn't have a hospital, and Tuttle had the closest level one emergency facility. This was definitely not Tuttle Medical and Community Care. Carefully, I patted around the sides of the bed for the call button, wincing as I pulled on the IV I hadn't realized was in the back of my hand, the layers of tape telling me I had probably tried pulling it out at some point earlier, some point I couldn't remember. My head swam when I turned it to one side, looking for some indication of date, time, location, and finding only a blank blue wall. The pillow under my cheek was far too smooth and soft to be hospital issue. I closed my eyes again and immediately felt the tug of a soporific in my system, the edge of drug-induced sleep still so close that even a long blink seemed able to pull me under again. Forcing myself to keep my eyes wide open, I shifted my head to the other side. There was a door in that wall, a pale blue against the stark white. A small window was set around eye level, metal mesh sandwiched between glass—no, I knew better, it was Plexiglass. Designed to keep patients from breaking through it, trying to escape from an otherwise locked room. I gingerly craned my neck to peer at the IV bag. There were no markings, and the fluid was clear. I hoped it was just saline or Ringer's solution.

The machines at my bedside definitely registered my changing vitals, but no one came to check on me. I shifted carefully, my muscles sore like I'd been running for miles. The bed was soft, almost too soft, and even though it lacked the typical controls of a hospital bed, it had rails along both sides, fully engaged and locked to keep me from getting out easily, and a railing at the foot where a glossy white tablet was perched on a stand. Who needs paper charts when you're apparently a very well-funded, expensive private clinic? Short of having some *Alice in Wonderland* level lucid dream, I had to be in some private facility, I realized, letting my head fall back—albeit carefully—against the way too nice pillow. "Hello?" I tried. My mouth felt sticky and raw. The word grated at my throat, and I had the disturbing realization I must have been intubated at some point. *Shit. Okay, take stock. What happened first?*

I hit my head.

No, wait... I didn't hit it. Something hit me.

Aunt Cleverly leaning over me. Did I get a bee sting?

What happened after that?

I tried to remember, retrieving only snatches of sound, the impression of a dark, bumpy ride in a car, muffled voices, then nothing.

Had I been kidnapped? What happened to my aunt? Shit... Ethan! Was he okay? It had to be Waltrip. I was an idiot, and this was my fault. He'd done something while he was in the house, maybe sneaked in one of his friends from before, someone who was waiting for me. For both of us, because I couldn't imagine them leaving Cleverly behind if she had seen what they did to me. *Fuck... she'd been there...* I pushed myself up to sitting and groaned as my head swam. Nausea roiled hot and acid in my gut, threatening to spill out. I groaned again, unable to stop myself. Eyes closed tight against the throbbing pain in my skull, I took several slow, deep breaths and ran a mental checklist on myself. *Headache, nausea, dizziness, light sensitivity: Concussion, probably a pretty decent one. Also signs of being drugged. No indication of breaks or sprains. Thank the powers that be, no catheter so they must not have been expecting me to be out very long. No hospital gown, but this is definitely not what I was wearing earlier.* The gray scrub set looked like the ones I'd seen morgue attendants wearing at Tuttle Medical, but they were softer than any scrub set I'd ever owned. They felt like super-luxe cotton and possibly angel hair and the tears of virgins. Same with the sheets. If I wasn't in the throes of panic, I'd have been trying to find out where to get my own. I opened my eyes and peered at the window in the door again. No sign of life on the other side. I tried to keep myself calm, or at least close to, as I gently slipped the cannula from my arm and pressed against the well of blood that rose through the puncture.

"Doctor Babin," someone chided from somewhere behind me. "That's not very smart, is it? You're quite dehydrated."

I was proud of myself; I managed not to squeak, but I did jerk, my head screaming in protest. "Hello? Where the hell am I?"

"A private clinic," they a few seconds later. Score one for me, guessing that one correctly. I twisted carefully on the bed and spotted the intercom set in a discrete panel just beside the headboard. It was flush and painted to blend in with the wall, making it easy to miss. *What else was hiding in plain sight? Cameras?* "Your aunt is doing well," the voice added. "You can see her soon."

My heart lurched painfully with relief. "Was she hurt?"

"She's fine," the man soothed. His voice was oily, sending twists of unease through my belly whenever he spoke. "Just stay calm, and a nurse will be there in a moment to assess your condition, Doctor Babin." There was no audible click to let me know he'd turned off the intercom, so I decided to function on the principle that he hadn't, that he was listening to me move, and I decided, looking quickly around the room again, probably watching as well. The room itself had no other doors but the one, no sink, cabinets, or even a shelf for personal items. I took a slow, deep breath and smelled nothing. Not nothing as in 'this place doesn't smell bad' or 'eh, it smells like a hospital but nothing out of the ordinary.' I smelled literally nothing. Not my own sweat, no antiseptic medical smells, not even the faint tang of my blood dripping along my forearm, which I knew should be flooding my senses by this point. I laid back against the pillows, my brain going completely blank for several long moments. Panic, I realized. Confusion. Time for my brain to reboot. *Have you tried turning it off and turning it back on again?* It must be the head injury, I decided, it had to be. For all my bitching and moaning about being broken somehow, my abilities being a burden, the idea of living without them made me panic. The monitors at the bedside bore this out, my heart rate shooting up, my blood pressure climbing even as I clawed at the cuff fastened around my upper arm. I ripped it off just in time for a short, pale-eyed woman to throw open the door and click her tongue at me.

"Really, Doctor Babin! You should know better!" she scolded, bustling to my side, and grabbing the leaking IV tubing, pushing the entire rig away from the bed.

"Sorry," I gasped out, my chest tight, "I tend to work with people who are past the need for a BP check."

She giggled, her entire face crinkling up like an amused bunny. "Oh, your aunt said you were funny!" She whipped out a penlight and grabbed my chin in a firm grip. "Now you know the drill, right? Even if your patients don't need this, either!"

Obediently, I followed the light with my eyes. She brandished a tongue depressor at me, then ran a fast read digital thermometer across my forehead. A quick pulse check later, she smiled again and patted my thigh. "While you were out, they did a quick scan of your noggin. No bleeding, so that's great!"

"Um, yeah, definitely." She had no name tag on her pale pink scrubs, no indication of the clinic name or her position or anything that could identify her as a medical professional. "I'm sorry, what's your name?" A frown flitted across her face, her happy bunny nose crinkle gone in a heartbeat. "I'm just really confused," I added, making my tone a little more pathetic (not that it was difficult to do). "I don't know where I am, and I'm worried about my aunt. Were we robbed or something?"

The nurse smiled again, but this one wasn't a cute, crinkly, happy woodland creature expression. It was cold, sharp. "I'm Rosamund. You're at the Garrow Clinic." A shock of recognition shot through me. I started to struggle up, but she pressed me back down with the flat of her hand. "We're a subsidiary of Bluebonnet Biomedical these days. You were brought here at the request of..." She trailed off, shook her head a little, then patted my knee. "Well, at the request of someone high up on the food chain, let's just say!" Her laugh was grating, not even a little like the silvery giggle of just moments before. "Give me just a few minutes, and we'll take you down to see your aunt."

I nodded, and she left me alone again, a definite, loud thunk telling me she had just locked me inside. *High up on the food chain? A private clinic...* The only person I knew who was high on any food chain was Ethan, but even as a clan leader, I doubted he had the resources to get me into a private clinic, much less my aunt. And even if he *had*, I wasn't flattering myself when I thought that he would be right by my side. Swinging my feet off the bed, I discovered a pair of slip-on canvas sneakers were waiting for me, ugly white but new, still stiff to the touch as I carefully slid my feet inside. Standing was an adventure in and of itself, leaving me clutching the foot of the bed as my head tried to decide whether or not to kill me for a few minutes. By the time I managed to stand straight and not want to puke my guts out, Rosamund had returned, professional smile firmly in place. Behind her, a young man with dark hair pushed a wheelchair, narrowly avoiding running over her toes as he eased it into the room. She shot him a swift, brutal glare that he seemed to ignore, bringing the chair to my side. "Well, Doctor Babin," she caroled. "Your aunt is ready to have visitors! We'll be taking you to the day room just down the corridor. Have a seat and let Jeremy give you a ride."

Jeremy, bless his heart, snorted softly. If I'd felt better, I'm sure I would've joined him in the conspiratorial wink he slid my way. As it was, I half sat, half collapsed into the wheelchair and leaned back, letting him flip down the footrests and take off the wheel brakes. "Just brace yourself," he muttered. I didn't miss Rosamund's sharp look between the two of us before she held the door wide and plastered a smile back on her face. "This way, y'all. I must say, Doctor Babin, your aunt is a lovely woman! Very kind to us worker bees!" The corridor was long, surprisingly wide, and had an ornate carpet runner down the center, covering a polished wood floor. Doors to either side of the corridor looked the same as the one to my room, but I had the feeling we were in a house rather than a place built to be a clinic.

"She's like that," I muttered. The movement of the chair was making me nauseated all over again. Not being able to smell set me off-kilter, and I found myself breathing too deeply, making myself dizzy as I tried to catch any trace of a scent, even the soapy tang of hospital antiseptic would do. Rosamund kept up a steady chatter about how amazing my aunt was, how she hadn't given them a speck of trouble even when she was worried about my injury. Jeremy grumbled under his breath, nothing I could make out clearly, but he seemed less than thrilled to be there. Not that I blamed him—I wasn't too excited, either. We reached a set of double doors, heavy wood with intricate knotwork carved over virtually every inch of the damned things. "Holy shit," I breathed, unable to stop myself. "Um, out of curiosity, did y'all make sure you're on my insurance plan because I'm really doubting I can afford this place." And I didn't just mean financially. This was it, the place that was the center of the shitstorm, I thought, trying hard not to let it show as my stomach turned itself into knots. *RunRunRun!*

Rosamund laughed again and reached for the brass panel beneath one of the doorknobs. She slid it to one side and began punching in a long series of keystrokes. "Garrow Clinic was, at one time, the home of Lucas and Delilah Garrow. They had it built during the railroad boom in the late nineteenth century here in Texas, and it's been in the Garrow family ever since. Forty years ago, Nelson Garrow converted it to a convalescent home, then later a private clinic. All of this," she gestured back down the hall, indicating the hospital-like doors on the rooms, "is courtesy of the Garrow family's generosity." She raised a brow and, for a second, I thought she was challenging me to disagree, but no, she was looking over my shoulder at Jeremy. He grunted in response, and she stared hard for a moment more before pressing in a few more keystrokes and turning the doorknob.

My aunt was sitting on a peacock blue divan beneath a picture window that took up most of the wall. Outside, it was dark, and I could make out the shapes of trees through the ambient light cast by the clinic's lights. She looked up as Jeremy pushed me in, Rosamund falling back to stand by the door. "Oh, thank God!" Cleverly gasped, struggling to her feet. Wearing dark scrubs that looked a lot like her work uniform but lacking in insignia, he looked otherwise just like she did every day of the week: heavy but neat makeup, her hair twisted back into a soft twist, gold chain around her neck, and all of her rings on round fingers. Cleverly rushed to me and grabbed my face in her hands, pressing pink-painted kisses all over my cheeks and forehead. "I was so worried! They told me you have a concussion!" She lifted her head to find Rosamund by the door, narrowing her eyes at the nurse before she whispered, "Are they lying to me, hon? Is there anything else wrong? Don't be afraid to tell me!"

"I'm..." I didn't want to lie. I wasn't fine; I wasn't okay. "I'm sore," I admitted. "And kind of freaked out. How the hell did we get here? And who did it?"

She nodded toward the divan, and Jeremy, whom I'd forgotten was still behind me, pushed me to join her by the window before stepping aside and doing a piss poor job of trying to blend in with the furnishings. "Bluebonnet does some work for the clinic," she admitted after a tense bout of worrying her lower lip between her teeth. "I called in a favor when I saw how badly you'd been hurt."

"What?" Words had stopped making sense. Maybe my concussion was worse than I'd thought. "The nurse said someone, er, high on the food chain got us in here? And you! Are you okay? I was sure..." I shook my head carefully, still wincing at the sloshing feeling it produced. "Aunt Cleverly?"

"I don't know how to tell you." She sighed, her eyes bright and shining. I hated it when my aunt cried and braced myself for one of her loud, wailing outpourings, but it never came. Instead, she inhaled deeply and took my hand in hers. "Your friend, the one that came by today? Mr. Waltrip? Well... I've seen him around quite a bit. And Lolly, from the café, she stopped me before I headed home and mentioned someone had been asking about you. Described a big ol' red-headed guy, and when I saw that Mr. Waltrip, well, I got worried. Why would this guy who'd been lurking around my work want to come out and see you? I thought maybe it had something to do with your dad..."

I winced. My father, whom I hadn't seen since I was two, had been a prolific gambler and drug dealer in our little corner of Texas. When he disappeared, everyone had assumed the inevitable had finally happened, and he was at the bottom of the bayou or drifting in pieces in the Gulf. But every once in a while, my aunt would get a phone call she'd take in hushed tones, locked in her room with the radio turned up so I couldn't overhear a thing. I had wondered, over the years, if it had something to do with my father, her brother. "Why would Waltrip have anything to do with him? He's been dead for half my life! And that still doesn't tell me how we got here!"

She smiled sadly. Before she said the words, I knew what was coming. Slick, thick nausea settled in my veins, and I wanted to cover my ears so I couldn't hear Cleverly's next words, but I was frozen, numb. "Honey, I know this is gonna be a real shock to you, but he's not dead. We just thought it best you didn't know.

He's... he's not a good man, baby. Your dad's been asking me for money for years. He's not dead. I think you already knew that, didn't you? In your heart of hearts. I've been sending him cash once every few months since you came to live with me. After your mama and grandma passed."

"Okay, so, full disclosure, I am not entirely sure I can deal with this information at the moment." The headache that'd come with my concussion now had a thrilling undercurrent of *what fresh hell is this* levels of tension. "So. Dad's not dead."

Her tiny huff of laughter almost made me smile, it sounded so familiar and homey. "I think you've known, haven't you? In your heart of hearts?"

I shrugged. "I... maybe suspected. Wished, when I was younger. But when I couldn't find any sign of him back when I looked in high school, I figured it must be true. And... and I made peace with it, I think." I thought. Maybe. Or maybe I just shoved it down so deep inside me, it was easy to ignore.

"He's always been very troubled, my brother." She sighed. "And we—I, really—thought it for the best if we kept him away from you. You were doing so well, and I knew he'd use you for leverage..." Cleverly smiled wanly. "I think maybe someone he pissed off is trying to kill you."

I let my head rest against the back of the wheelchair and closed my eyes. Not a great idea since that made my stomach swim, but at the moment, that was preferable to trying to parse everything out. "Okay," I said again. "One thing at a time. Your... boss? Supervisor? Manager? Just let us come here? Pulled some strings? Why is that?"

Cleverly blustered like she did that time I caught her all cozy with Doctor Mitchell at the church social. Just talking about Jesus, my ass. "Well, not... exactly," she hedged, not meeting my eyes when I finally managed to convince them it was okay to open. She sent a pointed glance Jeremy's way. He rolled his eyes again (at this point, I was kind of worried he was going to roll them so much, they'd pop out) and took a few steps back, in the direction of the still open double doors. Nurse Ratchet had her back to us, but there was no doubt in my mind she was listening. "I pulled some strings," Cleverly said, sotto voce. "As soon as we're home, I'm gonna have a lot of fires to put out so I don't get my butt in trouble!"

I nodded thoughtfully. It didn't seem too unlike Cleverly to do something like this, and Lord knew she was a huge fan of dramatics. She was the most practical person I knew when it came to raising me and making sure I didn't fall in with the bad shit that tended to happen to teenagers in our little town, much less gay teenagers in Texas, but she did love her flights of fancy in her personal life. "When we get home," I said, endeavoring to sound perfectly calm and not at all like I wanted to tear my hair out, "we'll have a nice, long talk about dear old Dad and just why you've decided we live in an episode of *Magnum PI* or something. For now, let's see what we can do about being discharged and calling an Uber or something. How far are we from home, anyway?"

She darted a glance toward the windows and looked distinctly guilty. "About sixty miles."

There went my fake calm. "*Sixty miles*? Good God! How the hell did we get here?"

She reached out to pat my hand again. "An ambulance!"

"Oh, Christ on a Pogo stick..." I was revisiting my opinion of Aunt Cleverly's common sense. I motioned to Jeremy. "Hey, so we're ready to get out of here. Who do we see for the discharge papers?"

Jeremy's dark eyes went wide, and he shook his head minutely. "I'll, um, ask," he said, the words halting. He gave Rosamund a furtive glance and murmured, "Don't freak out yet, okay?" before turning away and hurrying to speak with her in hushed tones just outside the doors.

My head still throbbed, but my awareness was starting to unfuzz just enough to feel that distinct kind of uneasy that had nothing to do with the weirdness of the place, of the entire day, but everything to do with my senses twigging to something. I wanted out. *Now*. I'd see my own doctor on Monday, thank you very much, one who wasn't working in some weird clinic that was probably the setting for some horrific hauntings. Cleverly was futzing with her rings, twisting them around on her fingers, tugging them, and pushing them as she worried her lower lip between her teeth. Jeremy was huddled with Rosamund, seemingly folding in on himself like a soufflé in a cupboard—arms tight around his middle, shoulders slowly hunching ever higher as his back bent in a painful-looking slouch. Rosamund was pinch-lipped and stiff-backed, rage pouring off her. Without even looking at her, my body had picked up on it. I was feeling the urge to run-no, need, not urge—and it was becoming increasingly difficult, with each passing moment, to keep myself still. I shifted uncomfortably in the chair—I was sure I'd be able to walk, albeit slowly thanks to the headache, but I didn't want to rock the boat too much just yet and staying in the damned thing seemed like a good way to appear compliant. I wasn't as subtle as I'd hoped when I moved, though, because suddenly, three sets of eyes were fixed upon me, each with varying levels of annoyance. Cleverly just looked miffed and embarrassed, but Rosamund was downright livid. Jeremy frowned at me but quickly erased the expression and had a very bland, neutral look on his face when Rosamund turned back to him. Rosamund said something to him in a tone so low, not even I could make it out and strode back to my side as Jeremy disappeared into the corridor. "I've sent Jeremy for the paperwork," she said through a tight smile. "If you'd like to dress, I can see you back to your room. You'll find your personal effects stored under your bed," she added, patting my shoulder. What the hell was it with these people and patting? She turned her attention to Cleverly, and her smile grew a shade more frosty. "You know how to get to yours, yes?"

Cleverly nodded, getting to her feet with a grim set to her jaw. "Yes, Rosamund, I do know my way around here." She gave me one of her sweet smiles and stopped just short of patting me herself. "I'll see you in a little bit, Landry."

I nodded. Rosamund hummed tunelessly as she unlocked the wheels to the chair and started pushing me back toward my room. We passed several other rooms on the way, their doors closed and the inset windows dark. "Is everyone else asleep?"

Her hum became a curious sound rather than a made-up song. "Oh, no, you and your aunt are the only guests with us right now."

"Ah." Okay, yeah, time to go ASAP. "Do you know if my phone made it with me? I'd like to call a friend to come pick us up."

"Oh, that won't be necessary! Arrangements have been made!" She stopped at my door and reached past me to slide open another panel and press in a quick code.

"With whom?" I had a brief, fleeting hope she'd say with Ethan, that they had decided the sheriff of our little town was the best option to come all the way out to Middle of Nowhere, Texas and pick us up. "And what time is it, anyway?"

"Oh, I'm not sure of their name," she fluttered, pushing me to the bedside and resetting the wheel locks. "There you go, nice and safe!" She moved to the foot of the bed while I pushed myself carefully to my feet. As she entered information into the tablet perched on the footboard, I gingerly reached beneath the bed and found a plastic bag tucked into a wire mesh shelf beneath the mattress. Inside were my jeans, t-shirt, socks, shoes, and underpants I'd had on that morning. Missing were the contents of my pockets: a few folded twenties I was in the habit of keeping handy and my phone. *That can't be good.* "I'm missing some things," I murmured. Rosamund stopped typing and frowned up at me.

"What's in the bag is what you were brought in with," she said, her tone brooking no argument.

Oh, I was gonna brook it, all right. "Yeah, no. When I was attacked, I had several items in my pockets, and not a single one is in this bag. Frankly, all I care about is my phone."

Her smile was supposed to be sympathetic, I think. "I'm sorry, Doctor Babin, but when the attendants brought you in from the ambulance, you only had your clothing on you. It's possible someone, ah, absconded with your possessions. If you'd like, I can bring you a complaint form with the other paperwork?"

I felt like I was being mocked. "I am honestly not sure if you're serious right now."

"The Garrow Clinic, though founded and maintained largely through a trust arranged by the Garrow family, also relies on financial and material support from Bluebonnet Biomedical and several private donors. If we allowed petty theft among contractors and staff, we would lose our supporters once word got out." She sniffed imperiously. "I'll be sure to bring a form for you to fill out in order to file a complaint regarding your missing items, Doctor Babin." She tapped at the tablet screen viciously before giving me a curt nod and striding for the door. "I'll be back in about twenty minutes, once the paperwork has been prepared."

I waited for the thunk-click of the door locking before I started pulling off the borrowed scrubs. My clothes felt stiff and a bit weird after the cloud-like softness of the scrub set but putting them back on was like a touchstone for my muzzy thoughts. A bit of normalcy, it helped brush away some of the mental fog and let me think a bit more clearly while I waited for Rosamund to return. Something wasn't fitting right in this entire jigsaw puzzle. I couldn't pinpoint why I thought so, but the idea that Cleverly was lying had sprouted to life at some point between the day room and my door and was sending out little runner-roots. I like to think that I'm not a stupid man, but I knew I could be blinded by loyalty at times, and I wanted to think the best of people I cared for. It's why I defended my mother and grandmother even long after I knew they'd abandoned me like a bag of trash, that they weren't just 'getting themselves together' somewhere. It's why I'd refused to believe my college boyfriend was cheating on me even after I'd caught his sidepiece naked in my apartment. Twice. Oh, God, maybe I was more stupid than I thought... I sat down on the edge of the bed; the breath virtually knocked out of me as I started to reorganize my day mentally. Waltrip had claimed his client saw me with Ethan and that I had been seen returning to town the night before. Cleverly said someone had mentioned Waltrip (or a man who looked a lot like his description) had been asking around about me. Ethan had... Well, he hadn't been lying to me, not really, more of a sin of omission. But had he known before Waltrip's visit to Cleverly's house that someone was trying to say he'd been failing as a clan leader? That he was at fault for a rogue were killing the Raymonds?

Wait.

Someone else knew it was a werewolf attack.

Someone else knew it was not just a werewolf attack, but a rogue were, not one of the clan members in the area, not someone they already knew even from one of the other communities, but rogue. Or at least that's what they were claiming. That's what they wanted Waltrip to prove, that Ethan was negligent and had caused the deaths by refusing to do his job as clan leader.

They claimed the Raymonds were weres. But I would have known, wouldn't I? I could tell when someone was. I *knew*. And Ethan... he'd grown up near the Raymonds. Hell, the Raymonds had been in Belmarais since it was founded, one of those old families that had come from a bit of money but never really rose up in the world, just sort of gently moldered more and more with each generation. There'd always been Raymonds in Belmarais, and none of them had ever been weres. The Stones would have known, would have either folded them into the clan or would have marked them as lone wolves (sue me—I can't resist a pun even when I'm in panic mode).

The Raymonds couldn't have been weres. It doesn't just pop up randomly in families. You have to be *born* were, with at least one were parent. No amount of biting or scratching from a were would turn a regular human. It'd hurt like hell and was just plain unsanitary, but I'm not going to yuck someone else's yum if they're into that with their were partner. But the Raymond kids being were after generations of non were family? It was impossible. Biologically impossible. Ethan's father, head of the clan for decades before his stroke, would have known the second a new were had come into the area, and if that were had married Jessup Raymond, then the family would have been watched extremely closely, just in case the offspring showed signs of the condition and needed to be brought into the community.

The Raymonds themselves didn't live like weres or even like someone who'd had weres in their lives. Weres tended to be fastidious to the point of obsession when it came to their living spaces and would never have lived in such squalor. Thinking of the Raymonds reminded me of the box I'd snagged from their bathroom. Bluebonnet Biomedical's creation. I needed to talk to Cleverly about it, see if she knew the name, if it had come across her desk in the phlebotomy lab.

Something was missing. Something really big and jagged, leaving a gaping hole in the puzzle.

The door swung open, and a jaunty Rosamund brandished a clipboard at me. Jeremy lurked behind her, lips pressed tight, eyes narrowed. "What's the matter, Doctor Babin?" she laughed. "You look like you've been caught with your hand in the cookie jar!"

"Just ready to go," I said. "Are those the discharge papers?"

"Mmmhmm. And your ride should be here soon. Jeremy arranged it for you."

I glanced at Jeremy, whose expression had gone from tense to downright miserable all in the span of a second. "Who did you call? Did Cleverly give you a name and number or something?"

Rosamund's expression didn't change, but Jeremy flinched as if she'd pinched him. "We have a driver," he murmured I wasn't sure what he was doing with his eyebrows, but it didn't look good. On any level. Great. Now I needed to figure out eyebrow semaphore before I got murdered.

"Ah. You know, if you don't mind, I'd really rather call someone I know personally." I stood, taking the proffered clipboard from Rosamund, and smiled as if she wasn't trying to flay my skin from my bones with her glare. "I'm just really particular about getting into cars with strangers."

"Oh." Rosamund sighed, clicking her tongue behind her teeth. "The driver is already en route, and there's a strict policy about answering calls while driving. It's too late to cancel."

I looked up at Jeremy again. He was back to being blank faced, but nervous energy was radiating off him. I wanted to hide, scurry away and tuck into some safe corner. Despite my best efforts, something must have shown because Rosamund's expression shifted from downright angry to amused and predatory in a heartbeat. "That's too bad," I said carefully, unable to keep the faint tremor from my voice, "but I'm really not comfortable getting in the car with a stranger. This entire night's been weird already." Rosamund's hard stare made my skin crawl. I looked at the paperwork in my hands and flipped through the first few pages, pretending to be unbothered. "Where're my labs? I'd like copies to take with me so I can show my GP back home."

"Jeremy, please go ask Franklin for Doctor Babin's lab results." She flashed teeth at me, not even bothering to pretend to smile now. "It will take a bit, as I'm sure you know, Doctor. Even on a slow night like this one."

I nodded. "Of course." The paperwork was all boilerplate stuff, nothing complicated or out of the ordinary in terms of discharge information and permissions. The facility's name was added in afterward, judging by the looks of things. Anywhere it appeared in the paperwork, the font was just a bit off, the positioning askew. Like someone did it in a hurry. "Did my aunt already sign herself out?"

"She's waiting for you in the day room."

"Still?"

"She enjoys the view." Teeth again.

"Ro," someone called from out in the corridor. She scowled, jerking around to face the door as a very tall, very built man filled the doorway. "Jeremy's asking for..." He trailed off, face coloring a nice shade of eighties pink. He looked familiar, but I couldn't place him. He was taller than your average person and striking to look at, almost too pretty, and someone I was sure I would have remembered.

"Doctor Babin's labs," Rosamund said tightly. "I'm aware."

"Um, are you sure?"

"Yes," she ground out. "Very."

He nodded, backing out into the corridor. He turned his face away for just a moment, looking back the way he came, and my stomach dropped to my knees. The profile flared my memory to life.

"How's Mr. Waltrip?" I asked, unable to stop myself. Yeah, I officially revoked my early statement that I wasn't stupid. I was pretty damned stupid.

Rosamund's face grew shuttered. She shifted on her heels to face the man in the doorway. "Mr. Waltrip?"

"Yeah," I said, staring him down. He was stock-still, not scared but wary. My senses screamed wolf, not just because I knew he was one from seeing him the other day but because he was radiating *were* like a sun. Were about to do something I'd regret, I realized, watching as his fingers slowly curled into fists by his side. "I know his... coworker? Boss? Friend? We met in town the other day, didn't we?"

He didn't nod, didn't even blink, just fixed me with a penetrating, wide-eyed stare that was somewhere between fear and anger. "Oh?" Rosamund said, voice slick and low. "Have we met Mr. Waltrip?"

"You're very invested in who he hangs out with outside of this place," I murmured. I didn't know what was about to happen, but I knew that I needed to be ready to bolt, to find a place to hole up until it was safe for me to find Cleverly and make a literal run for it. There had to be a major road nearby or a town or something. Though knowing my luck, we were in the Big Piney, and running on foot would just be a fun chase for werewolves before they tore us to pieces. A bit of light exercise before their evening entertainment.

"Sorry," the man said, offering a tight smile. "I think you're thinking of someone else. Head injury, right?" he asked, making a vague gesture toward his own head. "That's tough. I hear the memory problems usually go away in a day or so, though."

It was a horrible attempt at diversion. Like high school kid caught sneaking in at dawn while smelling of beer and actively smoking a joint and trying to tell their parents that they had just gone out to get the paper and found a lit doobie on the porch isn't that so weird levels of bad. Whatever you've heard about werewolves being all slick and suave? It's probably bullshit.

Rosamund's brows snapped together so hard, I was surprised we didn't hear the click. "I'm sure you're mistaken, Doctor Babin. David wouldn't lie about that, would he?"

"I have no idea what David would lie about," I said, shrugging. I was kind of feeling the asshole vibe and running with it. "But I do know that I need my labs, I need my aunt, and we need to go."

At first, I thought it was something I'd said. Rosamund and David both stiffened. They turned to peer down the corridor, away from the day room and back toward what I had to assume was the front of the building. If they'd had dog ears, they'd have been pricked up and swiveled forward. I was pretty sure David was just about to vibrate out of his skin. A second or two later, I heard it: the faint sounds of raised voices through closed doors. Shouting, something heavy hitting something else, and then, a crash. Voices spilled into the corridor, and I was forgotten, Rosamund and David speeding out of the room so quickly, I was surprised they hadn't left skid marks under their feet. I started forward but froze at the sounds of voices becoming snarls.

Fuck.

Weres. Fully transformed. And my aunt... *Fuck.* I had to get to her before they did. The anosmia was disorienting. I had never realized how much I relied on my enhanced senses, such as they were, until the most pronounced one was missing in action. It was impossible to tell if any of the weres were ones I knew, or worse, the one who had killed the Raymonds. Edging forward carefully, I took a deep, shaking breath. *Make the flight response work for me*, I chanted inwardly. *Run like hell, run to Cleverly. Get her and go.* My head was still throbbing and sloshing, but I had to run. The fighting was loud, terrifyingly so, and close. Snarls, snapping jaws, heavy bodies colliding drowned out even my own breathing. "Now or never," I breathed, closing my eyes for a brief second, trying to force myself to focus before opening my eyes and resolutely looking away from the sounds, down toward the day room. If I didn't look, I reasoned, I wouldn't freeze. I took a breath and bolted, teeth clenched hard against the pain in my skull as I sprinted toward the day room. The doors were closed—I could see that from the corridor. "Cleverly!" I shouted. "Cleverly, open the door!"

Behind me, there was a short, sharp bark. One of the weres (*Fuck, how many were there? I should have looked! Fuck!*) broke away and followed me. Claws clicked as it ran after me, its heavy breath louder than anything now. The day room door cracked open. I was almost at it. I threw myself forward and hit it with both arms outstretched, knocking Cleverly back as I tumbled in. I rolled onto my back and got my feet under me, lurching at the door to slam it shut as a large, dun-colored wolf tore—literally tore—down the corridor's carpet runner toward us.

Chapter Eight

My heart pounded so hard, I saw spots as I fell against the door. Cleverly was stiff and pale beside me, her lips pressed into such a thin line they were nonexistent. "What," she said softly, "the hell is happening? Are those dogs?"

I nodded, gulping air. "Yes, dogs. Wild dogs, very bad. Let's go. Now, Cleverly. We have to go now." I made it back to my feet and seized her by the arm. A frantic look around the room showed me a major safety violation: no emergency exit. The wolf on the other side of the door thumped against it hard, making it bounce slightly in its frame. I backed away, tripping over my own feet and going down hard on my hip. "Shit!" Cleverly bustled forward and helped me get back up, supporting me as I swayed. I wasn't sure how much was from my concussion and how much was from whatever worked in my senses trying so hard to keep me safe.

"Landry! Open this door! Fucking *now*!"

Cleverly yelped and ducked behind me. Because I, a wounded man standing at five foot eight and possibly one hundred and fifty pounds soaking wet, am a terrific human shield when faced with werewolves. A wereyorkie, I could take, but a wolf? Just call me puppy chow.

"Landry," Cleverly whispered, "who is it?"

The wolf had been dun-colored, but it wasn't Ethan. That much I knew. The were on the other side of the door had black tips to his ears and a white chest from what I could see before I closed the door in his face. Ethan didn't when he was shifted. "Landry Babin," the were shouted, "open this goddamned door or I swear to God, I will rip it off its hinges!"

Oh. Now I recognized the voice. I gently shook off my aunt and, after a deep breath that did nothing to help calm me, I opened the door just a crack. Tyler Stone stood, scowling and bloody, pressed against the door. Scowling, bloody, and *naked*. He pushed the door open wider, shoving me back and aside. He had it shut, locked, and a heavy armchair dragged against it before I could make my vocal cords work again. "Where's Ethan?"

"Hey, man, great to see you," Tyler muttered, voice full of false cheer. "Thanks for saving our asses. Wow, way to really put yourself on the line for your brother's ex, Tyler. Totally above and beyond. You're the best." He was dragging more furniture against the doors, his metaphorical hackles standing at attention. And yeah, still naked.

You didn't think weres kept their clothes on when they shifted, did you?

"You need pants," was all I managed in response.

"They're back in the car. Which is about two miles away, across the field and down along the bayou."

Cleverly was definitely distracted by this tidbit of information. And I will tell myself *that* was the tidbit distracting her till the day I die, thanks. The snarling and fighting in the corridor was definitely louder now, human screams mingling with canine barks and yowls. "Did you let them in?" she asked, tearing her eyes away from Tyler's... face... and pointing at the door.

His brows drew down, and he looked momentarily confused before shooting me a disbelieving look. "Seriously? I've heard of cognitive dissonance being a hell of a thing, but this..." He let out a low whistle. "This is some next-level shit. No," he said, turning to Cleverly and speaking in an exaggerated slow voice. "I did not let the big bad wolves in. They were already here. I just brought some friends of my own, and if we don't get the hell out of here *now*, someone will probably die."

From the look on Cleverly's face, I was pretty sure she'd checked out and was in a mental happy place. Which, considering where we were, wouldn't be that difficult of a task to conjure. Hellraiser's living room would be a happier place than where we were.

"How are we getting out?" I asked. "There's no emergency exit."

"Sure, there is." He strode past us and grabbed the divan, lifting it as easily as most people would a folding chair. Without breaking stride, he hurled it through the plate glass window. An alarm went off, shrill over the already mind-numbing din in the corridor. "Grab your aunt and go," he said, voice thickening, eyes taking on a golden cast. "Across the field. See that stand of pecan trees?" He pointed to a dark smudge some distance away, nails already lengthening, hands misshapen. "Head for those. Don't look back, don't slow down. You'll hit the bayou about a hundred yards past the trees. Go east, follow it till it makes a bend and the car is there. There's a dirt track. I left the keys in the driver's side wheel well. If I don't meet you there after ten minutes or if someone else shows up, go. Just get the fuck out, got me?"

He shoved me before I could respond. I grabbed hold of Cleverly and half-dragged her past the jagged broken glass spires sticking out of the bottom of the ruined window. She stumbled, slipped, and finally seemed to catch on that we needed to run. She was faster than I gave her credit for, shaking off my grasp as we ran hard toward the knot of pecan trees in the distance. Despite the pain from my injuries, I felt bone-deep relief. *Finally*, part of me was sighing. *You're doing what you're supposed to do. You're not like them; you're prey.*

I didn't realize I was slowing until I noticed Cleverly had pulled ahead of me by several yards. The sounds of the battle in the clinic were faint now but still audible, dragging my attention back. I craned my neck to look but saw nothing other than the light spilling out of the broken window and dark shapes moving across the grass toward us. I had no idea if it was Tyler and the friends he'd mentioned or someone worse.

"You okay?" I panted to Cleverly, forcing my legs faster. She didn't respond and, with a sickening lurch in my gut, I realized she was not in front of me anymore. "Cleverly? Cleverly!" There was no way she could have made it to the trees already, not unless she'd developed the power of flight, and I hadn't passed her on the ground. A sharp, high scream pierced the night sounds around me, and I stumbled to a halt. "Cleverly!"

"Help!" she shrieked. "No! Oh, my God! No!"

"Cleverly!" I was on my feet and running in an instant. Her voice sounded like it was ahead of me still, but I couldn't see her. She screamed again, and this time it ended in a gasping moan, loud and wet sounding. A howl, long and loud, rattled my bones and sent me to my knees. More howls joined in from all around me, rising up from behind hillocks, from the clinic, from the stand of trees. Something hit me from behind, and I went down hard. My entire body tensed and spasmed, trying to both curl into a ball and bolt at the same time. I succeeded in rolling onto my back as the were who had tackled me shifted away slightly.

"Tyler?" I panted. It looked like him, but it was hard to tell for sure in the moonlit dark, in the chaos. More wolf bodies hurtled past, and screams mixed with barks and grunts. Tyler—it had to be him—snorted, shook himself hard, and staggered a few steps away. I started to sit up, but he lurched back, leaning against me till I fell onto the grass again and pressed a paw down on my chest. He was breathing hard, rasping like it hurt to draw air. He fell to one side, his chest heaving, legs twitching, then suddenly went still.

"Tyler?" I reached out and pushed against his belly. He shuddered, sucking in a deep breath, but he did not get up. The sound around me was dying down, snarling replaced by grunts and low, canine huffs. A few human voices threaded through the wolf sounds. I felt detached, suspended between my own body on the grass and somewhere safe and far where I was just watching this like a bad dream. Everything was swimming and swirling, a sharp pain in my shoulder spreading down my arm and up my neck, dissolving into a too-hot sensation that slowly bubbled into lethargy. Hands grasped under my arms, yanking me up until I could be dragged.

"This was a noble effort," a familiar but roughened voice sighed. "I was hoping this would go more smoothly, but they have such a flair for the dramatic. That's what happens when you are not born to this but come into our world already tainted by humanity."

My head lolled back, but I couldn't make out the faces over me. Dark shapes moved around us—wolves I realized. Not everyone had shifted back. "My aunt," I managed, though the words were slow and thick.

"She is not your concern at the moment." We passed through a pool of light—we must have been closer to the clinic than I realized, moving through the glow of one of the tall lamp posts lining the drive—and I could see the sharp angles of David's face. I made an effort and was able to crane my neck to see who had my other arm. Jeremy. Damn it. I'd hoped... Well. I'd hoped.

My body was numb, and I felt like I was not quite all the way inside it, drifting in and out of near sleep as my heels dragged through pea gravel, bits of rock and dirt sliding into my shoes. "Take him away."

Away turned out to be some sub-level beneath the clinic. I faded in and out while they took me through the ruined front entrance with its blood splatters and a prone body, someone caught halfway between wolf and man. I supposed there was no point in trying to keep the facade going that they were normal humans there. We turned down a short, narrow corridor hidden behind a false bit of wall near the intake desk, ending in dull silver doors.

The elevator reminded me of the ones hospitals used to move patients on gurneys, the ones that opened up directly into the morgue. Stainless steel walls, large enough to hold two gurneys side by side, or one semi-conscious man and at least four werewolves. When the doors slid open, I was taken to a brightly lit room larger than my kitchen. It was set up like a triage bay in a hospital but with one crucial difference: the exam table was fitted with institutional restraints. I twisted, trying to buck free from Jeremy and David, but my movements were still sluggish, and I succeeded only in losing a shoe as they drag-carried me to the table and plopped me down. I couldn't even fight as my wrists were locked into the cuffs, Jeremy buckling them securely. He sighed something that could have been 'sorry,' but that was probably my addled brain trying to make things less terrifying.

David hovered near the end of the gurney, trying to catch Jeremy's eye, but Jeremy loped back to the elevator, his lanky form folding in on itself like a wilting weed. Rosamund was ensconced behind a low, steel-sided desk, tapping rapidly away at a computer. David gave up on getting Jeremy's attention, instead fixing a wide-eyed, unblinking gaze on Rosamund as he made a hash of tightening my ankle restraints. I held still, afraid to even breathe too deeply just in case it caught his eye. When he gave them a tug, he frowned, glancing at me quickly. I must have looked just as bad as I felt because he didn't even try to make them tighter.

"Thankfully, we were able to get your records right up as soon as you were en route," Rosamund said, smiling up at me from behind the desk as if this were just a pleasant day at the office. "Lucky for us, our system is the most efficient around. None of that off-site crap for us," she tittered. Clapping her hands together once, she pushed back from the desk and sighed, the very picture of a woman satisfied with a job well done. "You, Doctor Babin, are quite the pain in the ass."

"It's genetic. Runs on my mom's side."

"And your father's," she said, winking a little too broadly, verging on the Panto dame. "You're a dead ringer for him, did you know? Oh, maybe it's in bad taste to use the word 'dead.' Is it?" Her laugh grated again—I think she was aiming for a silvery trill and landed squarely in donkey braying through a moving floor fan territory.

I'd never been really good at shutting up. I mean, I like to think I can do it. I really made an effort during med school, holding back my opinions when an instructor was particularly *wrong* or keeping my mouth shut when a date or boyfriend chose a crappy movie or ordered well done steak (seriously, what kind of monster). But, overall, it's more of a bug than a feature for me to hold my tongue.

"I've heard more about my sperm donor in the past five hours than in the past twenty years," I said, my words sounding as lethargic as I felt thanks to whatever they'd dosed me with. I wondered if they'd gotten me with the same thing twice or if now, I'd have to deal with the side effects and symptoms from two, maybe antagonistic, drugs coursing through my battered body.

Rosamund's smile became very sharp. I wondered, for a brief moment, if she had been one of the wolves who'd hurt my aunt (I had to think she was hurt, not... not anything else, because if I'd let myself think she was worse than hurt, then I would lose my goddamned mind). She was still neatly dressed, not a hair out of place, not even a bit of dust on her shoes to indicate she'd tramped up that gravel drive outside. With a subtle nod to David and Jeremy who stepped into the elevator, she moved around the desk and paced toward me, keeping quiet until the elevator doors shut. "You are quite the little shit, Doctor Babin."

"Again, genetic." I half expected her to hit me or worse, but instead she just patted my damned knee again and smiled.

"Your aunt isn't dead, in case you were wondering. She was a marvelous distraction though, wasn't she? Some of the others thought you had planned this—the Stone clan trying to stop us—

but I assured them you are not nearly that smart. You"—she tweaked my nose hard enough to make me gasp— "are a broken bit of wolf, aren't you?"

The phrase made me jerk back in surprise. No one else, not even Ethan, had ever called that part of me a broken wolf. It was my phrase for it, something I'd figured out after meeting Ethan, after seeing how weres *worked*—at least as much as they let me see back then. My senses, my abilities, were all like theirs, just... less. Stuck halfway through the change, Ethan's father had said. Like my brain started to do it but gave up before it got very far.

Rosamund saying that, though, calling me that... I couldn't even try to muster a denial. We were pretty far past an attempt at *I don't know what you're talking about.*

"One of those drugs," I said carefully, my cotton mouth making it hard to enunciate. "The soporifics... are they what's causing the anosmia?"

"A bit," she admitted, looking pleased. "And the concussion has a bit to do with it, they think. All in all, it should clear up relatively soon. For now, though, it's been in our favor."

"Because one of you killed the Raymonds."

Rosamund shook her head, pouting like she was disappointed in her very spoiled puppy. "No, darling, not one of us. One of *you*." Roughly, she began a cursory vitals check. Fingers on my wrist, she glanced at her watch. "Bit high but not surprising. You've had a very busy evening."

"Is there any point in asking what you're going to do to me?"

"Please, Doctor Babin. We're medical professionals here. Scientists! We're not Bond villains!"

"To be fair, some of them were scientists, too," I muttered, the lethargy spreading once more. I knew I'd be in for a few more hours of drowsiness if my general reactions to being anesthetized held true. A few more hours of being useless and unable to do anything other than sleep or, if I did manage to get loose from the restraints, being unable to escape.

Who was I kidding? I wasn't going anywhere without Cleverly, even if a door opened right now and could spit me out directly into my house. And, I supposed I should try to find Tyler, too, if he was still alive.

"Speaking of Bond villains, I suppose I should make some sort of pithy statement or point out the obvious while you prepare to do some nefarious sort of experiment on me? Like the fact you have Sheriff Stone's brother here somewhere, and no matter what state Tyler Stone is in, Ethan and likely the rest of the Stone clan will come looking for him."

"That's fine," Rosamund murmured, moving away to enter my vitals into the computer on the desk. "Now, just sit tight." She smirked up at me. "I'll be back in a few minutes to collect more blood and some other stuff." She giggled again, that grating baying sound, and the elevator doors closed between us. There was no doubt in my mind I was being watched. If they were spying on me in my patient room, they would definitely be keeping several eyes on me in whatever level of hell this little room happened to be in. Still, I gave a few hopeful, firm tugs to the restraints. Even the half-assed job David had done on my ankles held.

Shit.

I could just nap for a little bit. That might help.

Or, you know, it could just let you wake up dead or something.

Whichever.

I couldn't sit up on the exam table, but I could wiggle around until I was tilted on my left hip, facing into the room. It bent my right arm back uncomfortably, but it wasn't unendurable. The closest thing to me, other than the table I lay on, was a low, stainless steel counter with a built-in sink. Cabinets lined the wall above the counter, glass-fronted and full of medical paraphernalia, mundane (blood pressure cuffs, thermometer covers, empty sharps disposal bins waiting to be used) and, frankly, sinister. While a bone saw and rib spreader would not be out of place in *my* exam room, seeing them just casually resting beside a large box of gauze pads and a row of bagged saline solution did not inspire feelings of calm acceptance in my soul.

I tugged again on my restraints. Nope, a miracle hadn't occurred. It was too much to hope that I could just slip out of the bonds and make a mad dash for it, but it didn't stop me from giving the ones at my ankle one more little yank.

Something gave.

It wasn't a lot, but the pressure eased a bit. I held very still, unwilling to glance down. Carefully, I pointed my right foot and flexed it back, trying to see if I could make the restraint ease a bit more. It held fast, but something was jabbing me through my sock. Resisting the urge to kick and yank, I rolled my foot again. If (who was I kidding, there was no *if*) they were watching, it would hopefully look like I was just stretching my joints out, trying to get feeling back in my feet.

Rolling onto my back again, a wave of exhaustion swept over me. It wasn't true exhaustion but that deep tiredness that comes with anesthesia, the feeling of standing at the edge of a cliff and tilting forward just enough for gravity to take over. I fought it for what felt like a long stretch of time but was probably a second, maybe two, my eyes closing and body relaxing into a deep, drugged drowse. Even when the door clanged open and voices flooded the room, my eyes wouldn't open all the way.

Part of me tried to fight as I was lifted onto another gurney, this one hard and cold. *Metal*, the tiny part of my brain that was alert supplied. *Like in the morgue*. That was enough to make me buck harder, shake off some of the tendrils of sleep trying to hold me down. Still, it wasn't enough. Strong hands held me, and a sharp jab in my neck sent me deeper into sleep, the distant awareness of movement sending a creeping thrill of panic through my limbs even as they grew heavy and useless.

Chapter Nine

It was hazy out; that kind of hazy that only happens in late summer and makes the entire day feel like some weird dream state. Or maybe that was because I was seventeen, and everything about the world felt weird and dreamlike, especially any time spent with Ethan Stone. "Come on," he murmured against my neck. "Try harder. It's not gonna hurt."

"Seriously, Ethan. This is it!" I twisted in his arms, not willing to break away but needing to see his face. He leaned back just enough to grin down at me. "What you see is what you get," I sniped. "All five foot seven, one hundred thirty pounds of me." Shaking my head, I added, "If that's not enough for you, then I'd better head back home."

"Oh, come on now." Ethan laughed, picking me up easily. I wasn't sure if it was just because he worked out a lot for all the sports he played or if it had something to do with that *thing* he'd done the other day, the thing I was pretending didn't freak me out, but he managed to carry me easily from beside his beat-up, shit-brown car to the steps of his front porch, not even hitching his breath as he set me on the top step. "You know you're more than enough for me, no matter what."

"I'm not sure if that's an insult or not," I said, squinting down at him.

Ethan laughed again, loud and ringing and not caring that his brothers were inside and would probably be out to bug the hell out of us in a minute now. "Well, I didn't mean it as one," he offered, moving to the step just below me. I frowned, back to being short again. Ethan tipped my chin up with his finger and kissed me before I could make some half-assed attempt at snark. What started as a quick attempt to divert me (I was on to his tricks, thank you very much, but that didn't mean I didn't enjoy them) turned into something much hotter. Within moments, his hands were sliding between my shirt and my skin, fingers tickling along my ribs as he pressed me back against the wooden railing of the porch. He grunted softly when I arched my back, rubbing against him like a cat as he deepened the kiss, taking my mouth and leaving me breathless, shaky in his hands. We hadn't done much more than kiss yet unless you count me dry humping him like my life depended on it (I counted the hell out of that, you betcha), but oh God, we both wanted to. He hadn't said as much yet, but I could tell. Or thought I could tell. Whenever we kissed like we were doing on the porch, he'd get this... rumbly growl thing going on. And his eyes... They always changed to this weird, beautiful golden color when he got worked up. Then he'd grab my arms, my wrists, whatever he could reach first, and hold me back a bit, ending things before we could really get started.

"No," I whispered, twisting my wrists in his grasp, finding it looser than anticipated. I worked my hands free and brought them up to his face. He had the barest bit of stubble, something my seventeen-year-old self found unbearably sexy (maybe, just maybe, in part because I couldn't grow a beard if you paid me). "We don't have to stop, Ethan. It's okay. I'm not..." I tilted my head back, trying to meet his narrowed gaze, "I'm not afraid of you."

Ethan sighed, pressing his forehead to mine so hard it verged on painful before he stepped back down to the ground and leaned against the handrail. "I don't get it," he said after a long, twisty quiet. "Everything about you says you're like us, but you can't shift, and you're scared of everything except me." He shook his head again, a gesture I was sure he'd cribbed from his old man. "Landry..."

My gut ached, arousal sublimating into nauseated awareness. "You want to break things off?" I asked, hoping I sounded braver than I felt. I might have been ass over tea kettle for Ethan Stone, but I wasn't about to drag this out just for a few more kisses, not if he was already trying to wrap things up.

"What?"

Part of me felt a twinge of gratification, seeing how startled he looked. "I'm not like y'all," I said, coming down the steps until I was on the hard-packed dirt of the Stone's front yard. "What you said? I'm nothing like y'all. I'm afraid of everything, though. That part you got right. Everything but you because I know you, you asshole." I tried to smile but judging by the grimace on Ethan's face, I didn't quite make it work. "What'd your dad call me? Broken? A broken wolf?" I reached out to gently poke his ribs, that spot just below his armpit that made him squirm when we were making out in the back of that awful car of his. He didn't squirm this time. He grabbed my finger and held it, staring at it, silent. "I'm not like y'all. I won't ever be."

"I think," he said carefully, "if maybe we tried it again..."

I closed my eyes. Nervousness washed away in a drift of annoyance and not a little embarrassment. We'd been 'trying' to see if I could shift, if maybe it was really just some mental block after all, for days. I had no weres in my family, not even a remote hint of one anywhere that I knew of, which meant the chances of me being able to change were in the single-digit percentages, if not lower, but Ethan was determined, more so than I was, to find out why I was the way I was. Why my senses were like the weres, why I was stronger (well, just a little), faster (quite a lot) than other non-weres. So far, every attempt had been frustrating, awkward, and embarrassing as hell. Though on the plus side, almost all of them had ended in kissing our faces off and a tiny, tiny bit of over the clothes groping. *Well, not so tiny, ha ha ha am I right, ha.* "Maybe your dad was right, and I'm the world's only were chicken."

Ethan stiffened in my arms but tried to make a joke. "Dude, have you ever seen a chicken in real life? They're not afraid of shit."

"Unlike me," I pointed out quietly. "I don't know," I went on, not letting him apologize. "My aunt wants me to see this shrink she knows through work, some guy who does consulting work with the lab. He works a lot with young adults." Ethan and I both made faces at that—we hated that phrase, young adult. It always felt like people were calling us 'little man' or something, pretending we had adult feelings while still treating us like toddlers. "Said maybe it's anxiety or something? Because of... because of my folks."

"Ah." He didn't sound convinced. "Does she know about..." He made a vague gesture at his head, his face.

"The sensing thing? Not really. I tried to tell her a few years ago when it was first real bad, but she started worrying I had some sort of personality disorder or something, so I stopped talking to her about it." It had been grim, honestly. She'd hauled me to Dallas to see a specialist. He stank of something sour, bitter. Something that had traces of metal and rot. He wanted me to talk about these heightened senses, asked me about harmful behaviors. I left with a recommendation for a special camp and a bottle of ADHD medication that I never took. "She's pretty set on this being an anxiety disorder now."

Ethan didn't say anything for a long time. His brothers were shouting at some game inside the house, and from one of the neighbors, the smell of barbecue started to drift. It was almost dinner time, which meant his father would be home soon, and I should get my ass in gear. Like he read my mind, Ethan tightened his arms around me and pressed a kiss against my hair. "Don't worry about what my father says," he murmured. "The old man's an ass."

"Wow. Seriously?" I tipped my face up to peer at him. "I mean, I know y'all have problems, but—"

"But when it comes to who I... who I'm spending time with," he said, his face flushing a delicious pink, and oh Lord, who had any idea that was a turn on for me. "He's an ass. Look, I promise we don't have to keep trying with the whole shifting thing, okay? This is who you are."

I huffed a small, tired laugh. The entire day was catching up to me, the peaks of frenzied make out sessions and the valleys of the shifting attempts wearing me out in one sudden swoop. "I'm glad one of us is okay with it." I sighed. "I'll see you tomorrow?" I asked, backing out of his arms and already missing him. He started to answer, but the front door banged open, and Tyler, the middle Stone brother, loomed in the doorway, rangy and dark-eyed, glaring down at us.

"You shouldn't be here, Babin."

"I'm leaving!" I darted in quick to kiss Ethan one more time and started walking down the drive, trying not to look like I was hurrying.

"Babin, what the hell? You're not supposed to be here!" He sounded close, and I frowned, glancing back. He was still on the porch, the haze of the day thickening. It was hard to see him and Ethan clearly, like looking through fog. I slowed my steps. Something jostled me, and my heart rate kicked into overdrive. "Come on, Babin. Talk to me, asshole."

Wait.

Wait, wait. That was over a decade ago, right?

Ethan and I broke up or split or whatever not-really-boyfriends do a few weeks later.

Tyler was yelling in my ear! "Babin, get the fuck up, you cocksucker!"

I wasn't on the driveway. It had been a memory. Maybe a dream of a memory. It hurt to open my eyes. They felt sticky and sandy, sore. The inside of my mouth was dry to the point of pain, my entire body trembling with the aftereffects of adrenaline and whatever I'd been dosed with. A passingly familiar face came into my blurred line of sight. "Tyler?"

"Fucking hell," he snapped. "What the hell is wrong with you, huh?" He shoved at my shoulder but, since I was lying on my back on a cement floor, it didn't have the desired effect. "You're not supposed to fucking be here!"

He was waxy-pale and sweat-slick. My sense of smell hadn't returned yet, but I knew, just knew, he reeked of sour-sweet-sharp fear and anger and pain. The back of my throat tickled with the phantom idea of that smell, familiar with it from my own body, from the lingering traces on the bodies of those I saw in my exam room. "Yeah, well, I'd argue that about pretty much everyone in this nightmare." I wasn't restrained anymore, but I was sluggish and heavy. The sedative had apparently been mixed with a paralytic, not uncommon in anesthesia. *But what did I need to be anesthetized for? Or had it just been the best way of making sure I didn't fight back?*

"Ethan said you were fast," Tyler sniped. "Said you were fast like one of us, not like a human." He rocked back onto his heels, squatting next to me. "What happened? Decide that was too hard, too? Fear of being one of us finally got so bad you can't even run anymore?"

"Hey, so, yeah, I get that you hate me. Totally get it, mutual feeling, no problem there. But"—with every ounce of effort I could muster, I pushed myself onto my side and did my very best not to vomit from the incipient vertigo that came with recovery from sedation— "could you, I don't know, fuck off for a few minutes or something?"

Tyler raked his dark, shaggy hair back from his eyes and glared, jaw set in something near a grimace. "Fucking hell," he repeated. I had the feeling it was sort of his catchphrase. "Ethan is going to shit bricks."

"That's an image I could live forever without." I tried to push up some more, but a wave of nausea was stronger than my will to be vertical.

"Fuck, fuck, fuck." Tyler unfolded smoothly, towering over me as he started to pace. From around us there came the murmur of voices, a few muffled groans. Fear, anger, aggression were all seeping into our tiny cell, creeping along the cracks in the wall, under the metal door. "That's two of my clan, some rogues from up near Dallas, and a rogue that came down from Baltimore when she heard you were involved."

"Huh?"

"The others. You were wondering who the others were." Tyler stopped pacing at the door, pressing his forehead against the postcard-sized bit of Plexiglas. pretending to be a window. "You cocked your head like a dog, tilted your face up like you wanted to sniff the air." His lips quirked into a knot of a smile when he turned his face toward me. "We all do it when we're not being careful. That whole"—he made a vague gesture around his face—"senses thing. When we're kids, we learn how to hide the tells around humans, but I guess you never had to, did you?" He turned, so his back rested against the door, and he could really get a good glower and tower going on. "Ethan always defended you, you know."

"I remember." With an almighty heave, I managed an upright position. Mostly upright. Kind of a forty-five-degree angle against the wall behind me, my neck doing that gelatinous wobble thing people tend to do when riding in the passenger seat and drowsing. "You were a real jackass." I smiled, mostly. "Well, I say *were*... I mean are."

Tyler's expression softened just a smidge. Or my vision was going. "Not against me. I just thought you were a waste of space. Still do," he added with a conciliatory nod. "Our dad. He wanted you gone."

"Ah. No." My legs still didn't want to work well. My ankle throbbed where the cuff had pricked me earlier, like a spider bite swelling and aching. I'd lost my shoes somewhere, either in the drag from outside or after they'd knocked me out the second time. My feet were cold, and it felt like there might be open cuts and blisters going on—I wouldn't be able to tell for sure until I could manage to reach down and take off my socks. "I get it, though," I said before Tyler could ramble on. "Ticking so many boxes for wolf, but not being one. I'm a genetic anomaly or something. If I hadn't lived in the same town as y'all, I never would have known about weres, I never would've known that these quirks of mine aren't just anxiety or some neurological disorder." I tried to wiggle my toes and winced at the pins and needles that erupted along the nerves. "Ah, fuck, there we go... I'll be up and moving soon."

Tyler's head thumped against the tiny window, his eyes closed. "We lost three," he murmured. "Cass and Nelly, from the Coopers in Dallas. And one of the rogues from Baltimore."

"I thought there was only one."

"Why?"

"You said 'the rogue from Baltimore' earlier, not 'one of,' and I assumed..." I trailed off and assayed a shrug. "You grammatically led me on."

"As she's the only rogue left, she is the rogue."

"There were two of them. Can you be rogue if you're in a set?"

Tyler opened one eye. "You're still an ass."

"It's one of my more pronounced qualities, yeah." I was able to bend my knees but not get my legs under me just then. I sat, crabbed against the wall, vision still fuzzy around the edges. "What did you mean, your dad wanted to get rid of me?"

"Not get rid of you. Just gone. Out of Belmarais. Out of Texas if possible." He pursed his lips, thinking. "I don't think he meant dead. He never made any threats about that sort of thing. Just kept saying you needed to be gone and gone far. That you were a threat to the clan."

Oh, hey, here was something I was familiar with, something that had nothing to do with the fucked up world of supernatural shit. "So, your dad thought I turned Ethan queer, is that it? I'd ruined his perfect son or something?"

Tyler's eyes popped open, and he gave me such an incredulous, confused look that I almost laughed. "What the... No! Dad gave zero shits about that. Hell, when I told him I was bi, he tried to set me up with one of the Mackenzie's nephews out in Baton Rouge."

"Very progressive," I muttered. I managed to roll onto my knees and slumped forward before I caught myself and executed a sloppy backward flop to rest against the wall once more. "Doesn't mean shit, though."

Tyler slid to the floor, face tipped up toward the ceiling. He was listening, I realized, watching his jaw work and his body faintly tremble with the need to *do something*. Any injuries he might have sustained in the break-in and fight were healed or well hidden, but he looked like he was in pain, the way he held himself, the way his breathing hitched. "The day you left, Ethan was going to go after you. Wanted to apologize, beg you to stay, offer anything and everything if you'd forgive him. He was even going to put off college for a year, if you asked, so he could be with you wherever you got accepted."

A weird little jolt zapped through my heart, and I frowned. "That's kind of creepy." I wasn't sure if I was telling Tyler that or reminding my inner seventeen-year-old.

"That's an eighteen-year-old trying to make things right." Tyler sighed. "Teenagers aren't known for their great decision-making skills."

"You lied to him about me screwing around?"

Tyler nodded. "Dad's idea," he admitted. "At the time, I thought it was a good one. Ethan was damn near out the door when I told him." He huffed a laugh. "No idea why that asshole believed me, but..." He shrugged. "Teenagers."

"Why are you telling me this? You realize I've lived my entire adult life with that whole incident nice and locked away?" I felt sick—what could've been, what wasn't... Would life have been better? For both of us?

Would I still be broken?

Or would Ethan have gotten tired of being with someone like me, wanted someone who was a were, too. Someone who understood...

I closed my eyes and let out a shuddering breath. "Fuck."

"You still love Ethan."

Ah. "Pardon?" I wanted to deny it, but I couldn't. The feelings were still there but stronger, more. Different but not. An adult's love, something beyond adolescent lust and affection and that desperate flailing feeling I'd had then. And it kind of terrified me in a way I'd need to examine when I wasn't about to die.

Priorities.

"Don't be like that. He never stopped loving you, either. That's why I'm telling you this." A muted howl distracted us both for a moment, and Tyler's lips crimped into a satisfied smirk even as it felt like my heart was trying to break into a thousand pieces. He still loved me? Really loved me?

"Cavalry's here," he murmured. "Pay attention. This is Plan fucking Z we're on right now, got it? Stick with me, and we'll get out of here. But listen, everything I'm gonna tell you? It's why the Raymonds ended up on the wrong end of someone's pet project."

Hello, fucking bombshell. Well, maybe not quite a bombshell, but definitely maybe a large firework or something. "Pet project?" I worked onto my knees, balancing myself against the wall.

"Emphasis on pet," he snarled. He rose to his feet, not nearly as smoothly as before, his neck bowing and body trembling visibly.

Shit.

A howl sounded again, closer but still muffled by the door. Tyler growled low in his throat, then flung his head up and let loose with an answering cry. My heart wanted to explode as it burst into damn near dangerous speeds—there was nowhere in the room for me to hide, but I shoved myself away from the wall as hard as I could, my still-heavy limbs making me half-crawl, half-lurch across the small room, cramming myself into a corner before

I really knew what I was doing. Tyler's eyes flashed amber as he shot me an openly annoyed, possibly disgusted glare. "Stay with me," he ordered, voice thick, teeth changing already. "I know what you want to do, Landry, but *don't*." He shook his head, eyes never leaving my face. "Please. Ethan—"

The door banged open, shoving Tyler in the back. "Damn it, Stone, come on!"

I didn't know the man's name, but he had been the second minion with Oliver the other day. Fuck me, was it only a few days ago? I never really got it when I'd hear about people not realizing how much time had passed during a crisis or thinking it'd been hours when it'd just been minutes. It truly felt like months, if not years, since I first saw the three weres while getting my lunch. And now, I was about to follow one of them, apparently, trusting in him and fucking Tyler Stone to help me escape. Correction, not me—us. Tyler slapped the man hard on the shoulder, jerking his head in my direction. "He's gonna fight. Grab him, and don't let go."

"Hey!" I barely had time to even get that single syllable out. The were was across the room and had me over his shoulder in a fireman carry before I could do more than gasp. "This is not fucking helping the whole *trust you* situation."

Tyler shrugged. "We need to move fast. The system will only be down for three minutes."

The were holding me nodded. "Dizzy, Lachlan, and Gio are already on the move."

"My aunt," I said suddenly, guilt washing through me because I hadn't remembered in several minutes, hadn't asked...

"Your aunt's not your problem right now," Tyler snapped. "Let's get."

"Contact's waiting for us," the were panted. He wasn't as tall as Tyler, but he still had several inches on me. He was built like a swimmer, all lean lines and lithe muscle, and carried me easily. We ran through a long, narrow room with bright white lights, open doors on either side of us. I had the impression of more small rooms like the one I'd been in and wondered how many people they'd kept down here regularly.

"Did you—" Tyler began.

"Got it, plus a bit of something I think you're really gonna love," he said, easily keeping pace with Tyler despite carrying me over his back.

We were moving fast through the long room, heading for a half-open door. Bright light spilled in, and from outside, more howls sounded, though distant. Like they were on another floor entirely. "Who else," Tyler began, then shook his head. "Never mind. If you tell me, I'll get mad."

The man laughed. "Probably."

We swung out into the corridor, and I was surprised to see an elevator standing open, barely ten yards away. Tyler and my erstwhile steed broke into long, loping strides, Tyler smacking the Door Close button as he cleared the gap between floor and carriage. I was set back down on my feet, pinned by twin glares as the elevator began to rise. "Are you going to be a problem?" the man asked sharply.

"He already is." Tyler sighed. "He was supposed to be gone already."

"They took Cleverly. I think she's dead," I muttered, swallowing hard against the need to cry. "I heard screaming—"

"They're not ferals," the man snapped. "They wouldn't tear her apart like that." He paused, glancing over my head toward Tyler. Some serious eyebrow semaphore went down before the man shook his head. "No," he said. "Not like that."

Tyler nodded. The elevator dinged loudly, and we all three went stock-still. My heart was rabbiting so hard I worried it might do something rash and decide to just stop altogether from exhaustion. I couldn't stop my shaking, even as I managed to keep myself from bolting as the doors slid open. "Fucking hell, they're going to smell him for miles," the man muttered.

"Nothing we can do about it, Charlie," Tyler pointed out, bouncing on his toes, ready to run. "Anything?"

Charlie (thank God someone finally said his name because it was about to be super awkward if I had to ask) shook his head. They both looked at me. "Anosmia," I said, tapping my nose. "But if it helps, something is triggering that whole scared bunny thing, so..." I shrugged. "Maybe?"

"Scared bunny?" Charlie muttered, brows drawing down. "What the hell did they give him?"

Tyler rolled his eyes, an expression so reminiscent of Ethan that my heart lurched hard, and tears pricked my eyes. "Less than two minutes. Charlie," he jerked his chin at me.

"Right."

I bit down hard on a yelp as Charlie hoisted me back over his shoulder. "It's just faster," Tyler said, and damned if he didn't sound just a tiny bit apologetic.

"I'm going to add professional gentleman in distress to my CV," I grumbled. Charlie had the decency to keep his laugh short. Tyler just snarled. He shifted as he stepped out of the elevator, clothes falling and ripping away as he moved. It took a lot of practice for a were to be able to do that without looking like someone's dog getting tangled up in the laundry. I had the feeling Tyler had practiced that move in front of the mirror like other guys practice their come-on smile.

"Show off," Charlie sniped. We were running again, howls echoing down the corridor, louder than before. We hit the outside at a dead sprint, the humidity of the night air stealing my breath as we went hell for leather down a gentle slope toward a gravel parking area that was really a wide spot in the back garden of the former residence. Two vans with Bluebonnet Biomedical emblazoned on the doors filled the space. One was running, sliding door cracked open just an inch or so, lights off. Someone threw the door open as Tyler neared, and he leaped inside to a chorus of "Shit! Fucking hell!" and for a moment, I was sure there'd be carnage, but the voices dissolved into gasping laughter and the rumble of a happy wolf's growl. Charlie threw me—literally fucking threw me, the asshole—into the open cargo area and scrambled in after me, climbing into the front seat as the woman driving slammed the van into reverse, and we crunched backward out of the parking area.

"This Babin?" one of the guys in the back asked, looking like he'd been rode hard and put away wet himself.

I unclenched my jaw enough to speak. "No, I'm a souvenir. Got me in the gift shop."

The driver grumbled something, and Tyler just shook his head. "Kinda had that one coming, Lachlan."

Lachlan—square-jawed and built like a spark plug—muttered something uncomplimentary about Tyler's preferred bedroom activities with relatives. He reminded me not so much of the wolf in his veins but a very angry rottweiler. Maybe a rottie mixed with something small and yappy.

"Fuck you," Lachlan snapped.

Oops. I said the loud part quiet and the quiet part loud. "Sorry," I murmured. "It's been a shitty day, and I think my last filter blew."

Dizzy, the woman driving, huffed a shaky laugh. "Shitty doesn't begin to describe it."

I closed my eyes, unable to keep them open as the drugs lingered in my system, and my mind gave up its fight against its effects and the stress of fighting against my own panic. We jounced down a long, gravel drive with the headlights off, my head bouncing against the metal wall of the van. Everyone's adrenaline chatter had faded to the occasional gasp of pain when we hit a particularly big pothole or a muttered curse when the road curved unexpectedly. I drifted in and out, only really coming awake for a few minutes when we reached smooth road, and there was an audible sigh of relief.

"We have to ditch it," Dizzy whispered.

"River Road," Tyler said just as softly. "Past the Raymond's place on the back end."

I dragged myself a bit closer. "No, not there. Whatever killed them, it was at the Raymond's when Ethan and I went out there."

Tyler's eyes were dark and sparking with something fierce when he jerked around to face me. "When did y'all go out there?"

"Um..." My memory swam and struggled for a moment. "Yesterday? What time is it now? The day Cleverly and I were taken."

"Yesterday now. It's three a.m."

"Fuck." That meant it was Monday, and that meant work. Yeah, I know, ridiculous thinking about having to be at work in about five hours, but I couldn't just no-show, and with Justin ill... "Tyler," I began.

He shook his head again. "I don't care. I honestly don't. Whatever it is, it's not my problem. Soon as we ditch the van, I hand you over, and we're done, got it?"

Sluggish words finally surfaced. "Hand me over? Wait, you promised me some information, asshole!"

Charlie gave me a gentle shove. I fell back against the rough carpet lining the van's floor. "Go to sleep, Babin. You're less of a pain in the ass when you're unconscious."

Despite my best efforts, I did as Charlie ordered. I slept, fitful and hot, waking when we rattled to a stop in the dark of the swamp off River Road. "Oh, Christ." Nausea roared to life in my gut, my overworked senses back on high alert already. The anosmia was gone.

"Back online, all systems go?" Gio, who had been quiet when I'd been awake earlier, seemed chipper as a mudlark now. Whippet-thin and vulpine, he was the physical opposite of Lachlan, though they seemed to be something of a set as they huddled close together in the open van door, sitting on the runner board and looking out into the dark of the swamp.

"Unfortunately," I groaned. Imagine every unpleasant smell you've ever experienced up your nose all at once. Yeah. That was stunningly awful to wake up to. Gio and Lachlan dove out of the way as I lurched out of the van and hit the ground, hands and knees stinging, heaving up bile and acid.

"God fucking damn it, it's an ouroboros of suck," I gasped after what felt like an hour of vomiting, then the smell hitting me and making me dry heave all over again. Dizzy, bless her cotton socks, had the sense to drag me away from the worst of it, but the smell lingered in the miasma of swamp-stench and werewolves in high blood.

"Sit here," she ordered, shoving one of her long, beaded braids back behind her ear. She'd produced a jar of mentholated salve from somewhere and shoved it at me. Looks like someone knew some morgue tips and tricks. "He'll be here soon."

"Who?" I took a deep whiff of the salve. It stung and verged on overwhelming but, thank the powers that be, didn't make me want to projectile vomit. They had all moved off toward the back of the van, except Tyler. "Hey, who's coming?"

They didn't answer. Tyler opened the van and set it in neutral, Lachlan and Gio getting behind to push. I scooted back out of the way and watched as the van with its highly identifiable paint job was swallowed by the thick darkness of the swamp, disappearing into the tangle of trees and grass and muck that spanned the distance between the road and the river. "It's not perfect, but it'll keep them off the trail for a bit," Tyler said, clomping back up toward drier land.

"I disabled all the trackers I could find before we left the clinic," Dizzy murmured, staring out into the swamp. "Hey, y'all..."

"Yeah, me too," Gio replied.

All of them were staring off in the same direction. I tried to see what they were seeing but got bupkis. I took a deep, slow breath through my nose and only smelled swamp and sweat and sick and fear, not even a trace of the Other One, the one who'd killed the Raymonds. "Okay, Scoobies, what's happening?"

Tyler scowled, ignoring the snort that came from Lachlan's direction. "Your Spidey senses failing you, Landry? Something's moving around out there."

"I don't think I can handle many more pop culture references before the last of the drugs wear off. And what is it?" I didn't even bother trying to be cool about it in front of Tyler—he'd seen me scream like a child and try to climb drapes when a large wolf (ha) spider had gotten into his father's house once. He knew I had zero chill about anything.

"He'd come from the road," Lachlan said. Glancing at Tyler, he frowned. "I mean, wouldn't he? He's not going to be walking all the way here, right?"

Tyler shook his head. "Y'all check, far as the river." He jerked his chin in my direction. "I promised him I'd stay with Landry till we make the hand off."

"Y'all realize this sounds more and more kidnappy in a bad way the more you talk? Right?" I shoved myself to my feet, woozy still but slowly coping. The smells were still a tangled mess, but my brain had come back online enough to start compartmentalizing and sorting, ignoring things that were relatively benign. My stomach gave a lurch of protest but settled as I picked my way across tussocks of grass and sucking mud toward Tyler. "Why couldn't you just take me to the station? Or was he waiting at home or something?" Even as I asked, I knew why he wasn't there. Not only would it have meant the end of his career if he'd been arrested, but he was clan leader for the Stones. If he was known to be involved in anything we'd done or had done to us, he'd be up that old familiar creek without a paddle in sight.

Dizzy straightened, eyes wide and dark, gesturing at us to be quiet. She was alert, her body quivering with the need to shift. Her nose even twitched as she sniffed the air, for fuck's sake. How these people managed to keep being wolves secret was sometimes beyond me. The others had fallen into a keen silence, metaphorical ears pricked forward, all eyes suddenly fixed on the dark of the road. "He's here," she murmured, barely a whisper, barely a breath. Gio and Lachlan rose as one, moving just slightly in front of me. Protecting me, I realized, protecting me as Tyler joined Dizzy near the road, still and watchful. My heart gave a queer little lurch behind my ribs. I was still nauseated, exhausted, shaking with anxiety and fear, but *Ethan was here*. Ethan was here, and that scared bunny brain of mine was practically sighing with the knowledge, singing things like *safe now, protected*. I pushed myself to my feet, wincing as cuts tugged open and bruises throbbed. I didn't want to be down in the literal dirt when he saw me again.

"Finally." Dizzy sighed, not bothering to keep her voice down as a dark shape resolved from the shadows of River Road. I exhaled shakily, starting forward, stopping only when I realized the shape was wrong. Ethan was tall, built like a football player, but this were was taller. Broader.

Fuck.

Tyler strode forward, doing that one-armed hug-back slap-forearm grip thing they must teach during rush week for frats or something. "'Bout fucking time. We're gonna ditch the van and scatter. You good to go?" He glanced back at me, and I thought a little sliver of guilt crossed his features before he turned back to my new custodian.

Waltrip smiled, the expression grim in the semi-darkness. "Leave it. I'll send Elio 'round to do a full-bore forensic scrub down within the hour. Get out of here. I'll be in touch." Gio, Lachlan, Dizzy, and Tyler all turned away, Dizzy and Gio giving me tight smiles and a nod, Lachlan hurrying to keep pace with Tyler as they all disappeared into the thick shadows of the swamp. Waltrip never stopped staring at me.

"No," I said, shaking my head. "No."

"It's either come with me or wait here for your new friends to come looking for their van. Which is it?"

"God damn it."

His smile became a bit closer to real. "It's not a long walk to where I parked. Ever been on a motorcycle before?"

Fuck my life.

Chapter Ten

I have a theory that the longer the hiring process is for a job, the quicker the firing goes. By ten past eight, just five minutes after I walked in the front door of the building, I was back on the sidewalk. Unmoored. Reba trailed after me, carrying a cardboard box that had once held copier paper but was now half-full of my personal items off my desk and out of my locker. My still-warm cup of coffee was wedged precariously in one corner. "I called you an Uber," she fretted, her eyes wet. "Doc..."

I shook my head, words stuck somewhere in my chest. Daniel Mansfield, one of the heads of the state medical board, had been waiting in my office when I clocked in. He had been with a vaguely familiar man, someone who pinged my senses hard, but I couldn't place. He wasn't a were, but he wasn't quite *right*, something not really human about him. I didn't get very long to puzzle it out, though. The fug of chemical berry cherry sugar body wash clung to him, making me gag as he reached to shake my hand as Dr. Mansfield introduced him. Nelson Garrow II (people with his kind of money never used 'junior'—only roman numerals for them, baby), owner and medical director of the Garrow Clinic.

Because of course.

When Mansfield introduced him to me, I forced a smile. "Of Garrow Clinic. Of course," I said. "I've spoken with several of your... workers," I said. "In fact, this weekend, I got to experience their particular brand of attention. Your clinic is a very unique place, Dr. Garrow. In fact, I'd love to learn more about it and just how you work."

Garrow bared his teeth in a wide, gummy grin. "I'm sure you would, *Landry*," he put emphasis on using my name, not my title. "But unfortunately, we at the clinic have a bone to pick with you..."

They made short work of my employment, apparently because I was somehow involved in a vandalism spree at the clinic after hours over the weekend. Resign my position at the coroner's office, and I'd receive a decent letter of reference with only the most oblique nod to the 'trouble' I'd caused. Refuse, and not only would I get dragged through all sorts of legal proceedings, but I'd also likely lose my license to practice.

The anxiety I'd kept on a fragile, slack leash since my rescue slipped free, and I'd folded in on myself, hyperventilating. Garrow had patted me on the back, his heavy hand sending sharp spikes of panic through me with each touch. Between his overpowering smell and my senses screaming at me to run, my body felt stretched and twisted, unsure where to go to what to do.

Mansfield moved back around the desk, already cleared of my things, and joined Garrow in patting my back.

They were both of an age—maybe that was something they taught when they went to med school. How to fake a bedside manner via hearty slaps on the back. "Look." Garrow sighed, his meaty palm resting against my spine, pressing me down toward my knees. "If we didn't have security footage of you at the clinic, tearing shit up, we could just let this go. Rather, we could be more lenient in how we addressed the matter. But, as it is," he paused and let his hand trail down my spine, then back up to rest at the base of my skull. He gave a short, sharp squeeze that Mansfield did not seem to notice, hurrying back around to the other side of the desk now that his quota of physical interaction with humans had been met for the week.

"I understand that you had been taken to the clinic at the request of your aunt, a longtime employee of Bluebonnet Research, one of the clinic's branches," Mansfield said carefully. "You'd been attacked?"

I managed a nod, my breath thin and hot, burning my throat and chest. Garrow's stench was choking me, his hand hot and hard against my back, keeping my spine bent and face down.

"Look." Mansfield sighed, "as far as the higher-ups are concerned, you're out of there. You were still on probation anyway, and there is a strict one strike policy. But..." He paused and there was some sort of unspoken back and forth between him and Garrow. Garrow's fingers curved, thin crescents of fingernails scoring my back even through my work shirt and undershirt. *What the actual fuck...* The pain was enough to cut through some of the anxiety fog, but only some. "I'd like to speak further with Dr. Garrow and the clinic board on your behalf, because frankly, Dr. Babin, you're one of the best candidates for this position we've seen in years. The violent trauma of a home invasion can..." He trailed off. "Well, play with the brain, really. I was mugged when I was an undergrad, and it took me years to stop using a nightlight!"

Yes, because these two experiences are comparable. I bit down hard enough to make my teeth squeak together. For once, the shrill little voice in the back of my head was being vaguely reasonable. *Keep quiet. Don't snarl, don't snark, just keep your fool mouth shut!*

Garrow's nails eased back, and his hand dropped away from me. "Don't give him false hope, Daniel." Garrow sighed. "But it's definitely something we can discuss. Just don't," he added, hand back on my neck, nails scraping, "think this means you'll get your job back, Dr. Babin. While we at Garrow are sympathetic to your trauma, the fact remains you destroyed thousands of dollars in property, scared the hell out of several of our employees, and we have it all recorded."

What about the weres? How'd you manage to avoid filming them, too? I didn't nod, no matter how badly my head wanted to move. Garrow's hand eased away again, this time in a slow slide that dropped away as he reached my belt.

Oh, ew. Bad touch time.

Dr. Mansfield sighed again. His (my) chair creaked as he leaned back. I finally braved a peek and found he had his eyes closed, hands folded across his middle. "Dr. Babin... Landry... My hands are tied, son. Until further notice, you're no longer employed here. Take your things and go."

Garrow rose as I lurched to my feet. He reached as if he wanted to take the box but stopped short, converting the movement into an awkward pat on the sides of the box and a tight smile. "We'll be in touch."

Reba must have intercepted me because I remember nothing from the wash of loud buzzing noise in my ears once I realized I was truly being let go and standing on the pavement as Reba and I waited for the Uber she'd called for me. "You go on home," she urged, pressing the box into my arms, waiting until she was sure I had a grip on it before letting go. "This whole mess is just a clusterfuck, Doc. I don't know what the hell they're thinking, but that can't be you trashing the clinic! Hell's sake, you're not that kind of person!"

A small blue Prius pulled up to the curb, and I smiled wanly at her. "Thanks, Reba. Text me, huh? Let me know how things go?"

She sniffed hard, her fire engine red ringlets trembling as she jerked her head in a sharp nod. "Don't go hide on me, hear? Call me tonight. Let me know..."

I nodded. There'd be nothing I could tell her, and we both knew I wouldn't call her. I couldn't. It was too raw, my whole life going to hell. Too raw and too much of a knot.

The ride to my house took less than ten minutes, even during the two-car pile-up that constituted rush hour in 'downtown.' I hauled my box inside, locking the door behind me. Numb, I did a walkthrough of the house, checking for anything out of place. Traces of Waltrip's smell lingered in the air, tangling up with the sweet-berry-plastic stink that had embedded itself in my senses from the office.

I should call Waltrip, I thought, before remembering his business card had been one of the things missing from my effects at the clinic. I realized I hadn't canceled my cards that had been in my wallet and, in a sort of daze, padded over to my computer and started going through websites for my credit card, bank, and even my bookstore rewards card, methodically reporting each one stolen. There'd been no activity on any of the cards, which was a small mercy, I supposed, but I knew that they hadn't been taken with the intent to use them but rather to just get information on me and make it more difficult for me to live my life. It took over an hour and a half, but I finally got a confirmation number from the bank and hung up, slumping in my seat, letting my head loll back, and closing my eyes.

Got rescued from a wackadoodle werewolf prison clinic, got fired, took care of some financial stuff... Yep, busy day. I deserve a bit of a nervous breakdown now. It wasn't quite time for Waltrip to pick me up from work, and the thought that he would lose his shit if he showed up and I wasn't there crossed my mind, but in a perverse streak I'm not too proud to admit to having, I decided not to try looking up his number or start a phone tree by calling Ethan and asking him to call Tyler to call Waltrip and get Waltrip to call me.

That would be some junior high-level shit, logistics-wise.

"Fuck." I sighed to the empty house. I'd just have to go back down to the office and hang around outside, hopefully intercepting Waltrip before anyone noticed I was back and lurking.

Three hard, loud bangs on the door jerked me to my feet, copper-bitter fear flooding my mouth as my senses kicked into overdrive.

This was my typical workday. I wasn't usually home. No one should be knocking, I thought, quickly followed by *Idiot, if you're usually at work right now, how do you know no one knocks during the day?*

The knocks came again and, with them, a tinge of something familiar. Nothing so overt as an odor or a specific sound, but a bone-deep knowledge about who was on the other side of the door.

Fuckity fuck. How had he found out I was home?

I opened the front door to see Ethan fucking Stone staring down at me, pale eyes crackling with fire, face flushed, body visibly trembling. I stepped back, already tensing to flee even though I knew that, if he wanted, Ethan could easily catch me even in his human form, and that, as much as my senses were telling me, *predator, run!* Ethan was not going to harm me. "Hey," I whispered the only word I could muster under his intense glare.

"Landry," he growled, moving fluid fast, kicking my door shut behind him as he strode to me, scooping me off the floor and pressing a hard, teeth-clacking kiss to my mouth. My legs went around his waist automatically, my hands finding anchor on his shoulders, grasping him so tightly my joints ached. He kissed me again, his breath a rough groan in his throat as he walked us the short distance to my sofa. We tumbled, landing half on the sofa with his legs on the floor and mine bent at an awkward angle between us. I broke the kiss enough to breathe, squeaking in a very virile and extremely unmouselike fashion when he bit the tendon between my neck and shoulder, sucking hard enough to bruise and sending thrilling waves of heat and need and *belong to me* through every cell of my body. I arched up, letting him tug my shirt free from my trousers, gulping in air as he frantically kissed my throat, my chin, everywhere he could reach without shifting positions.

"Ethan," I managed, his name thin and reedy. "Ethan, wait a sec."

He jerked back to sit on his heels, hands resting on his thighs. He was red-faced, breathing hard, looking at me like I was the answer to some big question, but still he held back.

It would have helped if I had more blood in my brain, but as it was, we just stared at each other for a long minute before words finally came out the way I wanted them to. "How did you know I was here?"

Ethan closed his eyes, visibly shuddering before answering. "I went by your work. Well, former work, huh? I heard... Tyler told me that last night..." He trailed off and scrubbed a hand over his stubbled, tired face. "Shit, Landry. I panicked."

"What did Tyler tell you? I thought you knew what was going on and... and I thought maybe I'd see you last night, honestly." My voice was small. Ethan's eyes snapped to my face, and I felt flayed, too exposed. Sinking back into the corner of the sofa, I wished it could just swallow me whole because Ethan's intense gaze was too much. I wasn't afraid of him, though that unhelpful little part of my brain told me I should be. "What did Tyler say?" I asked again. "Please."

"Last night went to shit fast." Ethan sighed, scooting forward so he was resting near my legs, leaning back over me again. "They were going to slip you and your aunt out, but something happened. Someone knew, and everything went to hell in a hand basket before they really got started. They had two moles inside, but they got made."

"One of them was with Waltrip the other day," I murmured. "David, I think?"

Ethan shrugged. "I just know Tyler went way off book with what he did. The fallback plan was to wait. I would come get him—get *you*—if the original plan fell through." He blew out a harsh breath. "One of the inside guys called me, like we'd arranged if things went to shit. But by the time I got out of Belmarais, he'd messaged me to stay away, that things were falling apart and there was no way to get y'all out."

Ethan's hair was soft between my fingers. I stroked and tugged, closing my own eyes then. "So, you came looking today?"

"Waiting was brutal. I never want to go through that again." He huffed, adding, "The idea of you going through it at all... it makes me want to tear things apart. Hurt them." He crawled onto the sofa and pulled me close, leaning back so I was against his chest. "What happened at work?"

I told him slowly, his fingers moving up and down my back nothing like Garrow's press and claw from earlier. Ethan snarled, demanded to see my back, letting out a string of curse words that blistered my ears to hear. "So, this asshole didn't show you the alleged video?"

"Um, no? But Dr. Mansfield saw it and probably members of the board..." I shifted, heat flooding my face and throat. There was that lovely Shame Tomato Red again.

"You were fired first thing on a Monday? If the state board for you folks works anything like the state level oversight for law enforcement, there's no way in hell they'd have convened before hours on a Monday and been ready in time to fire you by your shift start time."

"As far as they know, one of their employees—hi, me—went bananas and destroyed a private clinic!" I tried to lean back and glare, but he held me closer. I didn't have much fight in me anyway, and he was so warm, and I was feeling safer than I had in days...

"Even if Garrow or someone from his clinic went straight to the state board with evidence you did this, which is bullshit, how the hell would he have gotten in touch with them so early? Aren't these assholes all in Austin, anyway? That's hours away." He squeezed me tight for just a few seconds, less affectionate and more protective than anything. "This smells wrong, Landry. All kinds of shit." His hands started moving up and down my back again, his scowl new levels of intimidating. "You sure this Garrow isn't a were? That thing he did to you—it sounds like forcing obedience."

At my expression, Ethan sighed. "You ever seen an older dog pin a pup that's acting up? Grabs 'em by the neck and holds them down?" I nodded. "Some weres will do that kind of thing when they are trying to force a wayward were to come to heel, so to speak. It's considered extremely rude, and you don't see it much outside of super isolated clans, the ones who swear the old ways are best and all that crap." He reached down to tip my chin up, making me look him in the eye then. "Now, are you *sure* Garrow isn't a were?"

"What? No. I mean, he didn't smell like... Shit."

"Didn't smell like shit. Good to know. But was he a were, Lan?"

"He stank to high heaven like cheap berry body wash or something. Just damn near overpowering."

Ethan squeezed me again. "Like he was covering his scent." It wasn't a question.

"Maybe," I allowed, burrowing closer. The trope of big strong alpha male protecting his mate made me cringe in the worst possible ways nine times out of ten, but at that moment, I was more than willing to let Ethan just hide me and protect me from everything in the world.

I felt ashamed. Weak.

"Hey." His hands stopped moving. Shifting around, he sat up and pulled me onto his lap, so I was facing him, astride his muscular thighs. *Hello* emotional and hormonal whiplash in three... two...

"I know that face," he murmured, gripping my hips tightly. He slid his hands back just enough to squeeze my ass before leaning forward to press a kiss to the hollow of my throat. "None of this is your fault. It's not because of whatever reason you're imagining."

"I wasn't thinking it was my fault till now," I grumbled, letting my head fall back, exposing the line of my throat to his warm, wet kisses. "I was thinking I'm weak. Ow! Fuck, Ethan! That hurt!" I jerked back, but he held me tight. Rubbing at the sore spot at the base of my throat, I bared my teeth at him in a feral snarl. "What the hell?"

"You're not weak. And I'm not gonna sit here and give you an ego boost pep talk," he growled. He pulled me close again, and I went willingly, bending my head to kiss him hard, lips pressed to teeth, little thrills of pain dragging me out of the slide toward gloom and doom thoughts. At least for the moment.

"I never stopped wanting you," he breathed against my mouth. "Never. I thought about you every goddamned day. Christ, Landry, the stupid daydreams I had where you would just show up at the office. Or I'd see you coming up the walk." He squeezed my ass again, arching his hips up against me. His hips and his very obvious hard on. *Yes, please...* "Even when I knew you weren't coming back, Lan... Fuck."

He groaned and let his head loll back, pressing up again. "Swear I didn't come over to try to fuck," he whispered. "I just... I needed to make sure you were alive, that you weren't dead on the side of the road somewhere. I needed to see you, and when you opened the door..."

I ground down against him, drawing a gasp, then a hiss, as our cocks pressed together. "I know," I murmured. "I know you're not here to get laid. But we have like seventeen years to catch up on."

That startled a laugh out of him. "Fucking hell, Lan. This is the worst time for us to try hooking up."

I paused, mid-grind. He was panting, gripping me so tightly there'd be bruises. I hoped there would be, anyway. "Hooking up?" The phrase left a cold, empty spot inside me, like swallowing a bit of ice. "Is that what you want us to do now?"

"Huh?"

"I mean, it's not a no from me," I rushed because it really wasn't. Was it what I wanted? Not at all. But I'd take it. The years without Ethan had been lonely, even when I was with others. He'd made a space for himself in my heart, or maybe I'd made it for him, and without him in my life, it dragged, felt heavy.

I was doing lying to myself about it.

Ethan couldn't stop staring at my mouth, wanting to kiss again, but he spoke anyway. "No, it's not what I want," he said. "But trying to start something up again, start *us* again, in the middle of this shitstorm..."

I didn't want to hear anymore. It sounded too much like it was going to hurt if he finished that thought aloud. Moving quickly, I leaned in and kissed him again. After the briefest pause, he kissed me back. Fingers fumbling, we scrambled to unfasten our jeans, hands getting in one another's way as he tried to race for the prize. Laughing, we ended up on the floor, wedged between the sofa and coffee table, jeans pushed halfway down our legs, Ethan missing a shoe, my shirt rucked up to my armpits. I nearly howled when he bent his head to my tight nipples, sucking hard enough to hurt before laving the sting away with the flat of his tongue. "Fuck! More, like that!"

He laughed against me, moving to the other side as he dragged his fingertips down my ribs, over the soft skin of my stomach. I groaned, pressing against him again, the sound turning into a shout, ecstatic and sharp, when he slipped against me. His hand, strong and warm and only a little rough, slicked the copious precum leaking from both our cocks across the heads, around the shafts. My legs curled around his back, nonsense pleading tumbling from my lips as he started to stroke us together. It was messy and fast and desperate, his grunts of pleasure and gasping short groans of my name, of promises that weren't quite words, underscoring my own breathy, high pleas and sighs. I wanted to keep my eyes open, wanted to watch his face, see him fall apart, but he squeezed us together, his thumb pressing against my weeping slid, and I shattered. My orgasm raced through me, crashing down hard enough to steal my breath away.

Everything was white and blurred for a moment, a year. I felt my cries more than heard them vibrating in my throat as I arched up, the hot spill of my release between us, slicking us both. Ethan's own rough shout was muffled by my neck, his hand still moving, stroking us together even though we were both sensitive to the point of pain by then. Neither of us wanted it to end, but he slowed his hand, then stopped, moving his sticky wet fingers to my hip as he panted against my chest. I let my legs fall back to the floor, the ache in my hips reminding me I wasn't seventeen anymore. Without a word, Ethan rose and padded to the kitchen, coming back with damp paper towels. He cleaned us both and dabbed at an unfortunate spot on the carpet before smiling and tugging the coffee table over a few inches to cover it. "There," he said. "Good as new."

I laughed, feeling just plain happy for the first time in days. "Fuck," I groaned. "I don't want to get up."

Ethan started to say something, a smile on his lips, but paused, then frowned. "We're gonna have to. You got company."

"Fucking were senses," I muttered even as a heavy knock fell on my door and just kept falling. I hop-struggled into my jeans, tugged my shirt down, and checked to make sure Ethan was decent before heading for my front door, Ethan trailing behind me.

Waltrip was waiting on the other side. As soon as I opened the door, he shoved a flash drive and my phone against my chest and pushed past me. "If y'all are doing fucking, we've got work to do."

I fumbled the phone, almost dropping it. "Where the hell did you get this?"

"My mole has sticky paws," he said, wiggling his brows.

Ethan rolled his eyes so hard I was pretty sure he'd need an ice pack later. "For fuck's sake. Come on, let's take a look."

Chapter Eleven

When the flash drive's contents popped up on the screen, it was a timeline of my childhood. Four-year-old me with my chunky legs and round cheeks, wearing my favorite Spider-Man shirt and light up shoes. Seven, with a scraped knee and a gap-toothed smile. Me, age fifteen, hands shoved in the pouch pocket of my hoodie, earbuds dangling around my neck as I scowled at the man taking my picture. I was mad in that one, I remembered, because the man had made fun of the giant zit on my nose, called me Rudolph.

The flash drive Waltrip had shoved at me was apparently all about yours truly, in gloriously specific detail, in violation of what had to be a million laws and levels of patient confidentiality. Every specialist visit my aunt had trotted me off to, every doctor's office, had been recorded. Garrow, Bluebonnet Biomedical, and God knew who else, had been monitoring me as I grew and changed, watching how these medications worked on a child, then adolescent.

"It gets worse," Waltrip muttered, removing that drive from my laptop and inserting another. He brought up a directory of over two dozen video files, all several minutes long, each titled with a series of numbers that I assumed were code for the contents.

Ethan's hand shot out and stopped Waltrip from selecting the first one. "If these are Landry or, fuck, any kids getting hurt—"

Shit. I hadn't even considered... My heart rabbited hard against my ribs. Waltrip and Ethan both visibly tensed, predator instinct twitching, but Ethan slid his arm around my shoulders and tugged me close. I was still shaking, but a soft calm seeped through me under his protective touch.

Ugh. How... ugh. Let's pretend I don't sound like some soap opera heroine, okay?

Waltrip shook his head. "They're recordings of conversations. But," he paused, glancing at me and licking his lips like the words were sticking in his mouth. "Landry's not gonna take this well."

Ethan squeezed my shoulder again. *Are you ready?* I nodded. I was lying, but I nodded anyway. Waltrip hesitated a second more, then pressed play for the first video.

My aunt's face filled the small screen. She was younger in the video than in real life. Her hair was longer, worn in a thick braid over one shoulder with a hideous, fluffy clip-on bow at the end. "The official *I was a drill team captain in high school, y'all!* hairstyle of Texas," I murmured. Ethan huffed a weak laugh. Waltrip just stared grimly ahead. Cleverly's voice, made weird by the laptop's small speakers, pierced the room.

"Okay, so, you promise this isn't hurting him, right?"

Another voice, someone off-screen but whom she was facing, agreed. "Absolutely no pain, Miss Babin." The sound of a chair creaking as my aunt fussed with the end of her braid, looking away from the other person. "I do hope you're not going to try to back out of this. You've been a stellar employee, and you seemed quite on board with this before."

She perked up, glaring at the speaker. "I know that look," I muttered. "That's her *you just fucking tried me* look."

Cleverly tipped her chin, glaring down her nose at the other person. "I'm not backing out. I just want to make sure he'll be safe. I owe my brother that much."

"Your brother sold his own son, Miss Babin," the other person chided. "Do you honestly think he'd give a damn?"

Waltrip hit stop as I rushed to my feet. I made it as far as the kitchen sink before I cast up the contents of my stomach, meager though they were. Hunched over my sink, I couldn't stop shaking, not even when Ethan clomped into the kitchen behind me. "Thanks for stomping," I murmured.

"I didn't want to surprise you."

"I know. Not being sarcastic." Pushing myself to stand up straight, I rinsed the sink out, then grabbed a glass so I could rinse out my mouth. Ethan just watched, quietly looming in the doorway, his presence a comfort even while I felt squidgy about finding it so calming. "Okay. Let's do this."

"Landry—"

"No, let's do this. This is about me, right? My aunt is apparently some sort of... Fuck, is she a child trafficker? Shit."

Ethan moved as if he were going to hug me but stopped after half a step, his hands falling back to his sides. "There are so many videos, Lan. Let me and Waltrip look at them, okay? We'll—"

"No. No, this is me, right? Whatever the fuck is going on, it's about me. Or part of it, anyway. Those drives came from the lab. Your brother said they took them last night. That's what his friends were doing before we got freed, getting this info. Fuck, was it only last night?" A hysterical laugh bubbled up inside me, threatening to creak out if I didn't clamp down hard on the urge. "I'm a grown man, Ethan. Let me decide if I have to walk away."

He nodded slowly, thoughtfully, and stepped aside to let me pass. I grabbed his hand as I went, tugging him behind me. His sigh was soft and relieved. I pretended not to notice. Waltrip looked up at me when I sat back down, his jaw working like he wanted to say something, but he finally just grunted acquiescence and hit play on the next video.

The videos ranged in time from less than five minutes to

nearly an hour, depending on what they were discussing. We never got to see whom Cleverly was speaking with, and she never said their name, but it was always the same person. Low voice, nondescript accent. Someone she addressed only as *sir* a few times over the videos we watched. They discussed me, 'the subject.' Cleverly detailed my academics, my anxiety attacks, my habits down to how often I took a shit.

He asked her the same questions every time, mostly about any sensory issues, always sounding just a bit disappointed until, one interview sometime around my eighth year, Cleverly hesitated. The sound of the chair creaking was like a gunshot in my painfully quiet living room. "What is it?"

"It's just... he's acting out a lot at school lately. The counselor wants me to take him to his pediatrician, get him tested for ADHD and maybe some learning issues. She recommended he see a different shrink, someone the district sends problem kids to. They think it's to do with his living situation," she said, looking some mix of angry and embarrassed. "He keeps saying everyone is too loud, that he can hear them breathing too much, smell them too much."

There was a breath of sound, maybe a laugh. "And the medication?"

She nodded again. "Every night. Full dose."

"Growth is still below average," he murmured. "Hm. But the sensory aspect..."

Waltrip stopped the video. "Medication?"

"I was on some anti-anxiety meds when I was little. And a ton of allergy shots. I was allergic to everything East Texas has to offer."

Ethan and Waltrip exchanged looks.

"What?"

"Did your regular doctor give you the medications?" Waltrip asked.

"This shrink my aunt took me to gave me the anxiety meds. Doctor Pollard, I think. Pollard or Poland. I'd have to check my records. The shots..." I had to think for a few moments. It had been ages since I'd really given thought to them that dredging up the name of the clinic was work. "Cleverly took me to a specialist up toward Dallas. I forget the doctor's name, but it was in this big clinic, one of those professional buildings attached to a hospital system. I only went for a few years until they decided I was doing okay with just taking over the counter meds for my itchy eyes and sniffles. It was some pediatric specialist, that much I remember. There were always so many kids in the waiting room; it was like going to a play date or something," I added. Despite the shots, those visits had been pretty fun, from what I could remember. I always got to play with other kids, there were tons of really cool toys, and the nurse who took me back always remembered my name and asked how I was doing, making me feel like a big kid at the time.

Ethan leaned back on the sofa, closing his eyes and making that rumbly sound he always did whenever something was giving him a headache. Somewhere between a growl and goddamn it! "Fuck."

"Someone want to enlighten me?" I asked. Waltrip looked anywhere but at me. Ethan scrubbed his hands over his face and rumbled again. "Okay, I'm gonna count to five. Someone had better start talking, or I'll..." I trailed off, well aware there was no physical threat I could make against either of them that would be viable, even if I were tempted to hurt them. "I don't know what I'll do, but it'll be unpleasant for all of us."

"I didn't go through all the videos myself," Waltrip said, voice low and soft. "Lachlan, one of the guys who was there last night—"

"I remember him." Funny, built like a spark plug, scared shitless but handling it well. Clung like a limpet to Gio. "He was one of the ones who broke in?"

Waltrip tilted his head to one side. "Eh, kind of. Lachlan had been working in the clinic's IT department for nearly a year. He was one of our plants and wasn't supposed to be there that night, but a change in security protocols led him to stay on site in case the rescue team needed help."

"Wait up," I demanded. "A *year* ago?"

Waltrip made a negligent gesture, as if to wave off my outburst, but Ethan was on it before I could lay into him. He lunged, grabbing Waltrip by his throat and forcing him to the floor. A submissive posture, I realized. Ethan was showing dominance and yeah, okay, it was kind of (very) hot but at the same time, it triggered my own not-quite-wolf, that part of me that wanted to flee and run. It made me want to kneel, too. To show my metaphorical (maybe?) belly. To affirm Ethan was in charge of the situation.

Oh, no, fuck that, I thought with a flash of embarrassment and not a little anger. *No one is my fucking pack leader or whatever the hell it's called. Fuck. That.*

Waltrip didn't seem to be having that same problem, though. He'd gone still, his head bowed as Ethan loomed over him. "When I was approached by someone claiming to be Landry's aunt about a year ago, I knew something was off. They said their name was Sandrine Fisher."

"That was my mom's half-sister," I murmured. "She—"

"Died before you were born, I know," Waltrip said, wincing when Ethan gave him a little shake. "But I took the job because I knew they worked for Garrow Clinic." He lashed us a sideways smirk. "They're not as clever as they think they are."

Ethan let go of his neck but crouched beside him. His eyes were changed now, the wolf just below the surface. "Why did you let this go on for so long, asshole? Landry was in danger. He nearly died—"

"Because," Waltrip snarled, teeth bared ever so slightly, "I needed to find out who was behind this, what was happening. I needed to get closer. And someone from Garrow reaching out was like a gift in my lap. The dead kids from the first group? My uncle was one of them. He died before I was even born, but it haunted my father's family." He slowly raised his head, staring

Ethan in the eye. "I've spent years trying to trace the people who did this. And when I saw the chance to get my foot in the door, I took it."

"Why did they reach out to *you*?" I demanded. "Why you specifically?"

"Might be a surprise to you, but there are not a lot of weres out there in the PI game."

"Why didn't they connect you to your uncle?" Ethan asked.

Waltrip shrugged. "Different last name. Years had passed. And the fact my mom took off with me when I was a baby probably helped put some distance between who I am and who they killed." He flicked a glance my way before adding, "Their research isn't the greatest. It took me two minutes to find out Sandrine Fisher had been dead for forty years. But her name comes up when I google your mother's name. First page of the search."

Ethan's fingers flexed, the urge to grab for Waltrip again strong no doubt. "You said *we*. Who else is involved?"

"There's more than just me, trying to get to the root," Waltrip said, his expression shuddering. "Lachlan, Gio... we're all part of the same organization. And that's all I can say. I owe my loyalty to them, not you Ethan Stone."

"Tyler helped you," I said, realization dawning. "He knew? About you, about—"

"He knew there was a group hiring freelancers," Waltrip said. "Nothing more." I blinked. "If he hadn't been there last night..."

Ethan snorted. "If Tyler hadn't gone off half-cocked—"

"Then your boy here would be worse than dead," Waltrip growled. "Don't try to pretend otherwise." He snapped his attention back to me, ignoring the none too subtle snarl from Ethan. "Lachlan did a scan through the files, looking for some keywords based on his research while on site." He lost some of his steam, his strident tones easing back toward cautious. "You need to know that you're not the only one, Landry."

"Not the only one what? I swear to God—"

"You were experimented on as a child." Ethan sighed.

Turns out you can totally throw up even if you don't have anything on your stomach.

🐾 🐾 🐾 🐾 🐾 🐾 🐾

Ethan left me alone while I had my mini breakdown. I figured I'd have to pencil in a proper one later when this was all done because Lord knew I didn't have time for a good freak out. Once I was cleaned up and relatively composed, I padded back into the living room. Only Ethan was there, sitting on the sofa, frowning at his phone. "Where's Waltrip?"

"Out front. He's meeting Tyler down the way." He rolled his eyes. "Even if I didn't have the hearing, his voice carries. Someone named Dizzy called him, and he took the conversation outside. Tyler will be here in a few."

"Dizzy was there last night. Or was it morning? She was driving. Tall, blonde, looks like Legolas but with more earrings."

"Oh! I knew her as Desiree. Tyler's ex." Ethan shoved his phone into his pocket and motioned for me to join him. Curling me into his side, half on his lap, he sighed. "She's sweet but sneaky as fuck. They met when Tyler got arrested for, ah, a little bit of breaking and entering."

"A little bit? How can you do that a little bit?"

"The guy dropped the charges when he realized Tyler hadn't stolen anything but had witnessed him fucking someone most definitely not his wife."

"Let me guess—Dizzy was the not-wife?"

"That would be suitably dramatic for Tyler's purposes, but no, she was brought in around the same time for hacking University of Mid Texas' student database. She doxed her rapist. She and Tyler got on like a house on fire until they didn't."

My front door banged open, bouncing off the wall before Tyler caught it on the rebound as he entered. "We still get along," he protested. "Just better as friends. Or co-conspirators, according to the court documents."

Ethan didn't dump me on the floor at the sound of his brother's voice, but definite lurching happened. Tyler rounded the sofa, Waltrip following him back from outside. "Dumbass can't be subtle to save his life," Waltrip groused. "Just drove up like nothing."

"I think we can all agree that any sort of cover has been blown to shit," Ethan snapped, scooting me to sit beside rather than on him. My inner teenager was sulking but thank God that brat had learned to shut up during my undergrad years because there was no time for petulance just then. Tyler wedged himself between me and Waltrip, leaning out to talk to Ethan around me. "Dizz is in the wind right now but will be working on altering a few alarm reports that slipped out before Lachlan could catch them."

"Um, hate to interrupt, but you *do* know Garrow has video footage of last night? Or at least parts of it." I quickly detailed my morning to Tyler and was perversely gratified when Ethan slid his arm back around me and pulled me close again.

"That's impossible," Tyler protested. "Lachlan cut the security cameras before we started. Total blackout on all feeds external and internal. He blitzed their circuits to make sure none of them could be brought back online. Are you sure they weren't just bullshitting you?"

"My boss saw enough of it to know I was involved, but they kept saying it was vandalism."

"If there is footage of the aftermath," Waltrip offered, "they could doctor it, so it only showed Landry. A few seconds of a guy in front of a broken window, acting sketchy, or being hauled off by people in security uniforms? That's all a lot of people would need to jump to the wrong conclusion."

Tyler raked his fingers through his messy hair. "They didn't show it to you."

"No, didn't even offer." I slid from my perch on Ethan's knee and took up a seat on the coffee table. "Whether the video is doctored or not, the fact remains they have something, and Garrow was able to cost me my job. Why?"

"Retribution," Ethan suggested.

Waltrip hummed in agreement. "You took something from them—namely, yourself—and they take your livelihood."

"Hey now, I helped," Tyler sniped. "Not with the job part. That was all them. But..." he added, glancing at Ethan with a very pinched expression. One Ethan returned. Damned sibling facial semaphore.

"But what? Hey, if I'm gonna be torn apart by a werewolf, I'd like to know, okay? Whoever killed the Raymonds is out there still. They're connected to this clinic and—"

"Where's that box you found at the Raymond's place?" Ethan asked. His voice was quiet but heavy, cutting through my ramping panic.

Shit. "At Cleverly's," I groaned. "Under the bed in my old room."

"Fuck."

Tyler, succinct as always.

"What was in the box?" Waltrip asked, turning the laptop to better see the screen.

"It was some prescription medication. Nyc... something."

"Like one of those nicotine patch things?" Tyler scoffed.

"No, dumb ass. Nyc... No! Not nyc! Started with an L! Lycaon." The name popped out of my memory, bright and clear. "They had a stack of boxes in the bathroom, all sealed. I don't know if this Lycaon is an injectable or pill or what. The bedroom had so much shit in it, but I did see the discarded sharps." I quickly described the state of the garbage pit-slash-bedroom at the Raymonds. "I didn't take a close look at the needles, but I grabbed a few. *Safely,*" I added at Ethan's hiss. "They're bagged up with the box back at Cleverly's."

"Are you going to tell him, or should I?" Tyler asked, a thin slice of amusement coloring his words. "Fuck it, too slow, I'll do it. You don't recognize the name Lycaon? Didn't you have to take

World History with Mrs. Shelby in tenth grade? She was obsessed with Greek mythology."

"Yeah, I remember her little shrine to Apollo she kept by the window. Lycaon has something to do with Greek myths?" I shrugged. "A lot of meds have weird names like that. Artemis, that birth control thing," I ticked off on my fingers, "that sleep aide, what's it called, Hypnovere? Named after Hypnos—"

"Lycaon," Tyler said loudly, cutting me off, "is the first werewolf."

I sat back down hard. Ethan had his face buried in his hands while Waltrip had risen and was pacing a hole in my carpet. Tyler was the only one who looked relaxed, but I'd known him long enough to see the signs. He couldn't keep his foot still, he worried his lower lip with his top teeth, and he cracked his thumb under his other fingers. He was antsy, maybe downright anxious.

"Lycaon," I said slowly, a very faint niggle of memory coming back to me. "He... pissed off Zeus, right? And being a werewolf was his curse."

"He wanted to test Zeus," Ethan said, hands muffling his voice, "so he served him human flesh. Some stories said it was the flesh of his own sons. Zeus knew, though, and cursed him, turned him and some of his sons into wolves."

"Is this... is this like an origin story for y'all?" I asked slowly. "I mean..."

"It's just a story," Waltrip snapped. "I don't know a single one of us who thinks we're some sort of divinely cursed throwback to ancient Greece or wherever. We're mutants. An offshoot of human evolution somehow."

"And what does the myth have to do with medicine?" I wasn't going to like this. I knew it. "What does Lycaon have to do with the Raymonds?"

"Based on what we've found out," Tyler said, still jittering a mile a minute, "Lycaon is experimental. Something Bluebonnet Biomed was testing on a select few candidates based on their medical history and willingness to be human guinea pigs. You, and a handful of others, were the first run. But you were kids, unable to consent, you know? And you were early on in the experiment. Not all of you survived."

He was so blasé about it that I almost missed it. "Wait, they've killed children?"

Waltrip nodded once, grim. "Bluebonnet Biomedical wants to create weres."

Everything tilted hard to one side. "By... injecting them... us with something?"

"We're not sure what's in the crap they gave the subjects yet," Tyler admitted. I barely felt Ethan stroking my arm. My speeding heart must have been like a siren call to their wolf nature. I could smell the tang of my own fear and panic pouring off me in waves. But none of them so much as fluttered a lash in my direction. "Whatever is in it, the Lycaon formulation is the final or near-final form. Your group is the only one to survive long-term. They switched to adult subjects and have focused on them since."

My lungs didn't want to work. I was vaguely aware of Ethan pressing my head down, murmuring instructions to me, telling me to breathe slow and easy. Tyler kept talking, though, and my body just wanted to seize up. Tyler continued, "Of the three who survived, the best records are yours. You had some sort of surgery when you were ten, right?"

"Mastoid," I nodded, my voice reedy and high. "Here." Tilting my head to one side, I exposed the small spot behind my right here that was missing a square of bone. "Kept having headaches, turned out to be an infection." God, I just wanted to fucking *breathe* without it hurting, and if Ethan didn't move his damned hands, I was about to bite him. I growled, unable to stop myself, and he jerked back, holding up his hands so I could see them. "Sorry," I muttered. "I just..."

He nodded but didn't try to touch me again.

"They took a sample of your brain tissue," Waltrip said. "They took a small chunk of it to see why you survived and the others didn't." He gestured vaguely toward the laptop. "Your aunt mentions it in one of the longer clips, apparently. Lachlan was very thorough in his search."

"That's how they verify rabies, you know," Tyler remarked, stretching out on my sofa. "Lachlan thinks they were checking the survivors to see if y'all would turn on them."

"Wait, wait. If I was some grand experiment," I said, "why did they just let me leave? Why didn't I get dragged back to the labs or something?"

They all three exchanged uncomfortable looks. Tyler rolled his eyes and huffed. "Seriously, you two? Fucking hell, fine, I'll be the asshole. Because, Landry," he said in a sing-song voice you'd usually hear in a preschool classroom, "they wanted to see if you'd go nuts and start killing people when that little bit of wolf they left in you was let loose. You were on your own, no access to any sort of help from Bluebonnet, far from the labs just in case they needed to haul you into one of their friendly doctors who'd lie to you about a test or a new medication you needed."

Ethan tentatively reached out to lay his hand atop mine. "They let you go to see if you would finally turn, Lan. To see if you'd become one of us."

Chapter Twelve

Ethan made dinner. He set a plate of fried chicken, potato salad, and green beans in front of me with a glass of sweet tea. He'd plated it up like we were at a fancy restaurant, complete with a fancy carved tomato garnish and a sprig of rosemary tucked beside the chicken. At my praise and thanks, he offered a tight smile and took up the seat on the other side of my tiny kitchen table.

"When we were teenagers," I said after the first few surprisingly good bites, "you couldn't even handle boxed mac and cheese."

His grin was real this time. Quick and bright before he hid it behind a sip of his tea. "It's been a while. I learned to feed myself actual food and stopped living on takeout and boxed dinners sometime around freshman year of college."

"I think I figured out I needed to eat actual grown up food sometime around my first year of med school. Unfortunately, at the same time, I also realized I didn't have time to make anything other than instant noodles and whatever I could nuke in under five minutes." I speared a chunk of potatoes and popped it in my mouth. "Remember that time your dad was out of town?"

"And we tried to play house with that fancy dinner and shit?"

Ethan snorted. "Oh, God, I tried to make steaks. I remember the smell lingered for *days*. Mrs. Carroll from next door could still smell it when she came over that next weekend, and she didn't even have the senses the rest of us did."

It had been terrible. The steaks were burned on the outside but bloody inside. I'd forgotten to wash the spinach, so our salad was gritty and had one very scared little worm hiding under a chunk of tomato. Ethan had snagged some beers from his dad's stash in the garage fridge, but I tapped out after a few sips, the bitter-sour taste making me gag. His dad had been off at some meeting. Looking back, I know it must have been clan-related, but at the time, I was told it was for work. Ethan's brothers were gone for the night, off doing gods knew what. "I remember you wore that awful shirt. The shiny one? All... gray and shimmery?"

He blushed, looking down at his plate with intense focus. "I got it out of Tyler's closet. I thought maybe I'd dress up a little." The glance he shot my way was fraught with remembered heat, with the butterfly-laced excitement of two barely-men growing into their desires. "I remember thinking how *good* you looked. Um. I have to admit something. I burned the steaks because I kept staring at your ass while you made the salad."

I managed not to choke on my drink, but just barely. "Oh my God, Ethan!"

"Oh, don't act like you didn't know! You were dancing around, shaking your hips. You kept looking at me to see if I was watching."

"Never!" The serious expression lasted for less than ten seconds before I cracked, and then we were both laughing, pretending for a few minutes we weren't scared to bits. That Tyler and Waltrip weren't breaking into my aunt's house. Like we weren't waiting for everything to implode. Picking at the crunchy bits on the chicken, I glanced at the clock. "It's been two hours."

"It's going to take at least five," he murmured, back to snaffling down his food like he was afraid someone was going to steal it off his plate.

"What if Tyler can't find it? I mean, I told him exactly where it was but—"

"He'll find it," Ethan said flatly. He stood abruptly, his chair skittering on the old linoleum. "Want more? I'm gonna..." Gesturing toward the stove top and the still-warm food, he shrugged. "Being nervous makes me hungry."

He was kind of adorable when he blushed. I shook my head, picking at the chicken again. "I'm still working on this, thanks." The kitchen was quiet for another few minutes while Ethan refilled his plate and I moved the food around on mine, fooling neither of us. "Do you think..."

What did I even want to know? Did he think this would end well? Did he think Tyler and Waltrip were going to make it? Did he think that, maybe, when this all settled out somehow, we could make another go of it now that we were adults, and our heads were mostly out of our asses?

"Not often." He chuckled. "It scares the hamster off the wheel."

"Huh? Oh." I rolled my eyes, making a raspberry noise at him as he sat back down. He eyed me expectantly, but I kept my attention firmly on the remains of my potato salad. After a minute, Ethan tucked into his plate of chicken, and conversation slowly bubbled up again, meandering through mundane topics while skirting the edges of more dire ones. After we'd done all the damage we could to dinner, Ethan insisted on cleaning up, threatening to move me bodily from my own kitchen if I didn't let him.

"I like washing dishes," he lied.

"You're doing that nose crinkle thing you do when you try to convince people you're sincere about your love of diet soda or college ball."

"Am not. Now go before I duct tape you to the recliner." He held up one finger. "No. No sexy brow wiggles, racy comments, or suggestive looks. Go."

"You didn't say anything about salacious panting," I teased, sticking my tongue out and panting like a dog as I headed for the living room. Ethan's snort of laughter followed me into the dimly lit room. The TV showed the streaming screensaver, evidence of our attempt to watch a show to pass the time earlier. We'd given it up after neither one of us could stay focused for more than a few minutes, no matter how funny the comedian Ethan had chosen was. I flopped back on the sofa and grabbed for the remote to turn off the box, pausing mid-reach when I noticed my laptop was still open on the coffee table.

Still open, and flash drive still plugged in.

I felt like a kid sneaking out after Cleverly was asleep, jumping at every noise while I eased my laptop over and brought it out of sleep mode. It took seconds to open the drive and scroll past the things we'd already looked at. All that was left were some text-based files labeled with the initials B.D. and three numbers after them. Each file was a slightly different number, but all had the same initials. *Christ, what if this is about one of the other kids? My initials were on some of those files about me. This must be one of the kids who survived, too.* Or I hoped so. I hoped they'd survived and were out there somewhere, that thinking they had anxiety, or some sensory issues was the worst problem they faced in their daily life now, and they had no idea about what had been done to us.

Ethan was whistling some pop song I was planning on teasing him for knowing later, the sink running as he rinsed. *Now or never.* I opened the first text file only to be confronted with a wall of, well, text. It was gibberish, like someone had saved in the wrong format or something, but I scrolled down anyway. Six pages of the same mess on a file that showed it had seven pages. The last page was blank, which was a nice break from the nonsensical lines of blocky junk text but frustrating enough to make me growl like a dog.

Yikes. That's new... I glanced toward the kitchen. Ethan was still whistling about how some boy broke his heart, and now he was going to party, party, party all night, night, night with the sink still running like I didn't have to pay the water bill. Abruptly, the sink shut off and the whistling stopped. I fumbled the laptop and nearly dropped it when Ethan stuck his head around the corner of the kitchen door. "Hey, I was going to make some coffee. Do you..." He frowned and came out of the kitchen, crossing to me in just a few long strides. "Don't torture yourself with that, Lan."

"Bad choice of words there, Stone," I said shakily. I moved to set the laptop back on the table, avoiding Ethan's sharp glare. "It's nothing, anyway. Just a junk file from the looks of things."

"We'll have Tyler run through it, just to be sure. It might be coded or something." He looked at the screen, eyes widening and a soft gasp escaping. "Or hidden in plain sight."

When I'd fumbled it, apparently, I'd hit a few keys. The page was highlighted, a neat and tidy list showing up in clear, plain language. "They saved in white text on a white background," I huffed. "That's elegantly simple and painfully irritating."

Ethan dropped to sit next to me. "Those look like bank account numbers," he said after a few seconds. "No names but look." He tapped the screen where a column of numbers marched down one side of the list. "Decimals replaced by commas. They do that in a lot of European countries."

"It's a list of money they're getting from Europe? Or are they sending it?"

Ethan shook his head. "We need to get Tyler on this. Fuck, I wish I had Lachlan's number. I'd just go straight to him instead of dealing with my brother." Ethan took the laptop back and opened one of the other text files. This was the same, a page that looked blank but showed a similar list of numbers if you highlighted it.

"I was worried it might be about one of the other kids," I admitted softly. "I thought maybe if I could find their names, there'd be some way for me to track them down, and I could see if they were alright. If they... if they made it out in one piece." A shudder racked my body. I felt impossibly young and terribly old at the same time. Ethan didn't hesitate to wrap me in his arms, tugging me onto his lap and just letting me be there. His hands never strayed to more exciting areas. Instead, he tucked my head beneath his chin and drew his legs up to cradle me, making an Ethan-blanket around me.

I felt safe. I was still scared to hell and back, and the knowledge I could be killed relatively soon wasn't far from my conscious thoughts, but I felt *safe*. Ethan was what I'd been missing, or maybe what I'd been working toward. I thought maybe he might feel the same about me, but I couldn't think of a way to ask that would keep me from shattering into dust if he pushed me away again like he had back when we were kids. "Landry," he whispered.

"Uh oh. Landry, not Lan. I must be in trouble," I murmured. He tipped his head back, but I refused to move, keeping my chin tucked and eyes firmly on his shoulder. *Did he just read my mind? Does he know what I'm thinking? Or am I just that obvious, and he wants to nip this in the bud? We can go back to living close by and so far, pretending not to know the other is just an hour away.*

"Not that kind of trouble," he said, low voice sending shivery fingers down my neck. "Look at me."

His fingers tightened as my heart picked up speed. That stupid scared bunny part of me was nervous but didn't want to run. Not from Ethan. I tipped my face up and, before I could so much as breathe in, he was kissing me. Firm but not hard, he pressed his lips to mine. My microsecond of confusion made him tense, ready to pull away, but I was faster than either of us expected. Tangling my fingers in his thick hair, I held him in place, reveling in the feel of his beard rough on my cheeks, his tongue barely touching my lower lip. Opening for him, I felt his sigh rather than heard it. Maybe that was one thing to be thankful for, I thought, out of all this horrific mess. Whatever they'd done to me, however it had fucked up my senses, it made me able to feel this with Ethan in ways I'd never expected.

"Hey," I said, breaking the kiss for just a moment, "so, um, with you guys—"

"Us guys?" he asked, smirking. "I'm gonna guess you mean weres."

"Yeah, yeah. Weres. So, when you're *with* someone, is there any sort of..." I paused, not able to think of how I wanted to phrase things. I settled for waving the fingers on my left hand. "You know, woo?"

"Wooing?"

"No, like... *woooo*?" I waggled my fingers again, throwing in raised brows for emphasis.

Ethan looked like he was either trying to be subtle about choking on his own tongue or trying not to laugh. "Are you asking if we mate for life or have some sort of mystical bond or fated mates?"

My face felt hot. Ah, yes, there it was... that hideous telltale red flush that always gave me away when I was especially awkward. I'd managed to avoid it for years, at least since the pantsing incident during my clinicals. *Hello Shame Tomato, my old friend. I'd like if you'd fuck off again...*

"No," I drawled, sinking back against his chest, burying my face in his neck again.

"Liar," he chided. "And no, we don't. I mean," he amended, raking his nails lightly up and down my inner arm. *Hello, new erogenous zone. When did you get here?* "We tend to stick with other weres or people from were clans even if they can't shift."

"That's a thing? Is it a recessive gene or—"

"Easy there, Lan," he chuckled. "We don't know for sure, but the gene appears dominant. Once in a while, we have someone born without the ability to shift and completely lacking in any of our abilities. No one's really studied it, but I do know of a few families where a were had kids with a non-shifting were, and their kids were able to change and everything as they got older." He shrugged, the motion bumping my nose gently into his jaw. "Why?"

Ethan already knew why. I could tell. He was looking at me with a narrowed, satisfied gaze. I didn't let him smirk long. Shifting to straddle his thighs, I kissed him again, then again. The low groan that rumbled up from my chest when Ethan's hand slipped beneath my waistband surprised me, my startled jolt making him chuckle. I started to pull back, but Ethan was the fast one this time, pulling me hard against his chest and belly and moving us, my legs falling open to cradle his hips as he pressed me back onto the sofa. "We have a bit of time," he murmured, nosing my jaw and placing a sharp nip to the skin beneath my ear. My melting sigh was all the permission he needed. "Can I?" he asked, fingers picking at the button on my jeans. I nodded, arching my hips up for him. He had my jeans open and unzipped in a heartbeat, tugging them down with my boxers and tucking the waistband behind my balls. "Fuck, Lan." He groaned, looking up at me. "I want you in my mouth. Can I? Let me?"

"Oh, God, yes." A blowjob from Ethan had been the main event in so many of my dreams after I left for Baltimore. Feeling his hot mouth on me again after so many years was almost too much at once, my hips stuttering as pleasure shot through my veins. Ethan chuckled, damn him, the vibrations setting off more sparklers. He didn't give me time to whine about it, though, setting to work like he'd been starving for me. "Oh, God, oh God," I babbled, unable to stop myself from squirming. I usually had much better blowjob etiquette than that, but until Emily Post wrote a sternly worded column about it, I supposed I'd just have to accept the fact my bad manners were excusable if it meant Ethan would make that noise again. He took me nearly all the way to my root, his fingers stroking and tickling my sac as I gasped and made embarrassingly high-pitched noises. "Close," I finally panted. "Fuck, Ethan, I'm so close, baby."

He pulled away so fast it was a shock. Cool air hit my wet, hard cock in an unpleasant wave. I didn't even get the first word of complaint out before he was leaning over me, kissing me with the taste of my precum on his tongue and lips. "Can we... I mean, if you think we shouldn't yet—"

"Ethan, are you asking if I want you to put your cock in my ass?" I laughed, his awkward hesitancy wildly, weirdly endearing.

"No," he admitted, ducking down to bite at the tendon in my

neck, gently gnawing for a few seconds before he whispered against my throat, "I want you inside me this time."

Oh. "Oh." We'd never done it like that during our one summer together, though we'd talked about it in that jocular 'I only mean it if you mean it otherwise just joking' way teenage boys get around serious things. "Are you sure?"

He nodded. "I have to admit... it's something I've thought about a lot since that summer."

It was his turn to go all Shame Tomato.

"Oh, wow," I breathed. "Um. Gimme just a sec. I thought I wasn't so close now but hearing that? Fuck, I don't have any blood left in any other part of my body."

He laughed, sounding a bit relieved, before leaning up again to kiss the corner of my mouth. "Do you have supplies?"

I had to think a minute. "I think so. It's been a long while, but I wasn't exactly burning up the sheets before my last hookup."

Ethan's frown was deep and annoyed. "It's irrational of me because, no offense, I wasn't exactly keeping my own pants zipped up while we were apart, but I don't want to hear about your hookups right now, even in passing."

"I promise I'll keep the juicy details to myself until the afterglow." His scowl verged on the comical, though his eyes crinkled ever so slightly, telling me he was exaggerating his annoyance now just for my amusement. "My bedroom, top drawer in the nightstand."

Ethan reluctantly pulled away, trotting down the short corridor to my room. A minute or so later, he was back, his own jeans unfastened and open to reveal his cock hard and pressed against his stomach by the waistband of his briefs. "Well, hello, there. Looks like you brought a friend."

"I believe you've met," he replied dryly. He dropped a condom onto the coffee table and shucked his jeans, looking me over from face to chest to groin and back again as he knelt over me. "Do you want to do it, or should I?"

I grabbed the condom and tore the packet open. "You do you; I'll do me this time."

Ethan nodded, wasting no time in reaching behind himself and starting to prepare. The sound of his lube-wet fingers slipping in and out of his tight passage made my cock throb. I was afraid to touch it, even to put on the condom, for fear of shooting immediately. Ethan groaned and leaned forward, bracing his free hand on the arm of the couch next to my head. He started to thrust back against his fingers, and I just couldn't take it anymore. I quickly rolled the condom over my painfully hard length then reached a hand around to find his probing fingers.

"Is this okay?" He nodded frantically, gasping high and needy when I slipped one finger in beside his two. *Fuck*. We moved together for several long, breathless moments before he slid his own fingers out and took my wrist to move mine away. "Now?" I asked.

"Please!" He moved up a bit, one foot on the floor and the other braced on the cushion by my hip. I held my prick steady for him as he slid slowly down. When the head of my cock breached that first ring of muscle, he went still, head thrown back and chest heaving. "Christ, it's been too long since I've done this with another person," he breathed, half-laughing. "Toys aren't the same."

My cock gave a very interested twitch. Ethan groaned again, a strangled, breathy sound, as he took me the rest of the way into his tight passage. My fingers clasped his hips so tightly, I was sure there'd be bruises the next day, but Ethan didn't seem to care. He slid his hands down my shoulders to rest on my chest, his head dropping forward as he slowly began to move. Seeing Ethan above me, not as a teenage fantasy dragged through the years but a living, breathing, amazing man, was more than I'd ever hoped for. He rocked his hips, moving up and down just a little, tipping his head curiously when he caught my intense stare.

"I just can't really believe it," I murmured. "Goddamn, you feel so good," I moaned. "I can't believe you're… we're…" He ground down on me then, slow and filthy. My train of thought derailed, all souls lost, but I knew I'd be able to resurrect it later. After Ethan was done riding me like that, his body tight around me, moving tortuously slow. My balls ached with the need to cum, every stress and fear and inadequacy I'd felt over the past several days reduced to nothing but an annoying fly's buzz when compared with the rush of warm, heady love (why lie, that's what it was) and pleasure pounding through me as Ethan rode. His cock bobbed purple-headed and leaking against my stomach. He didn't stop me when I wrapped my fingers around it and started to stroke in time with his thrusts. Ethan's sharp breath was the only warning I had before his release spilled hot over my fingers. I wasn't long behind—the way he clenched around me, his body trembling, sent me over the edge in seconds. I cried out nonsense words, Ethan's name, and desperate sounds I'd have been mortified to make any other time. It felt like it would never end even while being over far too soon.

Ethan slumped forward, his head on my chest this time, both of us drenched in rapidly cooling sweat. "I have to be honest," he murmured, breath stirring my sparse chest hair, "I hadn't planned on doing this for a while."

"In general, or with me specifically?" His hair tangled around my fingers as I stroked it, making snarls and whorls that stuck out all over when he lifted his head to look me in the eye.

"Both," he admitted. "I've, um, been thinking about after this is over. I mean," he said. "I mean after we've figured out how to stop this mess with the rogue wolf and—"

"I know," I said. "I've been thinking a lot about it, too. I spent a long time thinking I hated you, Ethan."

"I spent a long time hating myself."

"I'm tired of it."

"Me, too."

We stayed in our uncomfortable tangle, quietly listening to the outside sounds as the night grew darker. Finally, I couldn't stand the feeling of the gross condom and itchy sweat anymore. "I need to shower. You want to try to squeeze in with me?"

Ethan's groan was far less sexual than the ones he'd just been making a few moments before, but it was definitely frustrated. "I want to so bad, but I'd feel safer if I waited until you were done before I got in so at least one of us can keep an ear and eye out for Tyler and Waltrip."

"Ugh, fine, make sense, be all responsible and shit," I teased, scooting to my feet and heading for my bedroom. I didn't have to look to know he was staring at my ass, so I made sure to put a little English on my wiggle before I disappeared into my room.

🐾 🐾 🐾 🐾 🐾 🐾

WE STAYED UP FAR PAST MIDNIGHT, THOUGH WE DIDN'T fuck again. We watched Netflix, made an attempt at checkers, avoided my laptop and the evening news. Finally, I made myself go to bed. Ethan decided to stay up a bit longer 'just in case.' I knew he would be trying to get hold of Tyler or Waltrip as soon as I had my bedroom door closed.

I'd swear I'd barely slept a minute, but I woke up to bright sunlight streaming through my window and the strong smell of coffee teasing my senses. "God bless you, Ethan Stone," I muttered.

"Sorry, babe. Wrong werewolf."

"Fuck!" I popped up like a jack-in-the-box, clutching sheets around me. "Tyler! What the hell? Where's Ethan?"

"Eating my fucking bacon if I don't get back to the kitchen," he said. "Here. Coffee. Drink. Get dressed then get your cute little ass in the kitchen. We've got some news."

Chapter Thirteen

When I walked into the kitchen, Tyler made a face and snorted like a dog trying to sneeze. "Stop being a dick," Ethan muttered, snagging a piece of floppy bacon from the plate in the middle of the table.

"Where did the bacon come from?" I asked, trying to pretend like three weres smelling me and knowing what I'd been up to last night wasn't weirding me out a little. "And who used my blueberries for pancakes? I was saving those."

"Your kitchen was seriously lacking in pork products," Tyler opined around a mouthful of meat. "I ran by Suprette to grab some bacon. And sausage." He snorted. "Though I think you—"

"*Okay*," Ethan snapped. He glanced at me, his cheeks faintly pink. I bit my lips and applied myself to the stack of pancakes Waltrip plonked down in front of me. Ethan waited until I'd managed a few bites and Tyler had brought out another plate of bacon before starting in on where things stood. "Last night, they were able to find the Lycaon and syringes at your aunt's house."

"Bad news is, the entire place stunk to high heaven of the rogue were," Waltrip supplied. He had one of my plain blue mugs gripped in his enormous hands, making the sturdy ceramic look like a dainty teacup. "I don't know your aunt's house, but nothing seemed out of place. No evidence of anyone tipping the place."

Tyler shrugged. "It doesn't mean they weren't snooping. The scent was pretty fresh. We missed them by less than an hour."

Those pancakes were super heavy going down. "You didn't see—"

"No," Waltrip cut me off. "No cars coming or going. Late at night, small town? Anyone out on the road would've stuck out. We parked at the U-Pump and shifted, took the back way 'round just to make sure we weren't seen."

I would think two large wolves running around in an area where no wild wolves lived would've been pretty eye-catching if anyone happened to look in the right direction, but I held my tongue.

"Without access to the clinic, we don't know what's in this." Tyler jerked his head in the direction of the counter where an innocuous brown bag sat, crumpled and grease stained.

"Did y'all use a takeout bag?" I asked. "Seriously?"

"Which is more suspicious to a cop pulling us over? Two guys with an empty bag from Dairy Queen, or two guys carrying vials and syringes?"

"You could have just put it in the glove box," I muttered, stabbing at a blueberry bubble in my pancake.

"At any rate," Ethan interposed, "we need to access a lab and the Raymonds' blood samples."

Shit. All three of them were staring at me. Waiting. I could play dumb for a few minutes, I knew, but it would never work. Besides, I could tell by the twitch of Waltrip's lips that he, at least, was expecting some push back and had something snarky lined up, ready to go. "You know I can't get back in there," I finally said. "They took my swipe cards, and all my access codes have been purged."

"And you know we're not talking about you going in," Waltrip retorted.

"I can't ask Reba—"

"Reba doesn't know the first thing about blood analysis." He sighed.

"I think you're underestimating Reba."

Ethan reached out and laid his hand atop mine. "Babe..."

"*Babe?*" Tyler threw his hands up in the face of our double-barreled glare. "I'll just be over here, getting more coffee then, *darlings*."

"I'm not asking Justin," I said flatly. "I can't. He's a sweet kid, but it just won't work. He's always sick, for one thing, so I doubt he'd even be able to come in, and for another, he's scared of his own shadow. He'd end up freaking himself out and running out of there before getting anything done."

"You're making excuses." Tyler sat back down across from me, coffee sloshing over the rim of his mug and onto the table. I shoved a napkin at him, glancing at the spill pointedly. He rolled his eyes and mopped it up, tossing the soggy napkin into the trash behind him without looking. He flashed me a grin. "Good, right?"

"You're a man of many talents. And none of them are convincing me to drag Justin into this."

Ethan squeezed my fingers again. "We don't have a lot of options right now. Not if we want to get this finished."

"By 'finished,' I'm guessing you don't mean have Garrow and everyone at the clinic arrested, the other survivors found and offered a shit load of counseling, and get me reinstated into my position with this whole thing expunged from my record?"

"Yes, but no." Tyler smirked. "Most of that, but more like finding who our rogue wolf is, where all the Lycaon has gone, and who they decided to give it to."

"Why not both?" Waltrip asked, his smile positively shit-eating.

"Fuck me," I muttered, pushing my plate away and ignoring Tyler as he fell on it with gusto. "I don't want to believe Justin is involved in this, alright? I barely know the guy but he's... he's fragile. He's scared of his own shadow."

"He's also the most likely avenue of help right now," Ethan murmured. "The safest route."

I wilted. "Fine. We'll go see him but I'm not happy about it."

Ethan shot me a soft look. "I know what you're thinking. You're hoping he's not home."

"Oh, so you're a psychic now, on top of being a werewolf?"

"I'm a man of many talents."

Tyler's groaned *oh my God shut up* was enough to almost make me smile.

"BE CAREFUL WHAT YOU WISH FOR," I MUTTERED. I'd spent the entire ride over to Justin's apartment wishing he wasn't at home. And it looked like my wish had been granted.

"No blood," Waltrip announced, emerging from the back bedroom. "Some piss, though. Few hours old."

Justin's apartment had been well and thoroughly trashed. Even the door locks—and Lord, there were a *lot* of them running down his door—had been destroyed, someone ripping them by hand or claw. "It wasn't the rogue wolf again." I was starting to feel real stupid referring to this killer as the rogue wolf. It sounded way too cool for someone who was a murderous fuckhead.

Waltrip shook his head, shaggy curls bouncing. "No, this is definitely someone different. The entire place has the smell of them, and it's not all fresh."

"Justin had a were over here regularly?" I edged further into the apartment, peering past Waltrip at the wreckage of the living room. "Christ, are those restraints?"

He grimaced. "Cheap sex shop crap," he muttered, bending to examine a length of what looked like black nylon webbing attached to a thick leather cuff. "This wouldn't do shit against a were in human form. And when we shift..." He held up the cuff to his eye and winked at me through the opening. "Our dainty little paws would slip right out of that thing."

"So was Justin... what? Fucking a were, and it went sour?" Goddamn, the mental images that idea created were terrifying. Justin didn't deserve an end like that. I pressed a hand to my roiling gut. "Are you sure no one is here?" I demanded. "I mean, they didn't do something to him and hide him in here, right?"

"No other living thing is in this apartment. Besides the spider I saw in the bathroom."

"Spider?"

"Calm down. Just a daddy long legs. At any rate, no indications of murder."

I felt a sharp spike of relief. Justin may have annoyed the hell out of me some days, and we weren't really close at all, but the idea of him dying like the Raymonds had... "Could he have escaped?"

"Could you? If you were trapped in an apartment with a were determined to tear shit up, could you have escaped?" He raised a brow and smirked at me. "Hmmm?"

"I don't think I like your tone," I sniped.

Waltrip laughed.

"I think," I said after a moment's thought, "it's possible. If I were highly motivated, I could run like hell. And Tuttle is small, but we're still in the middle of town. Even if he bolted at the crack of dawn, it would draw notice."

"From whom?" Waltrip asked, gesturing at the destroyed living room. "The neighbors? This place is a refurbished factory. It has thick concrete walls and floor." He pushed past me and opened the door into the hall. "And he's the only one on this floor. If he made it out through the building—"

"There're no signs of a were attack in the hallway," I pointed out. "It's possible."

"If he made it out through the building," he repeated through gritted teeth, "then what? Front sidewalk, facing a dress shop that's closed until ten a.m., a pet groomer closed until eight, and a parking lot."

I stared at the corridor for a few moments, trying to think around my instinct to flee. "No... No. If I were in here, if I'd been in Justin's place, I wouldn't have gone out the front door. The hall is too long, and I'd end up trapped on the stairs or the elevator."

Waltrip nodded, already moving toward the windows overlooking a wedge of what passed for downtown. "These are painted shut."

"Bedroom."

Acid burned in my stomach, my body wanted to shake apart, but I pushed through it and went into Justin's bedroom ahead of Waltrip. The stench of animal fear and a softer, earthy smell swamped my senses. "The window's closed. Shit."

"It's been opened, though," Waltrip murmured. He pointed but didn't touch. "The paint along the bottom's been peeled away."

"So, he took the time to pick off years of paint and close the window behind him when he fled?" I kicked at the pile of bedding on the floor. "Whatever happened in here, he wasn't going to make the were wait on him while he made an escape."

"No," Waltrip allowed. "But what if..." He narrowed his gaze, going very still. His breaths became deep and slow, drawing in the stink of the apartment, the regular smell of the place beneath the layer of fear and were. "Hmm. Okay. He's not here." He opened his eyes and gave me a searching look. "He's not dead. Or wasn't when he left here."

"That's not as comforting as you think."

"I don't think it is at all. I think it's a fact, though." He dropped to one knee and took a deep whiff of the bedding, his expression becoming thoughtful. "I highly doubt he's gone to work."

"You think?" I rolled my eyes. "Now we have to find Justin."

"No." It was a sharp, short bark of a word. "No, we let him be for now. We worry about the lab work first. Is there any other way to access a lab without having an in like Justin?"

"Um. No. Not really. Not unless I can break into a pathology lab somewhere like a hospital or send the samples off, which would be the stupidest thing we could do right now."

Waltrip grunted again. "These pathology labs, are they only at hospitals or..."

"Or? No. No, no, no. I'm already on suspension. If I do something like that, I lose my license and probably go to jail." I didn't know what would come next for me in terms of my teetering career, but I knew it definitely would require me to *not* go to jail.

"You didn't answer my question," he said a little too patiently. "Are they at hospitals or just morgues?"

"Bigger hospitals would have what we need. But the closest one is Dallas." Waltrip nodded, shoving to his feet and striding past me.

"Come on. We need to get moving. Tyler's gonna be back in a few hours, and Ethan's already on the way from Belmarais. Gonna meet at your house."

I followed him into the corridor. He was so far ahead of me, I had to jog to catch up as he reached the door to the stairs. "No, fuck that," I said. "I'm going in the elevator. Meet you at the bottom."

"I'm not leaving you alone, not now."

"And I'm not going down six flights of stairs. The elevator was good enough for the trip up; it's good enough for the trip down."

"I want to check the stairs for any signs Justin came this way."

"Then do it. I'll meet you at the bottom." The elevator doors had swooshed open while we talked, so I stepped inside and gave him a little finger wave. "See ya."

Waltrip made no move to get in as the doors closed, but I'm pretty sure he said a very specific word in reference to the veracity of my parentage. The elevator was slow and a little jerky, one of the joys of a building that had once been a lumber depot and converted to incongruously fancy apartments. My phone buzzed in my pocket, alerting me to an incoming text. I had a fairly good idea who it was but checked anyway.

Cleverly: *Where are you? I need you.*

My brain took an extra few seconds to process what I was seeing. Not Waltrip at all. "Holy shit. Holy shit!" I hit the button for the doors to open on the next floor and threw myself out into the thankfully empty hallway as soon as I could. Unlike the black-painted hallway on Justin's floor, this one was starkly blue, a bright robin's egg that made my eyes hurt as I staggered away from the elevator doors, thumbing open my contacts list to bring up Cleverly's number. It rang twice before her shaking voice answered. "Landry? Landry, where *are* you?"

"I'm... I'm in town. Cleverly, where are *you*? Are you safe? Tell me where you are, and I can come get you!"

"I'm at home," she admitted, laughing breathlessly. "I don't know how I got here. I... I remember going to work but then that's it."

"You don't remember someone breaking into the house a few days ago?" I leaned against one of the walls and slid down to a crouch, closing my eyes against the relentless pounding of the light. My body ached with the need to *do*. Every cell in my body was on fire with something that wasn't fear but a close cousin.

"*What*? No, I just... Landry..." Her voice was plaintive. "Landry, I'm scared! I don't know what's happening, and I feel *wrong*."

Shit. "Okay. Just stay put, right? Don't open the door till I get there." Waltrip would be waiting for me outside by now, impatient and annoyed. "I'll have someone with me, and I don't want you to freak out. He's... he's friendly."

"Is it Ethan? Maybe I should call Ethan. He's the sheriff now," she added, sounding a bit proud.

"It's not Ethan, Cleverly. I'll, um. I'll call him, too." I pushed myself back up the wall and made my way back to the elevator, jamming on the down button. "Just stay put and lock the doors." The elevator opened, but I hesitated a moment. "I'm going to hang up, okay? I want you to keep the phone by you and call me if something changes before I get there."

Cleverly's voice was clearer when she responded, the shakiness gone. "Of course, Landry. I'll be waiting for you."

🐾 🐾 🐾 🐾 🐾 🐾 🐾

Cleverly might have been waiting but Waltrip wasn't. I followed the sidewalk around the entire building, but he wasn't anywhere to be seen. Unless he'd decided to go to the roof, there was nowhere he could be hiding from me. His bike was still out front, parked sideways across one of the parallel parking spots, so it was obvious from the street. I ducked back inside to see if he was in the lobby, but the only person there was a cleaner with a sad-looking dust mop, making a desultorily pass at the wood floors.

"God damn it," I snarled. Waltrip's number rang out to voicemail when I tried him, the professional sounding greeting for his investigation firm sounding nothing like his usual rough, perpetually amused tones. "Way to be a dick," I snapped when the tone signaled me to leave my message. "If you're dead on the stairs, I'm going to find a necromancer to raise your ghost so I can punch it." I ended the call and looked back at the apartment building. The stair doors opened to the lobby, the only exterior doors being the ones for the entrance, a service door around back that required a PIN to open, and a metal security door on the east side of the building that had no visible means of opening from the outside. I stepped back into the lobby, where the cleaner gave me an annoyed glare before swooshing over with their dust mop to brush away the outside debris I'd tracked in, sighing audibly as I headed for the stair door.

I opened the door to a concrete landing with narrow, industrial-looking stairs rising at a sharp angle in front of me. They took a turn after about ten feet, jinking up at the same steep angle overhead. "Waltrip?" I called. "Hey, I need to go. Where are you?"

Nothing.

"Swear to God, dude, if you're just being a dick to make me climb stairs, I'm going to kick your ass." The door closed behind me with a thud as I took the first few steps. "Okay, I'd probably just have Ethan kick your ass because who am I kidding, but the spirit of the threat remains."

Still nothing. Not even a derisive snicker at the idea of me threatening to hurt him in any meaningful way.

I took another step up. Then another. I reached the first landing and froze. The stench of fear and were was intense, seeping through the door a few steps above. A big black number two was painted on the door, the soft sound of something scraping carpet barely audible through the thick metal. The sound stopped, and a rattling breath sounded, long and low.

"Landry."

I jumped at the sound of the low voice below me on the first floor landing. *Waltrip*, I thought, turning before I realized that the voice wasn't quite right, lacked that hint of roughness and humor. A white blur moved, snarling as it tackled me back onto the steps. My skull bounced off one of the concrete risers, pain exploding behind my eyes as the wolf pinned me down with its massive paws on my chest.

"Good, good," the low voice murmured. "Here we go." A sharp prick in my neck, and everything got warm and soft. "Careful of his head. If he dies, she'll raise hell again."

Someone lifted me, and I didn't care. All I could think was, I hope this many head injuries in a week don't leave permanent damage.

Chapter Fourteen

At least I wasn't in the clinic again. I was in Cleverly's living room, stretched on the couch with my feet propped on one arm, tingling with pins and needles. My head felt fit to explode like a dropped melon if I so much as twitched. Beneath the odor of the rogue wolf, of blood and piss and sharp-cold medicinal stink, I could smell the familiar scents of home, of coffee warming and something sweet just out of the oven, old books and sun-warmed wood. Cleverly's perfume wove through it all, growing stronger as she moved closer. "He's coming 'round," she murmured. "Get ready."

Showtime. But I'd been skipping rehearsals and didn't know my marks. I waited for some cue from Cleverly, from whoever was in the room with us, but everyone was quiet. They were close, though, their scent heavy in the air. My instincts shouted *wolftroublerunhide* louder than anything else in my head.

I must have twitched or shifted subtly, something I didn't notice my own body doing, because cool, beringed fingers clasped my wrist and squeezed just hard enough for me to feel the press of acrylic nails. "Aunt Cleverly," I said, barely more than a breath.

Her perfume smell washed over me as she bent close. Perfume and sour-sharp-earth-dog-wolf. Everything tilted sideways in my universe and pulsed itself inside out. I gasped, jerking away. The sudden movement sent a blinding hot shock of pain through my skull. I lurched sideways, nausea overtaking everything but the pain as my stomach heaved and spasmed. Cleverly cursed, and someone else in the room snarled. Someone already in wolf form, then, not human.

Cleverly released my arm and gave me a brisk pat on the back. "You always did have a weak stomach." She sighed. "Glad you hit the can and not my rug. These things are a pain to clean. Antique, you know." She nudged me with her knee, making me roll onto my back with a groan. The pain was still tangible, wrapped around my head with tendrils curling over my stomach and back, but I managed to open my eyes. She peered down at me, pink-painted smile tight and small. She looked like she was getting ready to head out to one of her club meetings, with her hair done up nice and makeup all pink and powdered as a doughnut. "Landry, darlin' boy." She sighed, sitting carefully by my legs. "You've really fucked things up, kiddo."

The oddity of her cursing, especially pulling out the high dollar word, made me laugh in an inelegant, ungraceful spurt. Her put-upon tongue click was jarring in its familiarity. I pushed myself onto my elbows, swallowing hard against the acid gurgle in my stomach. She watched me with the shiny dark eyes of a predator, a faint hint of excitement seeping through the perfume and wolf tang. "Did you kill Justin?" I asked, hating how shaky my voice sounded. "Is he dead?"

"Justin? Oh, DuBois?" She snorted. "No, he's just fine. Just fine, Landry." She patted the back of my hand, giving it a little squeeze. "He's getting better every day, isn't he, Doctor Garrow?"

The wolf gave a soft huff in response.

"Of course, it's Garrow." I groaned. "Of course."

Cleverly gave my hand a final pat before getting to her feet, lacing her fingers in front of her and giving me the *Landry, I'm not mad at you, just disappointed* look I'd seen so many times as a teenager. "I'd hoped you wouldn't be an idiot, Landry. I really did. When I realized you were determined to ruin everything, I tried my damnedest to get you untangled from everything, but Doctor Garrow was right." Garrow made a low, throaty noise I took to be agreement. "Even if I managed to get you to back off your little Hardy Boys adventure with Sheriff Stone and those... *people*"—she spat the word, making it an insult—"you're still part of the story. A very important part. We can't lose you."

Runrunrunrunrunhide! "Aunt Cleverly, I know about the... the experiments." The words were thick and slow, hard to say. Everything had become unreal. I was just a smidge too far to the left to be fully in my own body, I thought. This was some nightmare after getting clobbered the first time a few days ago. "I know what they did to me. And I know," I pressed on, hoping to make things true by saying them out loud and wanting them enough. "I know you had reasons you thought were good. And I know you must be scared. But please don't let them keep doing this, Cleverly. They've killed people. Killed *children*. And for what?"

"To perfect them," she snapped. "All of you were chosen for a reason, Landry. Children from defunct lines, children who were born to families who'd lost the wolf to time, to shitty breeding practices." She swiped a hand across her face, tired and frustrated. "I was terrified for you at first, but when you survived," she laughed, a remembered excitement and pride. "Your survival was a miracle. Only three of you made it. It was before they figured out how to adjust the dose. And that they needed to wait until the onset of puberty to mimic the natural shifting process."

Garrow groaned, the sound shifting from canine to human as it arced and fell. With the wet snap-pop of reshaping bones and the peculiar bloody ozone smell that came with a shift, he was no longer a wolf. Instead, he was a naked, panting, pained man on my aunt's floor. For a moment, I was seized with the idea, the *need* to throw myself on him and start throttling him while he was still weak, but Garrow was fast. He shook himself like he was still fully wolf before pushing to his feet. He grabbed a robe from the back of one of the recliners and tied it around himself before coming to stand next to Cleverly and peer down at me with open disgust on his face. Considering I'd just seen him naked, that definitely took a lot of nerve.

"Has your were friend ever told you about the wolf's mark? No? Well, it's not a very fun story, really. We tend not to like it. It reminds us of a time we were weak. Hunted. Everyone has these grand ideas of werewolves, how we're stronger and faster and just *more*. Where we originated, out in the wild lands before countries were made, we were hunted. If a shepherd or farmer caught one of us in sheep or pillaging the chickens," he made a whistling noise, slicing at the air near his head. "They wouldn't kill us. They'd mark us. So they could find us when we were human again. A quick nick of a knife across a soft ear, and you would see a man with a cut on the lobe the next day. We're easier to kill in human form," he confided in a loud whisper, a man telling a child a story. "Soon enough, some very clever sorts figured out they didn't have to kill us. We didn't want our secrets told, especially as the world changed and creatures such as us became the bogeymen in the woods rather than just another part of the natural world. So, you mark a were, you find him later. You know his secret and he'll do whatever needs to be done to keep himself safe."

He sighed and ran his hands down his face, pulling at the soft, aged skin. "You were special, Landry. We let you go to Baltimore and Denver and everywhere else because you were special. You were our test case. You"—he reached out and gently touched the spot behind my ear where I was missing the small square of bone — "were marked. Not just by this, but by your abilities. You were our walking advertisement. Do you know how many clans came to us, begging for help after they heard about you out in the world? Clans whose lines were dying? A human with the senses of a wolf! Though," he laughed, "you weren't our best example. But you showed the *potential*."

"Potential for what? A lifetime of neuroses?" I managed to sit up, swaying slightly as my brain protested all the tenderizing it'd gotten lately. "I'm *nothing*, Garrow. My abilities are shit."

"Your abilities," he chided over Cleverly's mutterings about my rudeness, "are *perfect*. You just lacked the strength to develop them. The others did better." He shrugged, glancing at Cleverly. "You were the first but definitely not the best. What's the phrase they use for those games? Beta version? You were the beta version."

Cleverly smiled kindly at me. "Landry, you think you were that irresistible to the clans? You were being tested, hon. Like buying a car," she said, pleased with her example. "When you get a new car, you want to take it out, see what it can do, right? Get on the freeway, do some loop-di-loops in the parking lot, that sort of thing!"

"Baltimore was desperate," Garrow added. "They haven't had any viable shifters in their clan for nearly a decade. Every new birth was a dud."

Baltimore was a bright red scar on my memories. It was terrifying, each day uncertain about my survival. Each day wondering if one of the weres would take me out, if I'd be torn to pieces by someone who thought I smelled wrong, didn't smell wolf enough to survive, not human enough to ignore. It followed everywhere I went. They'd find me, whatever weres lived in the area. Chase and retreat, stalk and observe. I thought they were scared of me somehow, of my strangeness, but they'd wanted it, or some version of it, for themselves. "The Raymonds?" I asked, lips numb. "Were they like me too? Were they being experimented on?"

"Only by themselves." Garrow sighed. "They were in our third data pool. Giving the drug to adults who showed no sign of were in their family history. They took to it well until they didn't."

"Tore each other up," Cleverly tutted. "Like watching one of those awful Pitbull fights they used to have in Delmit."

"What do you mean, they took to it? They changed?" I tried to get to my feet, but I wasn't quite ready yet. "They became... what? Wolves? Or something else?"

Garrow made a see-saw motion with his hand. "They could

shift to a point but never became fully wolf. It was a damn shame. They were going to be paid off. That whole family was going to see more money than the whole damn town put together. But they wanted the change too bad to see reason."

"They were self-medicating," Cleverly whispered loudly. "It was a problem."

The image of the Raymonds' bodies was burned bright in my mind. What they'd done to one another... "How? How did they kill each other like that?" I asked quietly. "They were torn to pieces."

"They were strongly motivated," Garrow chuckled. "Now, day's wasting. I want to get on the road before rush hour hits."

Cleverly helped me up with her hand on my elbow. "You want a drink before we get going, hon? Maybe a sandwich?"

"He can't have anything on his stomach, Cleverly," Garrow called from somewhere back in one of the bedrooms. "Anesthesia."

"Oh, shit. I'm sorry, baby boy!" She shook her head, pressing one hand to her soft cheek. "I don't know where my mind is."

"Anesthesia. For what?" Nothing good, I knew, but I needed to hear it.

"It's time to wrap up your part of the experiment, Landry," she said sadly. "I'd really hoped it'd go better, that you'd cooperate. But you got yourself tied up with Ethan Stone again and..." she trailed off, shaking her head. For a flickering moment I felt like I was seven again and tracking mud on her new carpet, like I'd brought home that D in biology, like I'd forgotten to thaw the chicken for dinner before she got off work. "Well. Sheriff Stone is a problem for later," she sighed with the hint of a smile. "He and Mr. Waltrip are further down our list of priorities. First things first."

Ethan. Fuck. He was on his way to my house. Was he there? Had he figured out something was wrong? They didn't let Waltrip go but was he dead, too? "Where did Oliver Waltrip go off to, after we left Justin DuBois' apartment earlier? I'm guessing you had someone take care of him before I was grabbed."

"Grabbed," Cleverly muttered. "Like you're a *thing*. You were retrieved."

"Whatever it takes to get you to sleep at night."

"Landry Babin, you do not talk to me like that!"

"Seriously? *Seriously?*"

"If I may interject," Garrow snapped. "Time's wasting. We need him at the clinic stat, Cleverly."

They managed to bundle me out and into Cleverly's sedan, mostly because I couldn't put up a decent enough fight. I was choking on the smell of them, on the tang of thick, cooling blood somewhere in the car, and my own fear. "Is Waltrip dead?" I demanded. "I want to know at least that much."

"I'm surprised," Cleverly said. "I thought for sure you'd be more worried about Justin. Or even Ethan."

Garrow manhandled me into the seat belt in the back seat. "One of your better qualities has always been your concern for others, Landry. Unfortunately, it's also your hubris, isn't it?"

"I don't think that's the word you want to use," I muttered. "I think you want the phrase *besetting sin*." I waited until he got into the driver's seat before adding, "That means something that's a fault." He glared at me in the rear-view mirror. I barely resisted the urge to stick my tongue out at him.

I dozed off and on during the drive, unable to stop myself. Whatever I'd been dosed with on the stairwell had worn off ages before, but the crack to my skull wasn't helping matters. *Two concussions in one week. I should start wearing a helmet whenever I get out of bed.* They brought me in through the front doors, parking directly under the portico. Whatever damage that had occurred during the fighting had been repaired. Everything smelled like new paint and apple-cinnamon air freshener. It was a truly disgusting combination that probably would have made me feel sick if I wasn't already feeling like shit on a shingle. The clinic was quiet, the only sound our footsteps on the new linoleum and the ding and hiss of the elevator as we went down to the lowest level. "In here," Garrow said, leading me by the arm into a patient room. Unlike the one I'd been in previously, this one was sterile white and blue, stainless steel trays and an IV. pole set up near one wall, waiting to be used. "It's just us this time. Well, us and a doctor friend of mine from Houston." He flashed me a grin that would have been attractive at another time. Now it was just too many teeth, too much threat. "Cleverly, step outside, please."

"But—"

"Cleverly. I've made you *many* allowances over the years, my dear. Don't press your luck today of all days."

My aunt shot me a wide-eyed look, lips pursed tight, but nodded and hurried out of the room, shutting the door behind her.

"I know you're expecting some big rescue attempt, aren't you?" Garrow paced, folding his hands behind as back as he peered at me with a narrow, amused gaze. "A knight in shining armor, all that crap?"

I really wasn't, not this time. Once was an outstandingly lucky occurrence. Twice would be some break in the laws of the universe. I just shook my head once, shuffling away from him to sit on the gurney, the only available surface in the room.

"Good, good," he said, "This wasn't planned until last night, to be honest. We'd always known it would happen one day but not this soon." He went to the stainless steel sink by the door and started washing his hands. The sharp tang of the green soap was strong, cutting through the fug of wolf and fear that was clogging my nose. "Cleverly made a lot of sacrifices for you over the years, son. After your father fucked off, she needed help and, luckily, knew where to come."

"She let you use me," I said. "I was a child. My father sold me to you, but Cleverly allowed these experiments to continue, even after she found out, after she got custody of me."

"She saw what you were," he corrected firmly. "Your father was the last of his family. A dud, like generations before him.

Null. Useless. Your mother had hoped you'd be different, but they knew before you were even walking that you were just like him."

"How?"

He tapped his nose. "Not one single wolf in the area took an interest in you. They'd paraded you around the Stones, the Dorians, the MacIntyres. Even took you to Louisiana. Not a single were batted an eye." He winked at me. "Weres know their own, son. And seeing a null and a human with a were baby? They'd have been all over that."

The jolt of realization—Ethan's father had *known* I had were in my history, that he likely was so against us being together not because I'm a guy but because I was defective in his eyes—made me sit upright. Garrow's eyes narrowed, and a small smile curved his lips. I cleared my throat and forced myself to try to look as if that hadn't just shaken me a bit more than expected.

"That sounds remarkably unscientific," I mused. "What if they were all just too polite to say anything? I mean," I was picking up steam now, every single fuck I may have ever given long gone and flown away, "I've known the Stone family for a while, and I never once saw them snorting and sniffing babies. And when I've seen weres in other towns, not a single one of them was creeping around to take a snort of a stroller or playpen." I slid to the edge of my seat and swung my legs a little, getting into it. "Law of averages says that all the thousands of children in the system for fostering and adoption, a small percentage must be weres, right? It has to happen somewhere in the world that a were baby or child ends up in the system. Are you telling me there's some contingent of weres that go around to foster homes and children's homes, sniffing babies to make sure they're all human?"

Garrow's face underwent such a rapid transformation from confused to annoyed to frustrated and angry that I was surprised he didn't hurt himself. "I take back everything I've ever said about how intelligent you are."

"I'm just saying a sniff-test is the least efficient method they could have chosen." I slid to my feet, reaching out to steady myself with the IV. pole. "So, I didn't smell like a wolf, and my parents decided fuck it, this parenting gig isn't our bag if the kid's totally ordinary and dumped me on Cleverly?"

"Your father needed money," he said. "A lot of it. He was stupid and owed the wrong people too much to cover on his own. Cleverly agreed to give it to him, a small gift from her employer, if he signed away parental rights. Your mother didn't even bat an eye, you know. She was tired of being a parent, especially to a dud, bringing shame on her family line. She was thrilled the day a job offer came in from a company she never remembered applying to. Don't you ever wonder where she is? If she's alive? She is, you know."

"I don't wonder, not really. Not anymore." The news was a punch to the gut, though. The little child inside me, the one who wondered where she'd gone, cried out and felt that sharp stab of grief all over again, but I swallowed down hard against it and straightened. Garrow was watching me, a small smirk on his lips. "So, I was in your first batch."

"You were in our third test batch," he agreed. "Our first even marginally successful one. When the others died, we were sure you would, too, but you and the other two survived. You never became what we'd hoped, but you survived with some traits intact. It was enough for us to start phase two."

"The Raymonds."

"Just so."

"Aren't you ashamed?" I asked as I swayed slightly, the pole tipping with me as I moved. "You're were too."

"And what? I should feel like I'm betraying my kind for trying to fix nature's mistakes? We're *correcting* what's gone wrong in our DNA. The wolf lines are dying, and if we can save them, build them back up to something truly formidable, then I've been part of something great. No, something *necessary* and world changing."

"It definitely changed mine. And the kids you killed. And the Raymonds."

"And Cleverly's," he said quickly. "Don't tell me you didn't smell it on her, Landry. The wolf all over her."

"That was you. The rogue, the one who's been lurking around. The one who's been stalking me."

"No." he laughed, truly tickled. "No! It's been Cleverly, you idiot. She kept away as much as she could. She was sure you'd figure it out quickly but thank God you're so naïve." He pushed away from the sink and moved toward me. "The final stage of development is perfect. It took the barest trace of wolf in your aunt and made it *sing*."

I gripped the pole so tight my fingers popped. "No. No, she can't be. She doesn't smell..." I trailed off. "Burned coffee. The long hours. Her perfume. Those damn plug-in oil burners." *Shit*!

"And," he chimed in gleefully, "that is one of the wonderful things about the Lycaon. It's a synthetic drug. It changes your scent but—"

"But it's different. Harder to detect unless you know what you're looking for." I remembered how Ethan had been so annoyed he'd missed the signs of a rogue wolf in the area, how Tyler had griped about the smell being hard to track.

Garrow nodded. "Now let go of that and get on the gurney. The room is ready for us, and the sooner we get this done..." He smiled. "Well. I think we both know you're not leaving."

"Well," I mimicked, "I think we both also know that I'm not putting the pole down, either." I swung it as fast and hard as I could, which, compared to a were's reflexes, wasn't very. But it was enough to clip him, make him spin away with a yelp of pain. I turned and brought the pole down hard again, across the back of his shoulders this time. He yowled, an inhuman noise from low in his throat, and fell against the gurney. The door opened, and my aunt gasped my name, skittering back as I brandished the pole at her, too.

Garrow lunged for me, tripping over the pole when I threw it at him, giving me a few seconds to get past my aunt and into the corridor. It wasn't the same one I'd been in before, and I was at a much higher disadvantage now that I was alone with no were on my side. I knew with all the certainty of a prey animal on the run that I was going to die. But I also couldn't stop myself from trying to live. I ran as fast as I could, adrenaline overpowering the pain, and headed for the stairway door. "Fucking stairs," I panted under my breath. Garrow's footsteps were heavy and close as I hit the release bar for the door and tumbled down a flight, rolling to my feet as he pounded after me. I threw myself against the next door and found myself in a brightly colored corridor lined with lockers and closed metal doors. I kept running, breath burning in my lungs, trying to keep far enough ahead of Garrow to at least find a door with a formidable lock.

A guy can dream, right?

I made it halfway down the corridor before Garrow caught me in a rugby tackle, both of us hitting the floor in a breathless, crunching heap. He hauled me to my feet, one arm across my throat as he dragged me toward the elevator doors. "For that," he panted in my ear, "I don't think we'll be using any anesthesia."

Chapter Fifteen

Cleverly was sobbing wetly in the corridor outside the surgical theater. The entire clinic was so quiet and still around us that it made me feel on stage, flayed open. Which, ironically, I supposed was about to happen.

"Your sheriff's been calling," Garrow commented matter-of-factly. He dropped me onto a surgical gurney, leaning heavily across my body to hold me down as he began looping restraints around me. "I don't know what kind of phone you have, but it's got amazing reception. Usually, I get shit for bars down this far."

Cleverly sobbed again, loud and theatrical. Garrow rolled his eyes, giving me a grin. "Seriously, she's the most dramatic woman I've ever met. But she's a good little pack member, very eager to please."

I really didn't want to think about the implications of that.

"I have to be honest with you, Landry. Your aunt keeps saying she hoped you'd be a good boy and fuck off, stop digging around with your cop buddy, but I'm glad you didn't. See, it's been decades since we started with you, and now that we've damn near perfected Lycaon, it's going to be a real treat to compare your changes to those of someone on the final version." He tapped one finger against the middle of my forehead. "Most of them happen here, you know? It's hormones and chemicals, and well, you *are* a doctor, so I bet this is all pretty simplistic stuff, right? You get it." He moved down to my legs and started lashing me down there. "Now, before we begin, I do have some questions for you."

"Is this where you ask me for my last words?" I closed my eyes, holding on tight to the shreds of hope I had left. What was Ethan doing right now? Was he okay? Would he be the one to find me? I know he'll come looking out here when he figures I'm nowhere in town. When he searches the woods, and there's no trace of me... I thought of Waltrip, of Justin, and wondered if they were dead and shoved into some supply closet at that apartment complex, or if they were tucked away somewhere here, maybe for poking and prodding later.

My aunt's sobs cut at me, severing my false calm. "Fuck's sake, what are you crying about? This is all your fault, Cleverly! You sold me to them, you kept this going, and you... what? Decided, hey, this looks like fun—let me try it for myself? And now you're one of them." I turned my head the little bit the restraints allowed and spat, "I hope it's fucking excruciating every time you shift."

She wailed. Garrow smirked. Any sympathy I had for my aunt, any worries and affection and love, were gone. That Cleverly, the one I thought existed, was dead now. The Cleverly I'd thought of as a mother figure hadn't actually existed. I was a commodity to her, and she was willing to let me be used for her own gain.

"Now. If we're done posturing. When was the last time you took any of the Lycaon? Oh, sorry, you'd know it as your allergy medications."

"I haven't been on them in years. I stopped when I realized they were slowing my reaction times at work when I lived in Houston." It hadn't been by much, but there were several instances during autopsies where I'd made a minor mistake in my incisions or nearly dropped materials because I was so foggy. "Shouldn't you know that? I'm guessing one of your doctors was my GP here."

He nodded, scowling. "They've been filled regularly, like clockwork, since they were prescribed." He paused, darting a glance at Cleverly. "Ah. I see." Smoothly, he turned away from me and paced toward Cleverly. "We'd wondered where the Raymonds were getting the extra from. How did you get it to them without being seen?"

Cleverly stuttered. In my limited field of vision, it looked like she was setting herself not to answer. Under Garrow's intense stare, she broke, though. "Church," she murmured. "Mrs. Raymond was in one of the clubs. Stitch-n-Time. I'd give her a ride sometimes. No one ever batted an eye. They all knew the Raymonds couldn't keep a car running nine times out of ten."

I thought of the smell of the rogue wolf around the Raymond's house, knowing it was Cleverly. If I'd had anything left in my stomach, I'd have embarrassed myself.

"You... what? Sold her the pills?" Garrow demanded.

"No! No, I gave them to her! She... she was desperate, and Landry wasn't taking them anymore. When he'd told me he stopped, I just changed the address in his file when I was at work," she admitted in a rush. "I was able to pick them up and say it was for him."

Garrow sighed, long and loud. "I see. Well. Thank you, Cleverly. This is a valuable bit of insight for me into some loopholes in the system." He moved fast, striking her backhand across the face. She cried out, falling to the floor as I shouted, trying to buck against the restraints. "Shut up. Both of you. Now," he dropped down out of my sight, to wherever Cleverly had fallen. "Do I need to know anything else? Any other details that are important? Because I can tell you, Cleverly, that as of right now, you have ruined *years* of work. *Years*." Another strike, this one crunching. Cleverly's cry was muffled as she choked on what was probably blood.

"Stop! Stop it!" I roared. "You needed me, right? Here I am! Whatever you need, do it. Leave her alone!"

"You'd forgive her? Just a few minutes ago, you were so mad at her, Landry." Garrow moved back toward me. Freckles of blood dotted his cheek. "Are you so easy in your affections, then? Is that another, what was it? *Besetting sin*?"

"I'm not forgiving her," I snapped. "That doesn't mean I want her to get beaten to death."

Garrow glanced past me, scowling. "Don't," he ordered. "You don't deserve to change." He looked back at me, shaking his head a bit sadly. "She's learning, poor old girl. But a true wolf, one who'd been born? They could have changed before the first strike. She'd have known; if she was truly one of us, she'd have known and fought back. Cleverly is our mascot," he said over my aunt's crying. "We can trot her out to show what a good girl she is, how well Lycaon can work even on a mature adult so long as there's a hint of the wolf left in them." He paused. "Well, I'm speaking in present tense, aren't I? Should be past tense." He snarled, arching and dropping to all fours. I screamed at Cleverly to run, flinging myself as hard as I could against the restraints, but it was no use. She shrieked, human voice changing to pained canine whine. I screamed again, and again, and again. I had to drown out the sounds.

When Garrow finally came back, buttoning his shirt, his face was a bit red, his hair out of place, but he looked like a man who had few cares in the world. Fewer now than he had a short time before, anyway. "Now. Another question for you, Landry. Do you ever experience sensitivity to light? Aversion to certain foods or perhaps a craving for them, things like rare steak or even steak tartare?"

The smell of blood, of wolf, of death was overpowering. My throat was raw. I felt apart from myself, floating. I could only stare back at him, unable to make words come.

"Well. I suppose that's a ridiculous thing to ask, isn't it? But it's one of the questions on the survey we're supposed to give you before the next phase. Some of our clients were concerned about the baser instincts that may present themselves during transformation. Our counselors have explained time and again that the whole idea of the werewolf eating livestock or mauling innocent humans is a fairy tale, something made up to scare rather than instruct, but I'm afraid the old prejudices are hard to shake."

He unlocked the wheel brakes with a kick, and we were moving. He pushed me out of the theater and into the corridor. "I'm afraid we need to move. This one's contaminated." Anger exploded in my chest. I howled, the sound raw and torn as it burst out of my throat. Garrow jerked back, eyes wide, then pleased as he peered down at me. "Oh, yes. Now, why couldn't you have done this ages ago?" He sighed and leaned in close. I had the urge —the *need*—to bite at him, to snap my teeth down on his throat, his face, anywhere soft and able to tear. He chuckled. "You always were a late bloomer." The elevator doors dinged softly, and he glanced up. "Good, you're here. We'll be moving to theater three. This one—"

Something pale and huge flew past me, hitting Garrow in the chest. A chorus of snarls and snaps rose around me, Garrow's cries transforming from shouts of anger to growls as he transformed again. A large wolf, tawny and bright-eyed, rose onto its hind legs beside me, teeth bared in a lupine grin. Fucking Waltrip. It had to be. He ducked down, a deep cut on the back of his head visible as he dove into the fray. Someone struck the gurney, and I went over, the fall knocking the wind out of me when I hit the floor. The bonds were looser but not by much. Still, it gave me literal wiggle room to start working my hands free. The thick webbing of the straps tore at my skin, but I was desperate.

The sounds of the fighting, the smell of wolf and blood, it drove me into a near frenzy that took me too long to realize wasn't fear. It wasn't my usual need to go, to flee and hide. It was different. New and heavy and painful in its insistence, it was a need to join. To attack and fight, to defend. Everything was too bright, too loud, too much, my eyes rolling back and body arching against the pain that ratcheted through me. Someone yelped, shock and worry in the tone. *Run.* This time, it wasn't the cry of prey in my thoughts, but the demands of the predator. *Go. Do it.*

Now. The straps were loose, easy to slip as my body relaxed out of the spasm, and before I realized what I was doing, I was moving.

Joy coursed through me. For the first time in ever, my body was *right*. Not just as a human but as the wolf, as the creature that had been hiding in me all this time. I felt good. No, more than good. Perfect. Colors had gone mute and strange, but I didn't need them to know what to do, where to go. Garrow, a large wolf with pale fur and a bloody muzzle, lay on his side. He was pinned beneath the massive paws of a wolf I knew to be Ethan, struggling to get out from under him. Garrow was already injured, bleeding badly from a wound on his side. Ethan's bloody fur told me who had done it. I paced closer, the cold of the floor a sharp feeling under my feet. Lowering my head, I peered close at Garrow's face, at his snarling mouth and dark stained teeth.

Kill. Protect the others.

No... If he's dead, there's even more who will be at risk. *Capture. Hold.*

I looked up at Ethan. Waltrip had moved to his side and was watching us both curiously, that wide grin back on his open, panting mouth. I made a sound, meant to say 'wait,' and 'don't,' but it came out as a throaty growl.

The fuck...

Waltrip snuffled, nudged Ethan's shoulder with his snout, and turned toward the operating room. He danced backward, yipping in surprise when he saw who was inside. Ethan bent low and bit the back of Garrow's neck. Waltrip made a noise like a muffled bark and moved away down the hall, where he shifted back to human form in a painful-sounding crackle of bone and muscle. Confusion held me in place, unable to look away from Ethan and Garrow.

"Hey. Hey, come on. Let me help," Waltrip said, gently placing his hand on my back. "This is gonna suck, but I need you to let me help you so we can get out of here. There are people coming, and we need to be gone when they get here."

Chapter Sixteen

"Start again."

"No." For the first time in several days, nothing hurt. Not one single part of my body was sore, throbbing, aching, burning... Pharmaceuticals were a wonderful thing.

"Stop," Ethan said quietly. "He's talked about it enough for now."

Waltrip huffed. "I was dragged into this shit under false pretenses and damn near got killed over it. All I care about right now is getting to the root so the vine can be killed."

I closed my eyes and let Ethan stroke my hair back from my face. We were all holed up at his house in Belmarais. It was not the one I'd imagined him in—the one he'd grown up in, all wood floors and dark brick with a screen door hanging on for dear life. This was a smart little bungalow with actual gingerbread trim and a pale green front door with a wreath hanging off it. Ethan had muttered something about Halloway at the station and his wife making these seasonal things for all the folks on the force, and he just put it up to be polite, but I knew he was really into that Martha Stewart type stuff and loved that he had a bunch of sunflowers and raffia dangling hanging there for the summer months. I saw him straighten the wreath as we all trooped into his tiny front room, smiling a little at the cheery flowers before shutting the door. I had still been in pain then, too tired and broken to say much about anything, least of all Ethan's wreath. Now, though, thanks to some heavy-duty painkillers and who knows how much sleep, I was slightly more alive, and a lot less busted up than I had when we first arrived. "Aren't you dead?" I asked Waltrip softly. "I was pretty sure you'd died."

He crouched beside the sofa to bring his face level with mine. "Don't you watch movies, Babin? If you don't see a body, don't assume they're dead." I must have made a face, or maybe he just took some pity on me because he sighed and sat back on his heels. "Some asshole were locked me in the trunk of a car after I got this beauty"—he lightly touched the gash on the back of his head—"at DuBois' place. They were going to make it look like I'd had some sort of accident, a wreck on a rural road somewhere. I'm not famous, but it'd definitely draw attention from the were community if I went missing." He winked, all false cheer over darker anger. "Always join the chamber of commerce, Babin. Networking is important."

"There's a were chamber of commerce?" I was so tired. Not sleepy, but definitely in the neighborhood of loopy.

"Mmhm. We're very organized." He rose to his knees and murmured something to Ethan. "You think you could eat something?" he asked me. "If this was your first change—"

"I don't understand," I said, cutting him off. "I'm not... I never have before. Even when they were dosing me with the Lycaon, all it did was make me squirrely. Why now?" I tipped my head back to look at Ethan. "Will it happen again?"

Ethan exchanged a look with Waltrip. "I don't know," he finally said. "And the only people who could maybe tell us are in the wind or dead, as far as we know. I'm thinking, and this is just me guessing, so don't take it as gospel truth—the, ah, stress of the situation triggered it. I'm going to go out on a limb and say you've never been in that kind of situation before, so close to being killed. Right?"

"I think I'd have mentioned it."

"Hmm. Well, I'm sure there's a lot of shit you haven't told me about from when we were being idiots."

"We?"

"Share the blame, share the love." He smoothed my hair again, making my eyes drift closed. "Most weres don't get our first big change until puberty, even when we already showing signs for years before. Our senses, speed, strength—they all kick in when we're kids. But the actual shifting?" He sighed. "Puberty is a bitch on many levels."

Waltrip rose to his feet and padded off into the kitchen, leaving us alone for the moment. I pressed my head against Ethan's hand and asked the question he'd been avoiding answering since we left the clinic just ahead of a whole horde of police cars and a few dark, unmarked SUVs. "How did you know where I was? Or did I really die, and this is just a weirdly boring but comforting afterlife?"

"Sartre-lite," he suggested. "All of the tedium, none of the existential angst?"

"I'm saving the angst for after dinner." I poked his leg with my finger. "You're diverting."

"So I've been told."

I jabbed harder. "Ethan."

He exhaled slowly, tangling his fingers in my hair to tug gently as he spoke. "Cleverly. She sent me a message. Said she'd fucked up, and you were in danger. She said she didn't think she could fix things like she'd hoped."

"Oh." The word came out as barely more than a breath. Tears stung hot and acid, burning my eyes before they started to fall. Ethan didn't pull me into his lap like he had before, just kept petting my head, letting me press my face against his thigh as I sobbed out everything inside. When I was empty and burning raw inside, he helped me sit up. Waltrip had come back sometime during my crying jag and placed a plate of sandwiches, a jug of water, and a large bottle of sports drink on the coffee table in front of me. Both men watched me as I took a bite of food, then another. "What?" I demanded around half a mouthful of cheese and tomato. "Are you waiting for me to shift again or something? Or is there some side effect of post-puberty changes that you're looking for, like I'm gonna burst into flames or something?"

"No, that only happens on your second shift," Waltrip popped off. "Drink. You'll feel worse if you don't."

Ethan pushed the plate closer to me, more for the need of something to do than to encourage me, I thought. He and Waltrip exchanged another one of those silent communication glances. "What?" I demanded. "Just fucking say it."

"When you're done, we need to get going," Ethan said after a beat. "We need to go see Garrow."

The sports drink did help me feel less queasy, but I wasn't going to admit that to Waltrip when he asked as I was getting into Ethan's truck. When I just grunted at his question, he smirked and pushed a fresh bottle into my hands with an order to 'sip, don't chug' and to keep a bottle going for the next few hours. "We don't know if this was a one-time thing or if you're going to be able to do it all the time now," he reminded me. "No use letting your body go to shit just because you're in a sulk. If you need to shift again, you want to be ready. Being dehydrated will just make it hurt even worse." He'd given me a wink, something I'd decided was a bad habit of his, and rapped on the roof of Ethan's truck before jogging over to his bike so he could follow us to Garrow.

"You stashed him out here?" I demanded as soon as I recognized the turn off. "What about the Raymonds? Er, the parents, I mean."

Ethan cut a glance my way, his jaw tight. "In the wind. Tyler's had eyes on the place for a few days now, and there's been no sign of life. It's secure enough for our purposes and the utilities are still on so he can access Wi-Fi and shit. Swear to God, I think he'd actually die if he couldn't do his hacker shit."

I made a small, noncommittal noise and sank back in the seat. We bumped up the rutted road to the Raymond's less than thirty minutes later. Ethan pulled the truck around to the side yard, following worn dirt tracks plowed into the grass by years of other cars parking there rather than the garage or driveway. Waltrip tooled up beside us and shut off his bike, face set in grim lines as we got out. Tyler opened the ratty screen door and stepped onto the front porch. "Y'all coming in, or should we move the party outside? Cause I gotta say, it's hot as balls out there, and we've got a/c running in here at least till they cut power next week."

Ethan took my hand and squeezed gently. I had a powerful jolt back to being seventeen, linking my fingers with his on his father's front porch, both of us pretending not to hear Tyler's mutterings about 'gross' and 'Dad's gonna kill you, Eth.' Now, Tyler didn't even blink, turning to hold the door open and let us troop past. Ethan kept his fingers wrapped through mine even as we navigated to the backroom, the one that had been wall-to-wall trash and used syringes when I'd been there before. It was still trash and used syringes, but everything had been pushed against one wall in a towering stack of awfulness, leaving an expanse of greasy carpet that may have once been blue or maybe gray but was now a color I'd forever think of as Rotting Whale Carcass. Against the other wall was a low table set with a jug of water, a plastic cup, and the remains of a fast-food chicken dinner. On the floor, on that greasy dead whale-colored floor, was Garrow. Someone, I guessed Tyler, had fastened a choke collar around his neck and run a heavy-duty dog lead to a metal spike hammered into the floor, through the carpeting, and into the under-flooring. "The real kicker is, that spike was already here," Tyler said gleefully. "I don't even want to think about what was going on in this room but judging by some of the shit in those bags, it was fucking wild."

"Just an FYI, I have a really sensitive stomach today, and I am not above ruining your shoes," I informed him, pressing closer to Ethan. "Is he still alive?"

"Yeah. He's just faking. Lachlan dropped his dinner off earlier, and the asshole chomped it down just fine. He just likes to pretend to be asleep whenever one of us comes to sit with him." Tyler nudged Garrow with the toe of his booted foot. "Hey, jackhole, open your eyes, or I'll re-enact that scene from *Clockwork Orange* on you."

Garrow grunted, pulling himself into a ball on his side. It should have been pitiful to see, but I was burning hot acid anger. Ethan's grip on my hand was tight enough to hurt. Beside me, Waltrip was fairly quivering. Tyler gave Garrow another nudge with his foot, maybe a bit harder than before, and jerked his head in the direction of the hallway. "Lachlan will sit with him until we're done. Come on." Lachlan darted into the room, squeezing between Waltrip and me to take up a perch on the table beside the remains of Garrow's dinner.

"Are you sure?" Waltrip asked.

Tyler nodded. "Lachlan can handle him. Want to show them?"

Lachlan grinned. "If he manages to slip his chain, I've got this." He pulled a police-grade taser from his hip pocket. "I've monkeyed with it a bit, so it goes up to eleven."

Tyler shook his head, smiling fondly. "Seriously, dude, if you weren't taken, I'd be all over you."

"Fuck off," Lachlan laughed. Tyler shut the door behind us, but not before we heard the sizzle-pop of Lachlan turning on the taser just in case.

"I need a soda," he said, moving toward the kitchen. "Don't worry—we're using coolers instead of the fridge. I don't know what died in there, but its descendants are currently developing a religion based around its corpse in the crisper."

"What are you trying not to tell us?" Ethan asked quietly. "Tyler..."

"Fuck, this is sucktastic," Tyler muttered. He swung a leg over one of the kitchen chairs, so he was facing us over its back, resting his arms on the high wooden slats. "Okay, first things first. As far as anyone else knows, outside of us in this room, your aunt was killed during a workplace break-in gone wrong. That's the official finding from law enforcement. No one is going to know anything else about what went down."

I shook off Ethan's grasp and sat heavily on one of the other kitchen chairs. "How are they believing that? She was... He..."

"They'll believe whatever makes paperwork easiest," Waltrip said. I looked to Ethan for denial, but he just grimaced.

"He's not entirely wrong," Ethan admitted. "Most of the time, you go with the easiest explanation. Finding Cleverly dead, obviously murdered and not just a heart attack or something? They're looking at hours and hours and hours of investigation and paperwork. Even a big city like Dallas is going to be thin on resources for a murder investigation. Throw in things outside the parameters of normal? Few, if any, cops are going to jump on that without putting up a fuss. Cleverly being murdered when someone tried to break into her workplace, maybe looking to score some drugs since it's a medical clinic and finding her working alone? The report practically writes itself."

"Suspect at large," Tyler intoned in a news announcer's voice. "No witnesses, but there's been a reward posted by the victim's family." He paused, then added, "Don't worry, you don't have to do that part, but it sure makes it sound realistic."

"I don't understand why..."

"She thought she was going to keep you safe, keep her brother safe. Your father made a deal. but he got greedy. What's that saying? Better the right hand of the devil than in his path?" Ethan said.

"Lachlan was able to do some digging and tracked her bank records back to around the time you moved in with her as a kid. She went flat broke virtually overnight. Cleared out everything from her 401k to savings, even her Christmas club account at Tuttle First National. The money from... from what she did would have replaced all of that, and then some."

Grief mixing and warring with anger and revulsion was a hell of a feeling. Do not recommend, zero stars. Ethan moved as if he wanted to take my hand again but stopped and settled back, letting me be the one to do the seeking when I needed it. "Glad to know I contributed to the household," I finally said. "No wonder she was never really on my ass to work as a teenager."

Waltrip burst out laughing. "Christ, that's grim. I think I do like you after all."

Ethan made a growling noise beside me, but I just shook my head. "It's fine," I muttered. "He's not wrong. It *is* grim. And I'm not going to get over it today, or tomorrow, or maybe ever. But it's there, and it's what happened. Cleverly is dead, but those remains in someone's cold storage drawer right now? That's not my aunt. That person never existed."

Tyler rapped his fingers on the table, nibbling on his lower lip for a moment before speaking again. "I wish you'd have saved that speech for a minute or two because there's a bit more. The good news is, it doesn't look like your aunt... um, I mean like Cleverly was passing out Lycaon to anyone other than the Raymonds. The only extra pills she had access to were yours, and since no one else she had contact with has turned up dead or, you know, a werewolf, we're pretty sure the Raymonds were it." He looked at Ethan, raising his brows expectantly. When Ethan nodded, Tyler reached into his jeans pocket and brought out a rather nice smartphone. "We were able to get Garrow talking before he realized we were recording. Once he cottoned, he shut up and started his Sleeping Beauty routine." He pushed the phone to me. "Hit play. Volume's already all the way up."

Garrow swam to life on the small screen. All those pixels, I thought, and he still looks like a blob with hair. The picture shrank then adjusted, whoever was holding the camera discovering some sort of focus mechanism because then, Garrow was full Technicolor and clear as day in front of me. Lachlan's voice came first.

"What were you intending to happen to Doctor Babin today?"

"This is a false arrest," Garrow spat. "Kidnapping, attempted murder, false imprisonment." He jerked, so the lead he was attached to rattled. "God knows what else they'll charge you with when I'm done here."

"What were you intending to happen to Doctor Babin today?" Lachlan repeated, sounding monotone and bored.

"Fuck. You."

"What were you intending to happen to Doctor Babin today?"

For nearly a full five minutes, it went on like that. Lachlan repeating the same question, Garrow hurling insults and threats until finally, Garrow snapped.

"Landry Babin needs to die," Garrow shouted. "He's a failed subject and should have died with the others!" He jabbed a finger at his own head, pressing hard enough on his temple to leave a red mark. "We gave him all the help we could, but he failed. Our later gens have reached perfection. Finally. *Finally!* We need comparisons between first-gen and new-gen. Doctor Babin," he said my name like it tasted bad, "is the only first-gen we can get hold of. And," he added with a smirk, "the fact he's a pain in my ass is an added bonus."

I pressed stop. Ethan started to rise as I pushed away from the table, probably had a good idea of where I was going, but Waltrip shook his head. "He'll be right back," he said. Ethan began to protest, but I didn't wait to hear.

The bedroom wasn't far. I made it to the door before I could second guess myself. Lachlan was still perched on the table, but Garrow had sat up now and was facing the door when I opened it. "I need a minute," I said. Lachlan hesitated but slid off the table and eased past me into the corridor. He pressed the taser into my hand with a murmur of, "Just in case," pulling the door almost shut behind me.

"What were you going to do once you took me apart?"

"You're a scientist, Doctor Babin," he said, voice more gravel than sound. My title was a mockery on his lips. "Don't you remember how these things work?"

"Were you going to do it to my aunt, too?"

Garrow's lips twitched. "I rather screwed that up, didn't I? We still have another, but I'm worried he's going to get himself in rather a lot of trouble before the end."

Oh. "Justin."

"Indeed. Doctor DuBois wasn't enthusiastic about the idea at first, but he was convinced by our counselor that it would be in his best interest."

"What did you do with him?" The taser was a nice weight in my hand. I wanted to use it, make him hurt, but I knew it wouldn't be enough. It wouldn't satisfy that howling deep down inside me.

Garrow's eyes flicked to where I was running my thumb over the Taser's button, not pressing it but feeling the possibility. "I have no idea," he laughed softly. "It was his first unattended shift. He must have been scared. Were you scared when it happened to you? I need to know how it all felt."

"I'm sure you're familiar with it. What are your clients going to do now that… now that everything's gone to hell?"

His laugh was sudden and loud. "Nothing's gone to hell. It's taken an interesting turn, but it's definitely not detrimental to our clients' interests." He started to lean forward before remembering the choke collar. He arrested his movement at an odd angle, a man caught mid-lean and wild-eyed. "You weren't supposed to change. For years, you were just this broken, *wrong* thing. You were a promise that never quite panned out. It was enough to give our clients hope, to let them see what we were working toward, but it took two more generations of Lycaon to get where we wanted to be, to show them their faith in us was rewarded."

Garrow was jerking, twitching against the chain even as it bit into the soft flesh of his neck. He wanted to shift. I could smell it on him, practically hear his bones crackle. The ghost sensation of my own shift, fast and surprising and confusing, tickled at my senses, itched under my skin. "Now what? Your lab is useless to you now the human authorities are involved. You can't run your experiments there anymore." I thought of the news story I'd managed to hear that morning before Ethan casually on purpose switched the station to some cable rerun of a college bowl game. Bluebonnet Biomed had been shut down by federal authorities due to unethical practices and poor worker conditions. Garrow Clinic, a subsidiary of Bluebonnet Biomed, was closing its doors temporarily during the investigation with plans to reopen as a substance abuse treatment facility. I imagined someone in the clinic's PR department thought that was a nice touch, make it seem like the organization really wanted to do good. Waltrip thought it was just the next thing to hide what they were doing. Waltrip was probably right, but I hoped not.

"Do you think we put all the eggs in one basket?" Garrow asked, his voice thick and barely human now. "Baltimore. Denver. Houston. You remember…"

"Landry." Ethan was on the other side of the door, pressed close to the opening. "Hey, we need to get out of the way. His ride's here." I stepped back, not quite able to look away from Garrow's grin.

"Why did my aunt decide to take it? Why did she… why did she want to be like you?"

Garrow spread his hands, grin even wider as Ethan tugged me back out of the way, and two large, barely familiar, weres moved into the room. "Age makes fools of us all."

The weres hefted him to his feet, one of them grabbing the end of the lead and the other slinging Garrow over his shoulder. "He got that wrong," one of them said. "It's 'time makes fools of us all.'" Garrow chuckled, giving me a small wave as he was carried past. We trailed after them, through the Raymonds' wreck of a house and onto the front porch.

Watching them load Garrow into the back of a white SUV with ridiculously tinted windows, it occurred to me where I knew them from. "Waltrip, are those your buddies from… Shit, was it just last week?"

He snorted softly. "They're my associates at the firm, yeah.

And they're taking Garrow to..." He trailed off and glanced at Ethan. "They're taking Garrow."

Tyler joined us on the rickety, rotting porch, giving the departing SUV a cheery wave. "Y'all don't come back now, hear?"

"You're such a dork," Ethan muttered.

"I'm a dork who needs to get on the road," he corrected. "I'll give you a call tonight when we get to our first stop." He hesitated, then leaned in and gave Ethan a hard bear hug. The brothers did that back pound jock hug maneuver but then just held on for an extra few seconds before Tyler finally pulled away. He looked between me and Ethan and sighed. "So, it was a bad idea when you were teenagers but for different reasons than I thought at the time. But it's less of a bad idea now, for what it's worth."

"Are you giving us your blessing?" I teased. Nervous butterflies were back in my belly, this time with tiny little knives.

"I'm giving you my 'eh, could be worse,'" he said, then surprised me by giving me a quick hug and a thump on my back. Guess I was really one of the boys then. "Waltrip."

Waltrip jerked his chin in a nod. "Stay in touch."

"Where are you going?" I asked belatedly. Tyler jumped down from the porch as Lachlan trundled out of the house with an armload of electronics.

"We got some chatter on a skittish wolf lurking around Houston. Scared the hell out of some neighborhood kids." Tyler made a wide-eyed face. "I wonder who that could be."

"Justin?"

Lachlan gave me an awkward thumbs up around his burden. "Got it in one. Dizz and the guys are on site already, trying to keep ahead of the Velazquez clan. Houston's a touchy area, and they don't like newbies."

Ethan groaned. "You gonna let me know if it all goes to shit?"

Tyler, leaning out of the driver's side of his truck, laughed. "Don't worry. I'll be sure to pull the *my brother's a cop* card if local PD picks me up for something."

"That's not what I mean," Ethan murmured, raising his hand in farewell as Tyler and Lachlan backed down the drive. It was a hot, sticky quiet as we stood on that rotting porch and looked anywhere but at each other. Finally, Ethan spoke again. "You heading back to Dallas tonight or staying around a bit longer?"

Waltrip rocked back and forth on his heels, humming low in his throat. A few days ago, I was terrified of him. Then annoyed. Watching him on the porch, I was going to miss him, I realized. He caught my eye and smiled. "I was thinking maybe stick around at least for the night. Traffic's gonna be a bitch, and I could really go for a beer right now."

"Beer sounds good," Ethan agreed. "Um, Landry?"

I nodded. Tomorrow would mean dealing with arrangements for Cleverly. Talking to people, making sure stories stayed aligned, figuring out what the hell to do next. I was her next of kin, I had her power of attorney, but what did that mean now? Her house was supposed to come to me, I remember that from helping her draft up her will, but I couldn't stomach the idea of living there now. The place I'd grown up wasn't a place of safety and good memories. It was the place where I was a lab rat, where I had my childhood turned into a science experiment. Hell, I'd have to talk to her bank, I realized. And what was I going to do with her money? Knowing where it had come from, who she'd worked for... I didn't want a cent of it. Even if it would help tide me over till I could get a job. Hell, did I have a job again? Or was I still screwed? Ethan looped his arm over my shoulders and pulled me to his side. I let my head rest on his shoulder. "Beer definitely sounds good."

Chapter Seventeen

"Again."

"I told you. I'm a freak. It was a one-time thing. Stress-induced."

"Again," Ethan drawled, leaning back in the camp chair he'd brought down from the house. The edge of the swamp was all sucking mud and buzzing flies, but he'd found a strip of firm, grassy ground that ran like a spit out into the water. We were far enough from any houses that we wouldn't be seen by a nosy neighbor, and the area was shit for fishing, so the chances of some weekend bass master trying his luck and stumbling across a werewolf and a mad man were slim. "Try again, and I promise I'll only make you try like ten more times before we head back for the night."

"Only ten, huh?"

"Ish."

"Ass." He laughed when I turned my back and sat on the ground. It was almost too cool out for shorts and a t-shirt, but I refused to stand out there with my bits hanging out, trying to shift into wolf form again. Since the incident at the clinic, I hadn't been able to change. I'd *wanted* to, but it was like a toothache. Dull and persistent need to press and bother that produced nothing but more frustration and discomfort. I'd roundly rejected Waltrip's idea that putting me in a high-stress situation again would trigger me to change, mostly because I was afraid of what his idea of a high-stress situation would be. If the stress of having to put my change away at the checkout line while the person behind me was already having their groceries scanned wasn't stressful enough to make me change, then nothing he could throw at me would do it. He'd just laughed and waved Ethan and me off to 'go do our little practice in the woods' while he caught up on work emails.

Waltrip had started visiting quite a lot since the summer, starting the day he'd brought me my missing phone with a muttered *found this at the clinic in your aunt's old desk*. At first, I was worried he had a thing for Ethan, then for me. After a few visits, I decided he was just lonely. I don't know what kind of cases he was taking other than specializing in weres, but he kept busy enough that he brought work with him. His two associates, whom I'd started referring to as Thing One and Thing Two, never came with him. After they'd taken Garrow—wherever it was, I apparently wasn't allowed to know—I'd only seen them twice. Once, when they showed up in the middle of the night at Ethan's house. Waltrip hadn't been on a visit then, but they met with Ethan on the front porch for a good hour, low voices rumbling so quietly even my sharp hearing couldn't make out what they were saying. When Ethan had come back in the house, he'd seemed lighter, somehow. Like he'd been relieved of a burden he hadn't remembered he was carrying until it was gone.

The second time I saw them, we'd gone to Dallas. Ethan had insisted on a weekend away just after Halloween. It'd been a busy week for both of us—he'd dealt with the usual teenager bullshit in a small town during the holiday week with the additional stress of a rash of robberies and two murders which, for a town like Belmarais, was unheard of in one year much less in one week. I'd been grudgingly reinstated in my position as county coroner, but I was starting to think it was time to move on. I couldn't do a thing without the state board breathing down my neck and sending an observer to second guess my every move. Besides, Reba had announced she was quitting after the new year. It would suck without her there.

Ethan took me to Dallas right after Halloween weekend so we could have a few days without work or people we knew bugging us for this or that. We went to a show and stopped afterward for dinner. While we were waiting for Ethan's car to be brought back around at the valet stand, I caught a glimpse of a towering brunet in a dark suit. A second look showed me it was Thing Two, playing on his phone near the hedges lining the restaurant's front path. He glanced up and saw me watching. After a brief hesitation, he winked and went back to his phone. Ethan followed the direction of my stare and sighed, walking over to Thing Two. They had a brief exchange, and Ethan was back, looking annoyed. "It's my weekend off," he said tartly. "It can wait until we get back to town." Waltrip showed up a few days later, and I didn't see him and Ethan for the entire weekend.

When I asked about it later, Ethan had tried to shrug it off as just a work thing. "You and Waltrip don't work together," I said. "Ethan, I already asked you to stop treating me like I can't handle this, okay? Being what I am, this whole... were thing."

He'd rolled his eyes, muttered *were thing*, but answered me. "Waltrip asked for some help looking for the others like you. There are some connections I have that he doesn't, so I'm putting him in touch."

After that, he'd clammed up on me, and did a damn good job of distracting me for a few hours after.

But back to my shifting practice. Four tries later, I flopped onto my back. "Nope. I'm done. Not doing it anymore today."

"Okay."

I rolled my head to one side so I could stare up at Ethan as he walked across the grass toward me. "Seriously? You're not gonna push?"

"Do you want me to?"

Part of me wanted to say yes. The rest of me, though... "I want to go home, shower, and take a twelve-hour nap."

He laughed and helped me to my feet. "Waltrip wants to go to that barbecue place over in Lashings."

"Good for him," I muttered, dusting my backside. "People who've spent the day trying to shift get naps, werewolves get barbecue."

We were halfway back to his truck before Ethan asked, "Do you think of yourself as a were? I mean, after the clinic... Do you think maybe..."

I stopped walking. "Does it matter?"

"To me, or in general?"

I threw up my hands. "Both? Look, I just need to know if this is going to be what makes you decide to break things off. If I can't change again, is that it? Or would you still want me if I was just Landry Babin, workaholic and nervous basket case?"

Ethan's expression moved swiftly between crestfallen and determined. Jaw set, he stalked across the few yards of grass toward me. I didn't run. That prey voice in my head was still there, but around Ethan, it was quieter. It knew he didn't want to hurt me. *I* knew. It was part of me, not a piece that had been taped on somehow. Not something broken I needed to make whole. And not something shameful I needed to beat into submission, erase from my entire being That fear, that drive, it was all part of who I was. And so was my trust in Ethan. But if that wasn't enough for him... He stopped just in front of me, towering over me like he had when we were kids. Those same flutters in my stomach and chest were there, maybe a bit more cautious now. He slid his hands up my arms to my shoulders, my jaw, and cradled my face. "If you never changed at all, you would be more than I deserved."

"Christ." I sighed. "Don't be so hyperbolic. All you had to do was say yes." I stretched up on my toes as he tipped his face down. His mouth was warm and pliant over mine, parting on a breath to let me tease the tip of my tongue along his lower lip. Ethan moved his hands down my back to cup my ass, pulling me close enough that our hardening cocks brushed. I groaned into the kiss, rocking my hips into his. He clutched me harder, pulling me up until I could barely balance and had to lean my weight against him, our bodies swaying together. He lifted me higher, my legs around his waist as he shifted, breaking the kiss so he could see where he was walking.

"I have a blanket in the back of the truck," he murmured against my neck. "No one's around for at least a mile in any direction."

I buried my face in his shoulder, giving my hips a little push into his stomach. He groaned and squeezed me tighter. "Waltrip will know. When we get back, he'll smell it on us."

"Waltrip can—" The shrill ring of Ethan's phone made us both groan. "Damn it," he snarled, setting me on the ground. "Swear to God, that man's made cock-blocking into an art form." He answered Waltrip's call, and I sighed, heading back to the truck with Ethan at my heels. We'd definitely be picking that up later, but for now, it was no use.

WALTRIP WAS WAITING IN ETHAN'S LIVING ROOM WHEN we got back. He opened his mouth to say something, an amused grin on his lips, but a soft growl from Ethan shut him up. Didn't stop him from winking at me as I went past on my way to the shower, though. "Hurry," he called after me. "You'll want to hear this."

They waited until I was done, sitting in the kitchen over bottles of beer and a pizza Waltrip had ordered before we'd arrived. "Is it Justin? Did they find him?" Justin had been seen around Houston for a few weeks, then disappeared. No sign of him in wolf or human form. Tyler had been working hard to track him down before Justin crossed the wrong clan, or worse, was seen by a non-were.

"Nope. But I think you'll still be interested." Waltrip licked his lips nervously. "Ethan thought maybe we should wait and be sure, but I thought maybe you'd want to know as soon as I found out." He reached for his laptop on the counter behind him and brought it over to the table, turning it so I could see. "Read it."

I scanned the email on the screen, scrolling down to the bottom before starting over again twice more. "I... Is this one of the others?" I reached for my beer, but my hand was shaking too hard to hold it. Shoving my hands under my thighs, I read the email again. "He's still alive?"

He nodded. "Mal Benes. Age thirty-two. Last known address was in Shootwell, Colorado. He was originally from Dallas." Waltrip took the computer back and opened up another tab. "Elio —the one you call Thing Two—found him about a week ago. I had to make sure his records matched with the ones Lachlan was able to retrieve from the clinic before it all went tits up. Mal Benes," he said, turning the screen back to me, "is one of the three who survived the first trials."

A man about my age stared back at me from the screen. He was caught mid-conversation from the looks of things, mouth open slightly, eyes squinting like he was making a face at whomever he was speaking with off-camera. He looked tall, but it was hard to tell without something to compare him with. Bright blond hair and sharp features made him look like a model. I felt like I should remember him from those clinic play dates, but I had no memory of him. Then again, I had quite a few holes in my memory of those days, and some things were blurred with the fog of childhood distance. Maybe we played together, I thought, and it was so long ago it's lost to me. "Is he okay? I mean... Does he have the same problems I do?" Admittedly, the problems weren't as intense as they had been, not now that I'd been able to work on my focus more and get on actual anti-anxiety medication, but they were still there, percolating beneath the surface all the time. Waiting.

"I'm not sure. His medical records are pretty thin, but there're indications he was showing some unusual traits before his family disappeared from Texas and showed up in Colorado. He's been on the radar of the local were clan for some time, but he's kept his head down and nose clean. They've mostly forgotten about him after a few changes in leadership. At least that's what Elio says seems to have happened." The next picture he showed me was a toddler, maybe around two years old. "This, though, is a bit of a problem."

"Oh, shit," Ethan groaned. "He's got a kid."

Waltrip nodded, grim. "I'm heading out on Tuesday. I'll be going to Denver and from there, going up to Shootwell. Benes lives on a ranch, works as the foreman. No one there is a were," he added before I could ask. "There's been no indication the kid is one, either, but he's getting to that age…"

Ethan nodded. "You know I can be there in just a few hours."

"You do remember you have a job here, right?" Waltrip asked. "And you," he said, turning on me before I could even offer, "are already on too many radars. I got this. It's just a check and see situation. Letting him know he's got options if things get hairy." He paused. "Heh. Hairy. I made a funny."

"Fuck's sake." Ethan grabbed the second to last slice of the Triple Hawaiian Fire with extra pineapple and ham. "Just for that, you get the shitty, floppy slice."

🐾 🐾 🐾 🐾 🐾 🐾 🐾

WALTRIP LEFT LATE THAT NIGHT, CITING THE NEED TO tie up some loose ends at the office and get Elio and Trey (Thing One) up to speed on a few cases before he headed to Colorado. I think he was just worried he'd hear me and Ethan going at it like rabbits. Ethan waited until I was throwing the last of the wash into the dryer before coming up behind me and wrapping his arms around my waist. "I meant it earlier. It wouldn't change anything. It won't change anything. If the shift at the clinic was a one-off deal just because of what was going on around us, then it was a fucking amazing one-off deal. If you wake up tomorrow as a wolf and find out you can shift back and forth like flipping a pancake, then great, we'll go on runs together and, shit, I don't know, get matching collars or something."

I snorted, leaning back against his chest. "Even if I could change again, there will always be things you can't let me know."

"Like where we sent Garrow."

"Mmm. And clan business. Even if I were considered a were, if they decided *yeah, look at him shift, you go Landry, way to be*, I'm still not a clan member. I have no clan. I'm a lab-created were in that case. As it is now, I'm just a—"

"Don't say freak," he growled, nipping at my ear.

"I was going to say I'm just a slightly tired but extremely horny man who wants his boyfriend to pound him into the mattress."

"Liar."

"Want to find out?"

Ethan pulled away, smiling as he reached past me to hit the button to start the dryer going. "Come to bed with me."

He took my hand, and I followed.

A sneak peek at Howl at the Moon
Marked Book 2

So... my boyfriend's a werewolf.

That's not really as much of a shock to me as people might think.

I mean, if they knew werewolves were real.

People would more surprised that I'm dating anyone, but especially that I'm dating Sheriff Ethan Stone, local poster boy for *unf*.

They have no idea that, behind closed doors, we're...

Well, we're doing plenty of that. But we're also tracking down others like me.

People who were experimented on as children, who have the faintest trace of wolf in our blood.

There were a handful of us who survived the experiments. A cohort of us who lived our entire lives not quite human, not entirely wolf.

And now, the others are turning up dead in rogue were territories, mutilated with parts missing, and the rogue weres have decided I'm the doc for the job when it comes to clearing their name with the recognized packs.

Some days, I'm regret going into forensics.

Also by Meredith

You can find all my books listed my website with links to buy at your favorite online retailers, or ask your local booksellers to order you a copy if you prefer!

The Bedeviled Series

The Devil May Care

The Devil You Know

The Devil in the Details

Speak of the Devil (Spring 2023)

Medium at Large Series

Bump in the Night

Ghoul Friend

Old Ghosts

In the Spirit

After Life (Winter 2023)

Book Six TBA (Spring/Summer 2023)

Science of Magic Series

Data Sets

Fuzzy Logic

Discrete

Scientific Method (2023)

Marked

Nearly Human (July 2022)

Howl at the Moon (Winter 2022)

Book 3 Title TBA (Summer 2023)

In The Pines

Fetch (Spring 2023)

Witch Bone (Fall 2023)

Conjure (Late Winter 2023/Spring 2024)

Stand Alones

Between the Lines

Shared World Series

Ring My Bell (Contemporary MM Fairy Tale Retelling, August 2022)

Leo (A Gaynor Beach Single Dads Romance, November 2022)

Final Days: The Calms (An apocalyptic romance with a HEA, October 2022)

Anthology

The novella, **Easy as Pie**, will be appearing in the **There Goes The Turkey** holiday anthology in November 2023.

About the Author

Meredith likes to write about sexy stuff, weird stuff, and sometimes weird stuff doing sexy stuff. Originally from Texas, they live elsewhere now with their family and two cats who think they aregods (the cats, not the humans—the humans know their place). Meredith writes queer-centered romances in various subgenres including paranormal, speculative fiction/alternate universe, contemporary, and historical. They firmly believe in happily ever afters and pineapple on pizza.

For sneak peeks at upcoming works and other goodies, check out Meredith's social media, Ko-Fi, and reader group.

www.booksbymeredith.com
www.facebook.com/groups/meredithsreadingranch
www.twitter.com/meredithspies
www.facebook.com/meredithspiesauthor
www.instagram.com/meredithspies
Support my Ko-Fi and get access to early peeks at upcoming works, first look at covers and promo art, ARC opportunities, and more:
www.ko-fi.com/booksbymeredith